𝔚𝔞𝔨𝔢 𝔬𝔣 𝔱𝔥𝔢 𝔅𝔩𝔬𝔬𝔡𝔶 𝔄𝔫𝔤𝔢𝔩

BOOKS BY
ALEX BLEDSOE

Blood Groove
The Girls with Games of Blood

The Sword-Edged Blonde
Burn Me Deadly
Dark Jenny
Wake of the Bloody Angel

The Hum and the Shiver

ALEX BLEDSOE

Wake of the Bloody Angel

AN EDDIE LaCROSSE NOVEL

TOR®

A Tom Doherty Associates Book
New York

WAKE OF THE BLOODY ANGEL

A Tor Book
Published by Tom Doherty Associates, LLC
175 Fifth Avenue
New York, NY 10010

www.tor-forge.com

Tor® is a registered trademark of Tom Doherty Associates, LLC.

ISBN 978-0-7653-2745-1 (trade paperback)
ISBN 978-1-4299-4731-2 (e-book)

First Edition: July 2012

Printed in the United States of America

0 9 8 7 6 5 4 3 2 1

To Jacob, for insisting that here be monsters

SPECIAL THANKS:

AC Crispin
Rhodi Hawk
Angus Konstam
Steve Osmanski
Mary Jo Pehl
Jarkko Sipila
Paul Stevens
Marlene Stringer
Miriam Weinberg

The Mount Horeb Public Library
Schubert's Diner and Bakery
Sjolind's Chocolate House

and Valette and Charlie

Wake of the Bloody Angel

chapter

O N E

There's a new client waiting to see you," Angelina said when I entered her tavern.

I shook off the warm summer rain and ran my boots over the mud scraper. I had just returned to Neceda from a job escorting a wealthy but timid merchant through a war zone to visit his invalid mother; the fresh sword cut on my side itched something fierce around its stitches, and the dreary weather didn't help. "Oh, goody," I muttered, and ran a hand through my wet hair. "Do they look like they have money?"

Angelina stood behind the bar, clad as usual in a low-cut gown that showed off her, ahem, assets. She was a mature woman, roughly my own age, but she still—and probably always would—turned heads. Some sexiness is eternal. She said, "You should be grateful people actually want your services, you know."

"I am," I groaned. The tavern was empty except for the two of us, and whoever awaited me upstairs. "I just wish they didn't want them today. I could use a little time to mend."

"Are you hurt?"

"Just a scratch." That's if you didn't count the pain in my forearms from blocking a dozen vicious sword blows that bent the blade on my Englebrook Jouster and ended only when I body-blocked the punk to the ground and cracked his head with a rock. He was a soldier, wine addled and bored, and deserved what he got for needlessly picking a fight. "I don't bounce back like I used to."

"Who does?" she said, her irony almost sympathetic.

I looked up the stairs toward my office. Having my place of business above a tavern made it easy for folks to contact me without drawing a lot of attention; after all, they could always claim they just stopped in for a drink, not to hire a sword jockey. Many of them did, in fact, have a drink—often several—before braving the stairs. Hell, so did I sometimes. "You think I have time for breakfast?"

"No. I think they're getting a bit impatient."

"How long have they been here?"

"As long as I have."

"Lovely. Okay, I'll go see what they want."

Angelina came from behind the bar and followed me up the stairs. I didn't think anything about it, since she kept odds and ends in storage outside my office. Even when she followed me inside, it didn't register as anything unusual.

But no one was waiting in the outer office, or the private inner one, either. I looked back at Angelina. "You said I had a client in here."

She said, "You do."

It took me a moment. "You?"

She nodded at my inner office. "Can we talk in private?"

"Sure." I closed the outer door and let her precede me into the small room where I kept my desk, sword rack, and what passed for my files. I opened the window to let in fresh air. The rain made a quiet swoosh in the background.

I gestured that she should sit in one of the two client chairs. "This is a surprise."

"For me, too," she agreed as she gathered her skirt and sat. She looked uncomfortable and nervous, two qualities I'd never associated with her before.

I sat and leaned my elbows on my desk. Water from my rain-soaked hair trickled down my spine and gave me goose bumps. I said, "So."

"So."

"You're hiring me."

"I'm here to talk about it, yes. Look, don't get weird on me, okay? I'm just somebody looking to engage your services. Treat me like you would anyone else."

"Usually I'd ask, 'What can I do for you?' "

"Ask, then."

"What can I do for you?"

She looked down at her hands resting in her lap. The rain continued to patter. When she spoke again, her voice was thick with uncharacteristic emotion. "First I need to tell you a story. Don't interrupt me until I finish, okay? If you do, I'll talk myself out of this and we'll have both wasted our time."

I nodded.

She looked up at the ceiling, took a deep breath, and began.

"There's a port on a western bay. It's not important where unless you take the job, in which case I'll tell you. Twenty years ago, there was a girl who worked in a tavern laying whiskey down. She was tough, reasonably attractive, and never wanted for male attention. She had no family, no past, no plans, and she liked it that way. Until the day *he* walked in."

I'd seen Angelina angry, happy, drunk, focused, and on rare occasions, wistful. In none of them had I seen the girl she must've once been. But now, as she told her story, I did. The smile lines faded, the wisps of gray in her hair vanished, and her body lost its wide-hipped maturity and reverted to the slender girl who drew every eye.

"He came on a summer's day," she continued, "loaded with gifts from all over the world. Just another sailor between trips, right? Nothing unusual about him at all. Except that the barmaid, that smart, tough, seen-it-all girl, fell for him. It was the first, and last, time in her life that she had anything to do with love."

Angelina looked out the window at the rain, but she wasn't watching the weather. I followed her gaze as if I, too, might see back in time. She continued, "He stayed in port for a month because of her. She used to spend hours watching his eyes while he told his stories. He brought the ocean to life for her, she could practically taste the salt spray and feel the waves crash against her. And he loved her." She chuckled coldly. "Well, she believed it when he *said* it, at any rate. But eventually, he had to go back to the sea. It was his life, and his real love. He promised to come back for her. And before he left, he gave her this as a token."

She placed a braided silver chain on my desk. It sounded solid against the wood. There was a catch in her voice when she said, "That barmaid kept this all that time, waiting for him to keep his word."

I picked up the chain. A locket hung from it, but I didn't open it. "Nice jewelry," I said. "A little pricey for a regular sailor, though. Was he a pirate?"

"Not when I met him. But later . . . yeah."

Pirate. That was not a word I liked to hear. Back in my mercenary days, I'd crossed both paths and swords with the so-called "Brotherhood of the Surf," and the thing that stuck with me most was the *smell*. Granted, an army-for-hire that had been in the field for a while was no bouquet of roses either, but the odor of these sea vermin—a mix of sweat, salt, fish, and blood—impressed me with its organic rankness. They seemed a separate species, governed by laws so arcane and labyrinthine that even looking at one of them risked sparking a violent confrontation. I avoided them whenever possible.

The wind shifted a little outside, and the rain began to splash off the windowsill and into the room. I asked, "What happened then?"

"He left, and she waited. New ships every day, new sailors, wondering which ones would bring a letter, or worse, news of his death . . . It was too much. The town didn't think very highly of her association with him, either, and made things even more difficult for her. So she moved inland, eventually ending up in a little town by a river, because when he returned, she knew it would be by water. She opened a tavern so he would hear about it and be able to find her. And she waited, holding her breath like a drowning woman with the surface six inches above her head."

She looked directly at me now. The smugness, the fire, the absolute certainty that she always presented to the world was gone, replaced by the countenance of that long-ago barmaid with a broken heart. "I want you to find out what happened to him, Eddie. I've waited as long as I can. Now I have to know."

"When's the last time you heard from him?"

"I got a letter from him about a year after he left."

As gently as I could, I said, "That's a pretty cold trail, Angel."

"I *know* it's a cold trail," she snapped. "I'm not an idiot. I accept that, and I don't care." She paused, looked down at her hands again, and said softly, "Here's the thing, Eddie: I trust you. The list of people I can say that about is awfully damn short. I know you'll see it through as far you can, and that whatever answer you give me will be the truth." She looked up and smiled her standard seen-it-all grin. "And *you* know I can pay your standard rate for however long it takes."

That was true enough. Angelina didn't *need* to run a tavern in Neceda; she could've bought half of Muscodia, and that's just with the gold I knew about, stacked in neat boxes along the attic rafters. Taking her case was a lucrative prospect. It was also doomed to failure unless I was very smart and got very lucky. *Twenty years.* I said, "Do you still have that last letter?"

She nodded, pulled it from her dress, and handed it to me. I'd never seen her handle anything with such tenderness. It was worn and creased from being reread.

It said:

My dearest:

I have crossed the line, and now have my own ship, the
Bloody Angel. *My crew is eighty strong and willing men,
and soon we will set out on our first voyage on the account.*

*When I return, I shall make you the queen of our own
island.*

Your loving,
Edward

"We have the same name," I observed.

"Except he was never an *Eddie*. Always an Edward. Edward Tew."

There was a little doodle in the corner, of an angel with a sword hovering over a skull. "What's this?" I asked.

"I don't know. He loved to draw. He always promised to paint my portrait one day."

She gestured at the locket. I picked it up and opened it. Inside, the inscription said, *You could steal a sailor from the sea. Your loving, Edward.*

I snapped the locket closed and tapped the letter. "And you're sure this letter came from him?"

"Of course I'm sure."

"You know what 'on the account' means, right?"

"Yes. I told you he turned pirate."

"And you haven't had any news about him since?"

"Some rumors. Nothing solid. Most people think he's dead. I want proof, one way or the other."

"This is a *very* cold trail," I repeated as I returned the letter.

"I don't expect you to find him alive," she said.

"Hell, I don't expect me to find him at all."

"But you'll take the job?"

"I'm thinking."

I sat back in my chair and watched the raindrops explode on the windowsill. There were two big professional downsides to this. First was the coldness of the trail, of course, and the other was more intangible but no less applicable: I'd be working for a friend. I might find out her boyfriend had died. I might find out he'd married someone else. I might find out he'd completely forgotten her. I wasn't sure how she'd handle any of that.

"I don't care if he's dead," she said as if reading my mind. "I don't care if he's settled down with some fat jolly bitch and raised a litter of snot-runners. I just want to *know*. So I can stop wondering."

That was clear enough. And it decided me. I said, "Okay. I'll do the best I can to find that out for you."

Her voice was as calm as if we'd been discussing the day's lunch special. "Thanks, Eddie." She stood to leave.

"Whoa, wait a second."

"What?" she said impatiently.

"I need some more information from you."

"Like what?"

"Like names."

"I told you his name."

"You've never told me *yours*. I don't even know your last name."

She stood still, but every muscle was tense, as if she fought the competing urges to run and to smack me. Then she took a deep breath and told me her true name.

"Really," I said.

"I didn't pick it."

"Why do you go by your middle name, then?"

"Because he used to call me Angel." She smiled. "Just like you do."

"He named his ship after you, too."

"I know."

"He could've changed a lot in twenty years. How will I know him if I find him?"

"He gave me that locket, I gave him a bracelet. It's made of gold, and has a heart in the center, with angel wings engraved all around the band."

She gave me the rest of the basic information I needed, then went downstairs when a customer started yelling for ale. I closed the door behind her, went to the window, and looked out at Neceda's muddy streets and the brown Gusay River beyond. The scent of water overwhelmed everything, and the rain hitting my face did nothing to wash away my doubts.

I knew Angelina took the afternoons off and left the place in the care of the barely capable, but definitely easy on the eyes, Callie. Young, gaspingly gorgeous, naïve as a bootheel, Callie was the reason a lot of men came to the tavern. She could disarm even the most determined mischief-maker with a sway of her hips and a smile.

It also helped that, in the fallow period between lunch and dinner, the tavern was mostly empty. At the moment, I was the lone customer, nursing my ale and pondering my new job. Callie knew to leave me to my thoughts.

When I first came to Muscodia, I hadn't planned to stay, certainly not in a small town like Neceda. Sevlow, the capital, might've been all right, but this muddy little river town was a great place to put behind me, or so I thought. As it turned out, its location was perfect.

I'd come to the tavern as a customer that first time, with no thoughts at all of making it my permanent base. It was packed that night, and I was lucky to get a place at the bar. Angelina appeared before me, blew a loose strand of hair from her face, and said, "What can I get you?"

I admit I stared. Her hair cascaded around her bare shoulders, and her face and cleavage gleamed with sweat. I hadn't been with a woman in a while, and suddenly I felt every moment of that time. I smiled.

My reaction was not new to her, and she had no patience with it. "Close your mouth and name your poison, friend, I got a lot of thirsty folks here. There's nothing under here that isn't exactly where you think it is, so let's pretend you've seen it and move on, okay?"

I ordered an ale, the same thing I was drinking now, and watched her sweep around the tavern with all the dexterity, skill, and composure of a soldier in the middle of battle. I'd never seen a woman so beautiful yet so single-minded in her task. And I wasn't the only one who noticed.

Between serving drinks, she took a big pot of slop out the back of the kitchen to dump in the ditch, and I thought nothing of it until that inner voice I'd long since learned to trust said she'd been gone too long. None of the other workers had noticed, so I discreetly slipped out and crept to the back of the building.

I was right. Two big, drunken young men had her backed up against the tavern's outer wall. The nearby kitchen door was shut, and no scream would be heard over the noise inside. They didn't physically hold her down, but that was clearly in the immediate future. One toyed with a knife and said woozily, "It ain't fair for you to look so sexy and be so ice cold."

"No one said life was fair," Angelina shot back, no fear in her voice.

The second man said, whining like a child, "Oh, come on, just show us a good time and we'll be out of your hair. You might even enjoy it."

I couldn't tell if she knew I watched from the shadows or not. She always swore she didn't. But she nodded in my direction and said, "You better watch it, or my husband might run you through. He's mighty possessive."

The one with the knife said, "Come on, how stupid do you think we are?" He slipped the tip of the blade under the laced cord that cinched the front of her dress.

I stepped out of the shadows behind them and slammed their heads together. They dropped silently.

Angelina tossed her hair from her face. "Thanks."

"My pleasure. Want me to tie them up?"

"No, they won't cause me any more trouble. I've seen them around; they're local boys who just had a little too much to drink." She picked up the empty slop bucket at her feet.

"That's awfully charitable of you."

"It's not charity, it's business. I want them back drinking at my bar."

"You own this place?"

"I sure as hell do." Then she looked at me steadily, with the kind of scrutiny that makes a moment feel like a lifetime. At last she said, "I think I can trust you, can't I?"

"You can."

She stepped over one of the fallen men, grabbed the back of my neck, and kissed me. Full on, with tongue. A lesser man might've burned to death on the spot. When she broke it, she said, "Anything?"

"Not really," I said honestly, which surprised me as much as it did her.

"Now I *know* I can trust you." She laughed.

It wasn't like the kiss diminished her sexiness; instead it was like I saw past it, to the integrity of the person behind it. I might have been her lover for years without seeing this, but once I had, I knew we'd never be physically intimate. In one kiss, we'd jumped over all that and become . . . well, whatever we were. *Friends* didn't quite capture it. Neither did siblings, or comrades-in-arms. It was all of those, mixed and applied as the situation demanded.

And this situation demanded all of them.

I'd taken a job at which I knew I'd fail. I'd never find this other Edward, the sailor and pirate, not after twenty years. But I *would* look as hard as I could. Because I knew that Angelina, whatever she might say for others to hear, would do the same for me.

OVER dinner that night, I told my girlfriend, Liz Dumont, about the new job.

We sat in our small second-floor room in Mrs. Talbot's boardinghouse. The rain had stopped, and the lamp burned as the overcast sky dimmed to darkness. Horses whinnied in the street, and someone yelled something in a language I didn't recognize. In the distance, I made out the distinctive clang of sword against sword and men's voices drunkenly raised in song. It was all part of Neceda's rustic river-port charm.

Liz was trim, with short red hair and freckles. She was also smart, brave, and tough, which she had to be since she ran a courier business that took her all over. She knew how the world worked, and how to navigate it.

She said, "You don't really think you're going to find him after all this time, do you?"

"It's unlikely."

"Then you're just taking Angie's money."

"I'm taking her money to *look*. And I will, as hard as I can, and as long as I think there's any point. She knows there aren't any guarantees."

Liz looked at me from beneath unruly bangs. It was a look that tended to make me agree with anything. "Is it a good idea to work for a friend?"

"I thought about that. I think it'll be okay. I also think," I added as casually as possible, "that I'm going to bring Jane Argo in on this."

Liz sat up, tossed her bangs from her face, and set her jaw. I knew that look, too. "Really," she said flatly.

"Yeah. She was a pirate hunter before she turned sword jockey, you know."

"And she was a pirate before that."

"Well, I'm *looking* for a pirate. It's her area of expertise, not mine."

"Is she still married to that worthless little weasel?"

"Miles? As far as I know."

"Didn't you have to go pull him out of one of Gordon Marantz's gambling houses last year?"

"Yep. Didn't change a thing."

"Amazing how some people can have such huge blind spots."

I didn't say anything. Jane Argo knew exactly what her husband was; she just didn't care. She loved him. It couldn't be explained rationally. Not by Jane, certainly not by me.

Liz continued, "I can trust you on a long trip alone with her, then. Right?"

"She's a colleague, that's all."

"But suppose your ship sinks and you get washed up on some desert island, just the two of you . . ." she teased.

"Do you want to come along?"

"Kinky. But I can't. I have to take a bunch of scrolls to the Society of Scribes archive in Algoma."

"Then you'll just have to trust me."

She grinned. "It always comes down to that, doesn't it?"

We both laughed. We drank some more wine. Then we abandoned our dinner for more intimate activities.

SOMETIME before dawn, I got up and walked out onto the landing. The stairs leading up to our apartment went down the side of the building, and I saw a lamp burning in old Mrs. Talbot's rooms on the ground floor. Neceda's riverside location gave her the perfect means to receive and dispose of stolen property, and it was no secret that she did so. Still, she was discreet, and I had no interest in knowing her business. She gave me the same consideration.

The clouds were beginning to break at last. I caught glimpses of stars behind the irregular blobs. Neceda was asleep; even the whorehouses and taverns were silent. Liz snored lightly, femininely, in the room behind me.

"Hey, what you doing up there?"

I looked down. Mrs. Talbot stood at the foot of the steps in a shapeless, too-short nightgown. At her age, I assumed it was for comfort against the heat and humidity. At least I hoped it was. I said, "Just thinking."

She took the pipe from her teeth and said, "About what?"

"Pirates," I answered honestly.

She laughed. "They're bad luck, you know."

"How so?"

"My second husband was a pirate."

"No. Really?"

"Sure as the moon in the night sky. Not a very good one, though. He lost a foot during a boarding, but he still got his share of the loot. Name a navy that would do *that* for him."

"What finally happened to him?"

"Got his peg leg stuck in the mud making a run for it ashore. A soldier cut him down and trampled him. That wooden leg was the only way I could tell it was him."

Chuckling, she went back inside. I heard male voices muttering before the door closed.

I looked up at the stars. Finding one pirate after twenty years was a lot like picking one star out of this sky. Just when you thought you had it, a cloud slid by and you had to start all over when it passed.

My star was Edward Tew. And my cloud was the two decades that separated us.

J ane Argo looked at me down the length of her sword. Her arm was fully extended and her feet spread wide for balance. From my perspective, I saw her face reflected upside down in the blade, distorted a bit by the accumulated nicks and dings. Sunlight sparkled from the numerous rings on her fingers. A strand of hair drifted into her eyes, but she didn't blink. Neither did I—the sword's tip was right at my throat.

I was hyperconscious of everything around me: the wind in the trees, the splash of a fish in the lake, a woodpecker's persistent knocking. Sweat trickled down my forehead. Not many men survived seeing Jane Argo from this angle. Offhand, I'd put the count at "none."

With a flick of her wrist, Jane knocked the bee from my collar and slapped it to the ground. She crushed it beneath the sole of one knee-high leather boot. "There."

My voice sounded reasonably normal when I said, "Thanks, but I could've just slapped it away myself, you know."

"Ah, where's the fun in that?" She looked at her sword longingly. "Was a time I could've sliced it in half before it hit the dirt."

"No, you couldn't," I said, wiping the sweat from my eye.

She laughed. If you spent any significant time with her, you realized she laughed a lot, and her voice was incongruously high-pitched and girlish for someone her size. She was my height, busty and wide-hipped but with a wasp-narrow waist. Her broad shoulders were as muscular as a galley slave's, and she wore a large ring on every finger. Her hair fell past her shoulders, and only the faint streaks of gray in it and slightly deeper smile lines indicated that she was older than she sounded. "Yeah, you're right, but it's nice to pretend we once had a mythical prime, isn't it?"

I shrugged. I tried not to pretend about anything, but that didn't mean Jane couldn't.

She turned to the young man tied to a nearby tree. He was scruffy, unshaven, and his clothes were often-patched rags. "So what did you think of my little trick?"

He glared at us and said nothing. The anger in his eyes was plenty loud, though.

"Kids these days are just so hard to impress," she said as she put away her sword. She wore a sleeveless tunic that showed off her shoulders and barely contained her bosom. She picked up the cape she perpetually wore in any weather and buckled the clasp around her neck.

I'd stopped by Jane's home, where her no-account husband, Miles, told me I'd find her on the road to Barre Dumoth, escorting a prisoner for trial. Miles was under house arrest, Jane Argo style—his right ankle was chained to a huge rock in the middle of the cottage floor, with just enough slack to reach the outhouse. Given Miles's penchant for drinking, gambling, and whoring, I thought it a wise precaution. I ignored him when he tried to bribe me to set him free.

I caught up with Jane and her prisoner in the middle of the forest, and we stopped by a lake to discuss my case. As we talked, a mule-drawn wagon driven by a white-haired old man made its slow way past on the narrow road behind us.

"So you're going to sea," she said as she settled the cape around her shoulders.

"Seems like the best place to look for a pirate."

"And his name is Edward Tew?"

"That's what he told my client. Don't know if that was his real name, or just what he called himself. Ever heard of him?"

"There's a lot of pirates in the world. What about his treasure?"

"What treasure?"

"Come on, you expect me to believe there's not a treasure involved? Nobody searches for a pirate just for the hell of it."

"If there is a treasure, I'm not being paid to find it, and I'm not interested in it. Only the guy."

"Assuming you're not bullshitting me about the lack of a treasure, why would you even *take* a job like this, anyway? It's hard enough to find someone who's been gone a week, if they really want to stay hidden. Two *decades* . . ."

"I like the challenge."

She laughed again and skipped a stone across the lake, getting an impressive six bounces. "Knowing you, Eddie, I'm guessing this is a favor for a friend. I'd say a *girl*friend, but I can't picture that skinny ginger-hair of yours ever tumbling with a sailor."

"Funny—I *can* picture Miles doing it."

That made her laugh even more, until we simultaneously noticed that the mule-drawn cart had stopped in the middle of the road, and its white-haired driver was nowhere in sight. Neither was Jane's prisoner. The ropes that had bound him to the tree lay in a pile across the knobby roots.

There was no exchange of words, no *You go that way, I'll go this way.* We simply drew our swords, she headed up to the road, and I ran into the forest.

I found them first. The prisoner led the way through underbrush still slick from the recent rain, and the older man tried to keep up. Mainly for Jane's benefit, I shouted, "Stop right there! No need for anybody to get hurt!"

The two men froze halfway up a slight rise. The older one leaned on the nearest tree and gasped for breath. The younger one said, "I didn't do anything wrong!"

"I don't care," I said, continuing to move toward them. I held the tip of my sword up so it wouldn't snag on anything. I knew Jane would locate me by my voice, and I wanted to keep their attention on me. "That's not my problem."

"Who the hell are you, anyway?" the young man demanded. "You show up, you jump into the middle of something that's not any of your business—"

"If you don't surrender now, I'm the guy who's going to see what color your intestines are." I sliced through a hanging tangle of vines for emphasis. "That's more of a chance than Jane Argo would give you."

"He's right, son, give up," the older man croaked. "We tried our best. We'll have to trust in Lord Corrett's conscience."

"Like hell," the younger man said, and was about to turn and run, when Jane's sword suddenly slipped under his chin.

"I *don't* like hell, since you mention it," she said as she grabbed him by the hair. "But I'll probably go there anyway. Now, don't move. Pops, get over here and tie your son's wrists. Do a good job of it and I won't have to hamstring him."

"He's innocent," the older man insisted, the words barely getting out. He was a disturbing shade of red, and seemed to be having no luck catching his breath.

"Then he's the one man in the world who is," Jane said. "Now, do what I say. Please, for everyone's sake, okay? You're both out of your league here. Eddie and I do this for a living."

The old man tried to say something else, but he had no wind left. His eyes rolled back and he collapsed beside the tree, rolling down the slight slope to land in the wet leaves at my feet.

I stuck my sword in the ground and knelt over him. I heard Jane tell his son, "Stay put. If you so much as *think* about running away, I'll catch you and geld you before sundown."

Then she was on her knees on the other side of the fallen man. She bent and put her ear to his mouth, listening for breath. When she found none, she put her lips over the old man's and repeatedly blew hard into his lungs.

Meanwhile, I ripped open his tunic to expose his pale, still-muscular chest. I put my palm flat over his heart and felt nothing. I drove my fist into the back of my hand, trying to get his heart going again, just as a moon priestess once showed me on a battlefield. Sometimes this worked; most of the time it didn't. And it was tricky not to break a rib and puncture a lung. But any chance was better than none.

And in this case, luck was with us. After the third whack, his whole body spasmed and he began to cough. Jane looked back at his son, still standing where she'd left him. "Go get the canteen off my saddle. And no funny stuff."

He left, while Jane and I helped the old man sit up. He was now a bad shade of pale blue, and I knew we'd just stirred the coals and not really restoked the furnace. "My son didn't do anything wrong," he wheezed. I admired his tenacity. "He's innocent, I tell you."

"Look, pops, let it go," Jane said patiently. "It's not for us to say. My job is to take him from point A to point B, that's all. Guilt or innocence is way above my pay grade."

He looked at me. "And you?"

"I just happened to be in the neighborhood."

The son returned with the canteen, and his father sipped from it. The younger man looked at Jane and said, "Now what?"

"Well, now we take pops back home and make sure he's comfortable, then we finish taking you to jail."

"How can you do that? You taking me to jail is what nearly killed him!"

Jane jumped up, grabbed the front of his tunic, and yanked him nose to nose. "I've about had it with you simpering barn swallows questioning my ethics. What nearly killed pops here was running uphill after cutting you loose." She shoved him back. "Now, if you want to help take him home, pick him up and carry him to his wagon. If you don't, you can just stay here tied to a tree until we come back. It's your call, so make it. *Now!*"

Sensibly, the boy gently picked up his father. He might really have been innocent of whatever crime he was accused of, but as Jane said, that wasn't her problem. And that was what I liked about her. She looked at the world the same way I did, and operated under the same rules.

AFTER we delivered the old man back home, where his wife shed copious tears both for his return and her son's imminent departure, we took the boy on to Barre Dumoth. We arrived at sunset.

It was an old manor town, where the population lived and died at the pleasure of the lord, who owned everything. There weren't many of these left in Muscodia, and the ones that remained fiercely guarded their power. We had to wait while the sentries at the town gate sent a message ahead to Lord Corrett.

When we got to the jail, Corett was waiting under the watchful gaze of two bulky, out-of-shape bodyguards. He was a tall, smooth-faced man with bad taste in expensive clothes. He regarded Jane with contempt as he paid her for her job, individually doling out each gold coin.

When he finished, Jane smiled and said, "Pleasure doing business with you."

The nearest bodyguard jabbed her shoulder with his fingers and prompted, "My lord."

Jane's glare could've melted rock. "Poke me again, lard bucket, and I'll fold you up so you can lick your balls like a dog."

"The prisoner is ensconced in his cell?" Corrett asked in a blasé near-yawn. His voice was like the tines of a fork scraping across a plate.

"Yes, sir," the jailer said. He stood at attention beside the cell door and gestured inside. The young man sat on the straw, rubbing at the metal collar clamped around his neck. When he saw Corrett, the boy hissed, "Proud of yourself, my lord?" He spat the last two words.

"My pride has nothing to do with this."

"This is all about your pride! Elaine prefers me to a dried-up prick like you, and your ego can't stand it!"

"Gag him," Corrett said with a casual wave of his hand. The jailer pretended not to hear.

I asked Corrett, "What exactly did he do?"

"He stole my best horse, not that it's any concern of yours." His accent on the final word carried enough contempt to bury a man standing up. He gestured at the portly escorts. "My guards found it tied outside his hovel."

"That's bullshit!" the boy yelled. "They planted that horse and you know it!"

"Gag him," Corrett said again, enunciating each word. "And now you must excuse me, I have a young woman to visit. She'll be delighted to learn that this rascal will no longer be forcing his attentions on her."

He and his entourage swept from the jail. The jailer sighed, took the uncomfortable-looking leather gag from its wall hook, and opened the cell.

Jane watched the jailer buckle it around the boy's head. She asked quietly, "You really didn't steal that horse, did you?"

The boy shook his head. Drool already trailed down his chin.

"Course he didn't," the jailer said as he emerged from the cell. "Doesn't matter, though. Man like Corrett can do what he wants with us commoners. He even owns the boots on our feet."

He froze when he felt the tip of Jane's dagger at his throat. I took the keys from his belt and went to unlock the gag. He raised his hands and said, "Just beat me up so it looks like I put up a fight, okay? I need this job."

LATER, as we sat in the nearest tavern, we heard the commotion when the jailbreak was discovered. There was lots of shouting, and eventually a half-dozen men on horseback tore out of town.

All innocence, Jane asked a stooped, bearded man who'd just entered, "Wow, what happened out there?"

"Horse thief escaped," he said. "Beat up Clyde over at the jail. Lord Corrett's guards went after him, but it looks like he's got a good head start."

Jane thanked him, then raised her ale mug in a toast and said softly, "To the good guys."

"If only there were more than just me and you," I added as we clinked mugs and drank.

"Guess we won't be coming back to Barre Dumoth for a while," Jane said. "So now I'm on your payroll. We're looking for a pirate, who may or may not be dead, somewhere in the whole wide wet world. Where do we start, boss?"

"At the scene of the crime," I said. "Where he met my client."

s we rode away from the Argo cottage, Miles watched us from the door. Jane had unchained him, since we had no idea how long we'd be away. Neither he, she, nor I harbored any delusions about what he'd be up to in her absence.

When he was out of sight, Jane asked, "Since I'm working for you now, trying to find a long-lost pirate and his treasure, shouldn't you tell me who our client is?"

"Not the treasure, just the pirate," I repeated. "And the client is—" I hesitated because I knew what her reaction would be. "—Angelina."

Her eyes opened wide. *"Angie?"* Jane barked, laughing loud enough to startle birds from the nearby trees. My horse, Baxter, tossed his head, annoyed by the sharp, shrill noise. "The great ice queen Angelina hired you to find her old pirate boyfriend?"

"Yes."

"That's crazy! I've been passing through Neceda and stopping at her tavern for years, and I've never seen her interested in a man. Or a woman. Or *anyone*."

"Yeah, she's been the reigning Miss Anthropy as long as I've known her. But I think this guy Edward Tew is the reason."

Jane giggled like a princess with a secret. "Crazy. That's the only word. Angelina in love. That's like imagining me cooking dinner. So where did they meet?"

"Watchorn Harbor in Cotovatry."

"I know it. Fairly big port. What do you think we'll find there after all this time?"

"Nothing, probably. But maybe somebody remembers them, and knows what happened to Tew. It's one end of the string that's tied to our man."

"And his treasure," she added.

I glared at her. *"Stop* that. Seriously."

She threw up her hands in mock surrender. "Okay, you win. But you know, pirates don't generally last twenty years. It's a tough trade. If he's not dead, he's probably changed his name and started a whole new life."

"Are you going to be such a beacon of optimism on the whole trip?"

"Just so we're clear, I get paid whether we find him or not, right?"

"That's the deal."

She sighed and shook her head. "That soft heart of yours is going to be the death of you one day, Eddie, you know that?"

I said nothing. My heart had once hardened beyond recognition, and I hated the man I became then. If being softhearted took a few years off my life, it seemed a fair trade for being human again.

FIVE days later, we stopped our horses on the ridge overlooking Cotovatry's coastal plain. Mine stomped around, refusing to stop until he'd reminded me yet again why I disliked all horses except the late, lamented Lola.

"I hope you handle that redhead of yours better than that," Jane said.

"Yeah, well, maybe you should consider gelding your husband, it might calm him down," I snapped back. She laughed.

Mile after mile of sand and scrub stretched away in either direction. Here and there, trees grew in tight-packed spots where the sand gave way to actual soil. Behind us stretched a vast woods crisscrossed with trails and roads.

In the middle of the vista before us lay Watchorn Harbor. The town's buildings clustered along the water's edge and spread inland from a central point like a lady's fan. A forest of masts and canvas filled the harbor, backlit by the afternoon sun that glinted blindingly off the water. The first gusts of evening wind brought the distinctive odors of salt and dead fish.

"How many ships do you think are out there?" I asked.

"About a hundred," Jane said. "See those two far out at anchor? Those are naval ships stationed to protect the harbor. And those little ones all in a row there? A fishing fleet."

"Any pirate ships?"

"Not in this harbor." She snorted. "Unless they're on the bottom. Those naval ships aren't just for show."

It was sundown by the time we reached the town, and people packed the thoroughfares, mostly men with the distinctive leathery look and rolling gait of sailors. On the dreary streets, the odors were much more vivid and considerably less pleasant, but like anything, we eventually got used to them. Languages both known and unknown blurred in my ears. Neceda was like this, but on a far smaller, slower scale.

Jane, though, was in her element. She tossed her cape behind her shoulders, pulled her hair up in a loose bun, and rode along, confident her way would be clear. It was.

First we sought the town magistrate's office. I always cover my bases by trying official channels first. Usually it gave me no direct information about my case, but it let me get a sense of the local constabulary. It also means people would know I was looking, and sometimes stirring the pot was the best thing.

We found the town's magistrate, a Mr. Tallarico, in his office going over a voluminous stack of shipping forms. The office was in a small building next to a warehouse and corral. A large one-eyed cat curled up on a corner of his desk. Vellum sheets were stacked everywhere, pinned down by rocks or anything else heavy enough to hold them in place. A lone neglected plant drooped in its pot on the windowsill. He had no secretary or formal guard; he just sat at his desk doing his job.

"Magistrate Tallarico?" I said.

He used a monocle to see the forms, and when he looked up at us, it made his right eye look huge. "Yes?"

"Sorry for interrupting, sir, but I think you might be able to help me." I gave him my most winning smile.

He looked at me, then at Jane, then back to me. "Indeed. You don't appear to be sailors, ship owners, businessmen, or officials. Those are the people I help. If you're looking for work, you'll have to talk to the captains of the ships. If you're here to report a crime, you're both in the wrong place and frankly wasting your time." He returned to his reports. "Good day."

We didn't move. The cattle in the nearby corral mooed through the window, glad to be out of some ship's cramped hold. At last he removed the monocle and impatiently looked at us. "All right, *what*?"

I smiled. "My associate and I are looking for a local family, and we thought you might be able to help us find them."

"Who?"

"The Dirnays. They had a daughter named Brandywine. Might've gone by Brandy." Jane stifled a laugh. I still had a hard time imagining Angelina as a "Brandywine," let alone a "Brandy," but as she said, she didn't choose it.

"Dirnay?" he repeated. "I don't recall ever meeting anyone by that name in Watchorn."

"How long have you been here?" Jane asked.

"Four years." The way he said it implied it felt much longer.

Jane leaned on the desk and looked down at him, using her size, in every sense, to intimidate him. She said through a humorless grin, "Then who might be able to help us?"

Tallarico sat back in his chair and held up the monocle. "You know, they say a wizard in the court of King Haviland once mounted a series of polished glass disks like this in a tube so that the king could observe things so small, they were invisible to the naked eye. And even if you had two of those devices and attached them together, you would still be unable to locate my interest in your problem." He waved his hand toward the door. "Now, good day to you, ma'am. And sir."

Now I stepped forward. "Where's the records office?"

"What records do you need?"

"Shipwrecks. Specifically any record of the *Bloody Angel.*"

If anything, his expression grew more contemptuous. "Ye gods, you're treasure hunters, aren't you? You think you'll be the ones to find some missed clue and discover Black Edward's treasure." He laughed with the contempt of middle management. "Fine. The records office is three doors down. Tell the old harpy that I sent you. I wonder if she's still growing her mustache?"

Three doors down I knocked, and a loud female voice said, "Enter!"

The smell of vellum and ink filled the little room. Shelves lined the walls, holding rolled-up sheets and bound volumes. There was a table with two chairs by the single window, and a desk where a round-bodied little woman with gray hair piled high on her head sat squinting at a map on her desk. She looked up and said, "What do you want?"

"Don't get mad," I said.

"Why would I get mad?"

"We mentioned the *Bloody Angel* to the magistrate, and he got mad."

"That man is a blot on the good name of Watchorn. I used to have his office, did you know that? All that space. Now he's got me in a damn closet." She narrowed her eyes at me. "Why do you want to know about the *Bloody Angel*?"

I liked her casual air and the fact that she agreed with me about the magistrate. "If I say I'm not interested in the treasure, will you believe me?"

"Sure, because there is no treasure. Lots of people have looked, but it's been twenty years and not so much as a bead has showed up."

"Has anyone looked lately?" Jane asked.

"Not in at least five years. We get the occasional inquiry, but mostly it's just sailors thinking they're unique in their interest. When they find out they're not, they wander off. Also, not too many of them can read."

"So you do have records," Jane said.

"Of course we've got records. And maps. And detailed reports." She stood and took a large bound volume from a nearby shelf. On the cover it was titled THE WRECK OF THE BLOODY ANGEL AND WHAT REALLY HAPPENED.

She handed it to me and gestured at the table. "It's all in there, all gathered up neat and nice for convenience. Have a seat. Read to your heart's content. Make notes, copy maps. Just don't damage the book; if you do, I'm within my job description to kill you."

Jane put a hand on my shoulder. "I'll let you handle this. I'm going to go find a drink. I'll check back in an hour."

I nodded, sat down, and began to read.

The texts were legal, which meant they were also boring. There was a description of the storm, and a map showing where the *Bloody Angel* supposedly sank. Then there was testimony from people who were on the beach when pieces of the wreck began to wash ashore. They were referred to only by their initials.

The official report was written by a man named Cyrus Northack, special envoy from the Cotovatrian court, and his contempt for the locals was palpable. He excoriated them for snatching up everything that washed ashore without reporting any of it. He asserted that no hint of treasure had been seen or mentioned, but he suspected that if any had, he'd be the last to know. The final straw was when the local gravedigger presented him with a bill for the burial of the dead pirates scattered along the surf.

But there had been a lone survivor, initials WM, who explained what happened. Driven into the shallows by the storm, the ship hit a sand bar and the wind snapped its mainmast. She rolled over, and the weight of everything in her hold—including treasure, one would assume—broke through the deck and led the way to the bottom. Black Edward Tew was last seen clinging to the upside-down ship's rudder, shaking his fist at the sky.

"Anything useful?" the clerk asked me when I closed the book.

I shook my head. "Just confirms the story I've been told."

"It's an old story well known," she said sadly. "Are you giving up your treasure hunt, then?"

"I told you, I'm not hunting the treasure."

"Of course. And I'll turn down a shepherd's pie. Want to see something?" She opened a drawer in her desk, reached beneath some papers, and brought out a piece of wood. It was light and faded from age, and either end of the plank was ragged where it had broken. There were a few darker spots on it that could once have been bloodstains. Or mildew.

"They tell me this is a piece of the *Bloody Angel* herself," the woman said. "My predecessor snatched it up right off the beach, the morning after the wreck."

I turned it over. There was no hidden inscription, no markings or carvings. It could have been from anywhere. Yet I felt the truth of her assertion along the back of my neck, where the hairs rose in warning.

I handed it back. "Thanks." Then I gathered up the book and returned it to the shelf.

"My God, you've got manners," she said.

"And you should see me dance."

She batted her eyes. "Is there anything else I can help you with, kind sir?"

"Do you know a local family named Dirnay?"

"Alas, on that topic I'm like the end of a worn-out sounding line." When I looked blank, she added, "I'm a frayed knot."

"Ah. Nautical humor."

"It's all we have here," she said with a smile.

"Then I believe I've learned all I can. Thank you."

"Thank *you*. A gentleman is always welcome."

Outside Jane sat on the wooden sidewalk, watching the people pass. She got up when she saw me. "Anything?"

"Nothing I didn't already know."

"So now what, boss?"

I looked at the crowded street, the mélange of races and nationalities, and felt the impending weight of my likely failure. What the hell had I been thinking? Finding anyone after twenty years was unlikely, let alone a sailor, let alone a pirate. "We ask around. Angelina was a barmaid when she met her man, so we start with the bars."

"Hey, this job just got a whole lot better," Jane said with a wink.

Angelina had told me she worked in a place called the Floating Coffin, but we found no one with any memory of it, and it certainly wasn't around now. So we started closest to the water and methodically tried all the bars we did find: the

Crossed Harpoons, the Sword-Fish Inn, the Trap. In each we bought a drink and asked as discreetly as possible about Brandywine Angelina Dirnay and the Floating Coffin. And in each we came up blank.

Finally, as we were leaving the Cuttlefish's Embrace, an old salt called out to us, "I say, I couldn't help overhearing your question to the bartender. Was that place you were asking about down by the waterfront?"

"Yeah," I said. I had no idea, but it seemed reasonable, and this was the first positive sign we'd gotten.

He smiled wistfully. He had teeth only on the right side of his mouth. "Ah, the Floating Coffin. I used to go down there in my younger days, when I first went to sea. I got drunk for the first time there. Not even the harpoon that took out my teeth hurt as bad as my head did the next day. I couldn't keep down solid food for a week."

I exchanged a look with Jane; she rolled her eyes, but this was all we had. "Is that why you remember it?" I asked the old man.

"Partly. But what kept drawing me back was a girl. They had a lass slinging drinks who could make a dead man poke a hole in his burial shroud, if you take my meaning. 'The swan was in her movements and the morning in her smile'; I forget who said that." He almost shivered at the memory. "She could reduce the strongest man to a simpering pup with just a glance. To this day, I've never seen a woman who could compare." He nodded at Jane. "No offense, ma'am."

"She sounds like something," I agreed. "What was her name?"

"Brandy," he said with a sigh, his eyes closed. "I think it

was a nickname, but it's been a long time." He shook his head at the memory. "Wonder what ever became of her?"

Well, I thought, *the good-luck fairy just unloaded on us.* I asked, "So is the Floating Coffin still around?"

"Goodness, no. Every time I return to this port, everything has changed owners and names. But there's still a tavern there."

I held out a coin. "Show us where it is, Mr.—?"

"Quintal, Derrick Quintal, harpooner's mate," he said with a little bow.

"Well, show us where it is, Mr. Quintal, and you can put this toward some new teeth."

"My pleasure," he said, and took the coin. Jane caught my eye, and I shrugged; it was the first lead we'd had, after all. It did seem a bit overly convenient, and I wasn't entirely sure we weren't being led into an ambush for robbery. If we were, though, they'd get a whole lot more than they bargained for.

We left our horses tied at the Cuttlefish's Embrace and, alert for trouble, followed harpooner's mate Quintal on foot. But the old sailor was on the level. After several twists and turns, we reached a corner a block from the ocean and stood before a tavern called Lurie's Wharf. It didn't look like much, but the noise from inside testified to its popularity.

Quintal sighed as he looked at it. "This is it. *Was* it. I don't suppose she's here anymore. Long gone, to either her family or her grave."

"She's probably old, fat, and gray by now," Jane said dismissively. "That's what always happens, isn't it?"

Quintal smiled his half-toothed grin. "Now, I hope your man here won't take this wrong, but you've got little to be jealous about. You may have a touch of snow on the mountaintop, but the peaks look in fine shape."

She kissed him on the top of his head. "That deserves a tip." She looked at me. "Right, my man?"

I gave him another coin, which made him laugh. He touched the brim of his cap in salute, then strode away whistling. The crowd swallowed him by the time he reached the next corner.

"Think we just got taken?" I asked.

"Only one way to tell," Jane said, and unbuckled her sword. "I'll handle this one. You go in there and start asking about a girl that used to work here, nobody'll say anything. They'll think you're her husband or her pimp. Give me ten minutes to get settled, then come in and watch a master at work."

She handed me her sword belt and scabbard, and I needed both hands for the weight. She undid her hair and shook it around her shoulders. She pulled the strands down close to her face, which made her look younger. Then she changed her whole demeanor, opening her eyes wider and somehow draining the maturity and tension from her face. She looked as innocent and vulnerable as a woman her age and height could possibly look. With a wink, she went into the tavern.

I put her sword belt over my shoulder and walked slowly around the block to give her time. The masts of the big sailing ships towered over the low buildings, darker shadows against the now-starry sky. A lone sailor with a lantern tightroped across one spar, checking the rigging. The rolled-up sails looked like the cocoons of enormous insects. Cargo was being unloaded even this late, and men sang work songs in languages I didn't know.

I imagined standing on the deck of one of these floating warehouses and seeing the black flag of piracy atop an approaching ship. Merchants seldom went unarmed, but they also rarely employed real fighters. A man who could lift cargo all day could still be useless in a fight against an experienced sword arm. I knew pirates often left the crews and vessels unharmed after pillaging them, unless the crew resisted. Then all bets were off, and everyone on board might die. It was good motivation for standing quietly in the corner while your riches were offloaded.

I'd given Jane her lead time, so I went into Lurie's Wharf and took a seat at the bar. Jane's sword caused me to get more elbow room than I might have otherwise. I spotted her at a table with a half-dozen men around her, all with fresh mugs of ale or rum. I felt a twinge of professional annoyance—*Hey, I can buy drinks for sailors, too*—when I heard her loudly blow her nose. I listened without being obvious about it as she said tearfully, in a voice so demure, I had to check twice to confirm it was her, "Thank you, sir. Thanks to all you gentlemen. I just don't know where else to turn. I'm at the end of my rope."

Most of the men were too young to have known Angelina back then, but a couple were wizened with age and experience, and they regarded Jane with clear compassion. I ordered a drink and settled in to eavesdrop.

"It's been a long time since this place was the Floating Coffin," one of the younger men said. "My pappy mentioned it back before he died, but that would've been, oh, twenty years ago."

"That's about right," Jane said. "She was my much older sister. I was a sunset baby, you know."

"Was she as pretty as you?" another sailor asked, masking his lasciviousness with a gentle tone.

"Oh, sir, you're being kind," Jane said. "Brandywine was very pretty. All the boys liked her."

"I knew her," one old man said suddenly.

"You did?" Jane said hopefully. "When?"

"Like you said, twenty years ago. We just called her Brandy, but I remember her. Beautiful girl. Had a smile that could guide a ship through a storm. But . . ."

He trailed off. Jane prompted, "Please, sir, continue. I *must* know, no matter how bad it is."

The old man looked down at his hand on the tabletop. He was missing his middle finger and pinkie. "I dunno, I'm speaking out of turn."

"Oh, come on, Racko," one of the younger sailors said, "you can't stop once you've started."

Racko sighed, pushed back his cap with his intact hand, and took another drink. "All right. Miss, I'm sorry for what I have to tell you, but it's the honest truth. Your sister had every man in this port under her spell at one time or other."

"So she was a whore?" Jane asked, playing the hurt perfectly.

"No, that's not what I meant. I meant 'spell' literally." He took another drink and this time looked up at the ceiling before he said, "She was a witch."

Silence fell over the table. In the back of the room something crashed, and I heard the grunts of a close-in fight. No one, including the men with Jane, paid any mind. They all stared at Racko, waiting for more.

At last Jane asked meekly, "Are you sure?"

Racko pulled out a pipe and packed it. Another man passed him a burning stick from the nearby hearth so he could light it. One thing about sailors: they respected a good storyteller. Everyone waited patiently, an island of calm and silence in the crowded tavern, while Racko got his thoughts in order.

At last Racko looked directly at Jane. "Do ye know the tale of how your sister got her name?"

I tensed. The old man was testing Jane's story before beginning his own.

"No. My parents barely spoke of her."

That wasn't good enough for Racko. "Seems odd they wouldn't tell you."

"Not if you knew them," Jane said, her tone conveying secret knowledge of her mythical parents.

"Either swim or drown, Racko," another man said.

"Yeah, you got us all wound up, now drop anchor and offload your tale," another added.

Racko sighed and took a long drag from the pipe. "All right, here's the tale. Seems her parents—*your* parents—were coming to Watchorn Harbor on a merchant ship when they were captured by pirates. Old Captain Cloche, to be specific. Ever heard of him?"

Jane shook her head.

"The fright affected your mother, and she had the baby even as the pirates were taking the ship. When Cloche saw the woman had just given birth to a daughter, he told her that he'd release the ship with no harm done if she'd name the girl after his own long-lost mother. So they did. And that's how your sister got the name Brandywine."

Jane began to silently cry, and smiled through the tears. "Thank you, sir. I didn't know that story." She dabbed her eyes. "But please, what of Brandywine when she worked here?"

I fought the eye roll that built in my head. *What of Brandy-wine?* Jane was laying it on thick.

Again Racko took a puff before continuing. "Your sister never suffered for attention. I know, because I tried to catch her eye, too. I was old enough to be her father, but many seafaring men had young wives. She was kind to me, but she made it clear I wasn't the one for her. She treated us all equally, and kept us at an equal distance. Look all you want, but don't touch, she said with her eyes."

"So she wasn't a whore," one of the young sailors said, trying to follow the subtleties.

"No, she wasn't," Racko agreed. "But she used herself to gain favor and fortune, just the same. A beautiful girl can get a drunken sailor to do pretty much anything, including part with his gold and make him glad he did it. Some say she used more than her beauty, as well."

"I can't believe she was a witch," Jane said.

Racko blew a puff of smoke at the ceiling. "Perhaps not. Beauty is its own witchcraft. But in either case, one day it didn't matter any longer. Because *he* walked in."

"Who?" another sailor asked.

"He was young, handsome as the very devil who makes the tides, and she saw at once he was the one. Everyone else knew it, too. They fell for each other with a crash that could be heard for miles. At first we all thought he was just another sailor, but in time we learned the truth." Again he paused for a puff. He sure knew how to hold an audience. "He was Black Edward Tew."

The sailors exchanged glances. Jane played dumb. "Who?"

"Black Edward, the pirate?" one of the younger men asked.

"Aye," said Racko. "The very one."

"Did he . . . kill her?" Jane asked, her voice trembling.

Racko smiled without humor. "Hardly. He wasn't yet a pirate when he arrived, but he was hers from the moment their eyes met. They set up in a cottage out on the dunes. Everyone knew they weren't married, but they carried on like they were, if you get my meaning. Then one day, he was gone."

"Where?" another sailor asked.

"Back to the sea, to find his fortune," Racko said. He patted his stomach. "But he left something behind here in Watchorn."

I was in mid-sip, and almost poured ale all over myself. Angelina kept a lot of her past hidden, but at no point had she ever mentioned *children*. She was the least maternal woman I knew.

"She had a child?" Jane asked, and her surprise was also genuine.

Racko nodded. "A son. The spitting image of his father, too, so there was no doubt who sired him. But I'm getting ahead of my story. Brandy continued to live at the cottage alone, but she had to come into town eventually, and by then there was no hiding her condition. Watchorn was a lot more strict back then, when the Captain's Federation still had power. They liked all the improprieties out of sight, including barmaids knocked up by passing sailors. But she paraded about with no shame at all. So she was arrested and thrown in jail."

"Wait, they locked her up just for being pregnant?" one of the young men asked.

Racko smiled. "It was a different time, lad. A woman living out there alone was suspicious enough. The Captain's Federation, especially the Wives' Auxiliary, had a low opinion of women not legally bound to a man. But to be so brazen as to publicly carry a child without a husband, that just couldn't be tolerated. Next thing you know, women would be owning businesses and commanding ships."

A couple of the younger men chuckled nervously, watching Jane's reaction. She just listened.

"As I said, I don't know if she was a witch," Racko said. "I suppose it's possible Black Edward would've turned pirate anyway, whether he'd met her or not. But the fact remains he was an honest seaman before, and a notorious blackguard after. Make of that what you will."

"So did she die in jail?" Jane asked timorously.

"No, she didn't stay in jail. The rumor was that her witchcraft was so powerful, no cell could hold her. But I think it was more likely that the warden's deputies—young men, sailors who through accident or inclination no longer wished to serve the sea—simply felt sorry for her and kept letting her slip out. The Federation, of course, insisted she cast spells on the lads, and the boys probably went along with it to keep their jobs. She escaped three times, and each time she returned to her cottage. She was terrified of being taken away from the sea before Black Edward returned. And then she had the baby."

He stopped, swallowed the last of his ale, and raised the mug for a refill. A harried young woman saw him, nodded, and went to fetch a jug.

"Oh, come on, there has to be more," someone prompted.

"Not really," Racko said. "She gave the baby to a local couple who did all they could with him, but he was his father's son in more than just looks. Black Edward never returned, although there's not a sailor who doesn't know how he met *his* end."

"I heard he's not dead at all," a young man said.

"Aye, the mate on my last ship said he saw him once, years after he supposedly died."

"Probably another one of his bastard sons," Racko said dismissively. "I bet they all carry his look, just like Brandy's son does."

"And my sister?" Jane asked with just enough desperation to elicit pity.

"As far as I know, she disappeared after that. I'm sorry I don't have more news. But her son . . ."

Then the noise from the fight in the back grew too loud for me to hear any more of the conversation. Eventually Jane stood, and astoundingly so did all the men around the table. One even pulled back her chair for her. She dabbed her eyes, hugged a couple of them, and went outside. I discreetly followed.

I caught up with her a couple of blocks away. She said, "That was all pretty interesting. Who knew Angelina was so complicated?"

"I overheard a lot of it, except there at the end." I mimicked her high voice. " 'She was my much older sister. I was a sunset baby, you know.' "

"The apple of my parents' dotage." Jane chuckled. "Besides, I'd heard just about enough about how sexy Angie was. Did *you* know that she also had a son?"

"No, first I've heard of it. I wonder if Tew ever knew about his child? Or cared?"

Jane stopped, looked around to make sure no one on the crowded street was eavesdropping, and leaned close to me. "I don't know about that, but I *do* know something about the boy," she said with a triumphant little grin. "He's all grown up, he's the spitting image of his father, and he still lives here."

"In Watchorn?"

Still grinning, she nodded. "And I know where to find him."

The next morning, after a night in an inn better suited for livestock (yes, we shared a room, but I slept on the floor), we set out to find the bastard son of Black Edward Tew.

Well, Jane had slept; I lay awake most of the night pondering the day's events. Mostly I wondered why Angelina had not mentioned the fact that a child was involved in all this. I had no firsthand knowledge, of course, but it seemed to me that giving birth was the kind of event that would stick with you, whether or not you gave the kid away. So why didn't she mention it? Did she think I wouldn't find out about him?

I didn't put any stock in the witchcraft talk. Sailors in general saw magic and omens in everything, and this was no different. Besides, in all the time I'd known her, Angie had never expressed any sympathy for either the belief in or practice of magic. She was a thoroughly down-to-earth woman.

But there was an inherent contradiction in the two stories, Angelina's and Racko's, that I couldn't resolve. Angie claimed that her Edward became a pirate on his own; Racko said she pushed him into it. She also didn't mention that he'd become famous—Black Edward was the kind of nickname you got only when a lot of people knew about you. The difference might not ultimately matter, but discrepancies always got my attention, and when added to Angelina's serious omission of her son, it made me wonder what else she might have left out, or tweaked to her own benefit.

And unrelated to all this was something that nagged me, another discrepancy that I couldn't coax to the front of my brain. I let it go for the moment; I had enough to worry about.

In the street outside, someone drunkenly began a song, and in moments an impromptu chorus had formed.

Ashore in Boscobel, a lady I did meet,
With her baby in her arms as she strolled down the street,
And I thought how when I sailed, the cradle stood all ready,
And how my lovely little son has never seen his daddy.

I rolled onto my side and closed my eyes.

"THAT'S him, huh?" I said.

"Must be," Jane said. "This is where they said we'd find him. Duncan Tew, part-time farmer and full-time ne'er-do-well. Nobody expects much from him, him being the bastard son of a witch and a pirate, and by all accounts, he lives up to those expectations."

We sat on our horses in the shade of a pine tree and watched a young man wrestle with an ox and plow. He was tall and narrow-shouldered, with black wavy hair tied at the nape of his neck. At this distance I couldn't tell anything else about him, except that he wasn't a very good farmer. The soil was little more than shallow half sand suited for growing only the tough grass that anchored the dunes near the water. You couldn't see the ocean from here, but the farm was well within its reach for wind and storms. Trying to get crops to take hold here was a real exercise in futility, and from the looks of his pitiful results, Duncan Tew was well aware of that.

"Not exactly the revelation I expected," Jane said.

"No, but we can at least talk to him. He might know something about his father. Orphans get curious. And persistent. Maybe he's already done a lot of our legwork."

"You're the boss, boss." Then she added, "There he goes."

The boy walked away from ox and plow without bothering even to unhitch the animal. The ox bellowed its annoyance. Tew kicked at the ground as he strode across the field toward a small cottage, where smoke trailed from a chimney. His bellowed curses were loud enough to reach us.

"That sounds like Angie, all right," Jane said.

I said, "Let's go."

The cottage was as well put together as the field was plowed. Beside it, a ramshackle stone ring and a bucket on a frayed rope indicated a well. The lower walls of what had once been a barn loomed jaggedly from a patch of high weeds. Chickens pecked at the grass and a skinny dog saw us, growled once, and skulked away. The lone flower pot beside the cottage steps, its blue blossoms waving in the wind, seemed both pitiful and somehow noble.

Then we heard the screaming inside.

A man said, "You call that breakfast? Starving pigs would run away from this!"

"Yeah, well, I can't make a chef's salad with nothing but the moss and rocks you manage to raise, you know!" replied a female voice.

"You couldn't make a chef's salad with the chef standing over you!"

Something breakable crashed inside. A baby began to cry.

Jane laughed. "They sound like me and Miles, only in reverse. And without the baby."

"Miles cooks?"

"He does if he knows what's good for him. I can burn boiled water."

"Is he any good?"

"Not a damn bit, but he does it on purpose, because he thinks it'll make me stop asking him to do it." She dismounted, strode up to the door, and pounded on it. "Hey! Duncan Tew!"

There was silence; then the door opened and the young man peered out. He had a strong jaw, cleft chin, and striking blue eyes. His patchy immature stubble was the same color as his black hair. He looked no older than twenty, which made him the right age.

His glare was not encouraging. "Who the fuck are you? What do you want?"

"Is that one of your other girlfriends?" the woman's voice taunted from inside. "She here to tell you she's carrying another of your bastards?"

"Leave the kids out of it!" he yelled over his shoulder. Then to us he said, "And you two, whoever you are, get out of here."

"Sorry for interrupting," I said. "We'd like to talk about your parents."

"I got no parents," he snapped, and was about to close the door. Jane stepped forward and blocked it. "Get out of my face, bitch," he warned.

Jane laughed. Then with one hand she grabbed a handful of his tunic and yanked him bodily out the door. She tossed him head over heels onto his back in the bare-dirt yard. The chickens scattered in clucking outrage. He rolled onto his stomach and tried to push himself up, but she put a boot on the back of his neck. She said, "You've got a lot to learn about talking to a lady."

"Hey, you! Get off him!" A small, wiry girl stood in the doorway, a baby on one hip and a paring knife in her free hand. She was barely out of childhood herself, but life had already aged her.

Jane drew her sword and leveled it at the girl. It was almost as long as she was tall, and the blade did not waver. Sunlight reflected a vertical bar across the girl's face.

"Best thing for you and your snot factory there is to go back inside and shut the door," Jane said coolly. "The light of your life won't get hurt if he starts behaving." She twisted her foot for emphasis. "And you're going to behave, right?"

"Yeah!" he snarled through the dirt.

Jane stepped back and, still holding her sword ready, said, "Get up."

He did so slowly, head down, spitting dirt from his lips. He brushed the front of his tunic. He glared at me and said, "Your wife's a bitch."

"Why does everyone think we're married?" Jane asked, and winked at me.

Tew stumbled to the well, drew up the bucket, and poured it over his head. He sputtered as it washed away the dirt. Without looking at us, he said, "Just so you know, my real mother died when I was born, and I never knew my real father. So you got me muddy for nothing, and you wasted your own time."

"Who told you your mother died?" I asked as I climbed down from my horse.

"What the fuck difference does it make?"

"Manners, hot stuff," Jane said warningly.

He sighed and nodded. "The dog under the porch, who do you think? The folks who raised me."

"What did they tell you about your father?"

He turned the bucket over, sat on it, and glared up at us from under wet strands of hair. "Why do you care?"

"We're looking for someone."

"My dad?"

"Maybe."

"He was a pirate who fucked my mom and left her to deal with the consequences. Or, if you take the other side, she was a witch who made a nice young sailor turn to piracy to keep her in gold and jewels. It's for damn sure everyone in Watchorn believes one story or the other. Doesn't make a difference to me."

"Yeah, you're a no-good bastard either way," the girl said, and slammed the door.

Tew laughed harshly. "Guess that makes it unanimous."

I held out a coin. "If you know anything else, I'm willing to pay for it."

Jane shook her head at me. "Where do you keep getting those? Do you pull them out of your ass?"

I ignored her and waited for Tew's reaction. He stared at the coin like a bird hypnotized by a snake, seeing the possibilities in it. He said, "They tell me my father was Black Edward Tew. People who knew him say I look just like him. It doesn't make it easy around here."

Jane asked, "Why do you stay?"

"I got my reasons," he muttered.

"Do you have any idea," I asked, "where your father is?"

Before he could answer, a small boy emerged from the back of the house, brandishing a sharpened stick. He was barefoot, dressed in tattered clothes, and looked maybe five years old. "Twouble, Dad?" he said, staring fearlessly at us.

Immediately Tew's whole demeanor changed. He sat up straight and said calmly, "No, son, just visitors. C'mere." The boy eased over, keeping the sharp end of his stick pointed our way. "This is my son, Sido. Say hello, son."

"Hi," the boy said flatly.

Tew kissed the boy's dirty cheek. "I'll be done here in a minute. Go back inside and finish your lunch, okay?"

"You sure you don't need me?" Sido asked seriously.

Tew smiled. "I probably do, but you need your lunch more so you can be big and strong. I'll be along, don't worry."

The boy went back inside through the front door, giving us his best tough-guy look the whole way. When he was gone, Tew said, "No need for him to see you kill me, is there?"

"We're not here to kill you," Jane said.

"Then what do you want?"

"Anything you know about your father," I said, and waved the coin for emphasis. "Like we keep saying."

"And his treasure," Jane added. I stared javelins at her.

"I don't suppose he ever stops by for a father–son chat when he's in port?" I asked.

Tew laughed. "Yeah, sure. He brings me presents from all over the world. One day I'll sail as his first mate."

I fought not to smile. His sarcasm sounded just like his mother. "What about the Dirnay family? Do you know them?"

"Is this a trick question?" he snapped. When I didn't answer, he said, "They're the jerks who raised me. Look, I got nothing to add. Neither one of my parents stuck around to change my diapers or watch my first steps or teach me a goddamn thing." He stood, adjusted his clothes, and with as much dignity as he could muster, said, "And you can shove that money back where she said you found it."

With that, he went inside and slammed the door. The bar slid into its slot across it.

Jane chuckled. "That was pointless."

"No, it wasn't." I put the coin on the middle of the top step, careful to avoid the smeared manure. "We know what Edward Tew looks like now."

"We do?"

"Junior in there didn't get that cleft chin and blue eyes from Angelina."

"Wonder what he did get?"

"Definitely the warmth," I said as I got back on my horse.

Jane laughed as she did the same. "So now what, boss?"

"Your friend Racko sounded pretty sure Black Edward was dead. He implied it was a well-known story."

"Some of the other guys disagreed."

"Yeah. I think we need to find a more reliable source."

She chuckled. "A more reliable source for pirate gossip?"

"Pirate *history*. I want to know what happened to Black Edward and why some people think he's dead. There must be a better authority than some drunks in a tavern. Maybe the Society of Scribes, or some royal archivist somewhere."

Jane looked down thoughtfully. "There is. It's a bit of a ride, but we don't seem to be in a hurry."

"Who?"

She said in a whisper, "The Sea Hawk."

I repeated, "Who?"

She snorted at my lack of knowledge. "You land crabs. I mean *Rody* Hawk. Captain Hawk of the *Poison*."

I knew *that* name, all right, and it sent a rush of apprehension up my spine. I'd heard all the stories about this particular scourge of the seas, and if only a fraction of them were true, Hawk was the worst of the worst. "I thought he was dead, too."

"See? You can't trust any stories about a pirate's death. Rody Hawk has enough treasure hidden to buy Langlade and most of Algoma for dessert. He's in prison in Shawano until he tells where it is, or dies, whichever comes first."

"How do you know so much about him?"

She grinned triumphantly. "Because I'm the one who *caught* him."

chapter

FIVE

Shawano was six days' ride from Watchorn. For a guy looking for a pirate, I was spending an awful lot of time in the saddle.

Two nights we stayed at inns, but the rest we camped along the way. The third night I spotted another fire behind us, and crept back to check it out. Granted, it could have been anyone who happened to be going the same way, but the hackles on my neck told me otherwise. By the time I got there, the fire was out and the camp abandoned. Whoever it was didn't show themselves again.

The prison outside Mosinee, capital city of Shawano, was known as "the pirates' graveyard," because if a pirate was captured and not executed, he ended up here. After a few weeks in this facility, most pirates would welcome being hanged, their tarred corpses displayed as a warning. The prison was smack in the middle of a stretch of desert, isolated by a range of low mountains. On the other side of these slopes stretched miles of verdant countryside leading down to Mosinee and the ocean. Here, though, there was nothing but heat, dryness, and death. For a man of the sea, there could be no closer approximation to hell.

Only one road led to the pirates' graveyard, and it ran straight across the open desert. This made sense tactically, since no one could approach without being seen. I'd picked up a wide-brimmed straw hat for the occasion, but this early in the morning, it wasn't needed. Some weird weather inversion had drawn moisture across the mountains and bathed the area in a heavy mist. It wouldn't last, but while it did, the temperature was almost pleasant.

Queen Remy of Mosinee led the international coalition that supported and funded the Anti-Freebootery Guild. Her goal was to make it more lucrative for these sea bandits to turn honest than to keep raiding ships, and it worked for a lot of them. I didn't know the exact circumstances that turned Jane from pirate to pirate hunter, but she became as legendary fighting on the right side as she had on the wrong. I also didn't know what had caused her to leave the sea entirely and turn land-bound sword jockey, but I could accept that none of it was my business. She never asked where I'd come from, either.

The prison walls were twenty feet high, with guards stationed at each corner. The only thing that rose higher was a single round tower, stretching into the mist so that we couldn't see the top. Jane looked up at the tower and sighed wistfully.

"Sentimental about prison?" I teased.

"About my old job. Rody Hawk was the toughest son of a

bitch I ever crossed blades with. When they sent me out to find him, I almost peed my pants, both because I was excited and because it scared me to death. For the first three weeks I hunted him, I was afraid he might be a ghost, the way he'd appear and disappear, like he was taunting me. Which he was."

She'd shared many stories of the man known as "the Sea Hawk" on our ride. By the time she finished, I was really glad they were about a man who was locked up. "He knew you were after him?"

"He knew *everything* about me," she said distantly, then came back to the moment. "He was a mean bastard anyway, but he got much worse when he heard I was after him. Like he was trying to pack in all the evil he could while he still had time."

"Really?" I said. Jane wasn't above a little self-aggrandizement, but something in her tone told me she wasn't doing that here. Her intensity sounded almost religious.

"Yeah. I found one ship he'd hit, a little merchant vessel carrying settlers along with a cargo of rum. He killed the crew, then tied all the civilian men together around the mast. He hung the women and children by their ankles and drilled tiny little holes in their foreheads, so they'd rain blood down on their husbands and fathers. We heard the screams across the water before we even sighted the sails." She shook her head. "Not many of the hanging ones lived. And a lot of the men forced to watch died by their own hand before we reached port."

"I'm glad you finally caught him," I agreed. We were close enough now to see the archers along the wall, and the long curves of their bows. They watched us with the silent composure of men secure in their profession.

Jane said, "Do you know what the hardest thing about catching him was, though?"

"What?"

"Leaving him alive when I had him under my sword."

I knew that feeling for sure. The fact that she *did* leave him alive reinforced my opinion of her. "And now where do they keep him?"

She pointed at the tower. "Up there. Permanently. No way in, no way out, and no visitors until he tells where his treasure's hidden, or dies."

"Then how do we talk to him?"

"Don't worry," she said. But she didn't explain.

We tied our horses to the empty hitching post outside the gate. Behind us, only our tracks disturbed the sand. I couldn't imagine they got many visitors. A guard in leather armor watched us through the gate's thick iron bars.

"Hey, Louie," Jane said as she shook dirt and sand from her cape. "How's tricks?"

"Same as always, Captain Argo," Louie the guard said. He spoke to her but kept his eyes on me.

"I'm not a captain anymore, Louie, just a plain Jane. But we *are* here to see the Hawk."

Louie pondered this. "I'll have to get the warden."

"You do that," she said.

The whole area was silent, except for a lone crow cawing somewhere in the mist overhead. Given the absence of trees, it must nest somewhere on the grounds. I asked quietly, "You ever been in prison?"

"Nope. If I get arrested, I try not to stick around for the trial."

"Me, neither." I'd been in jail on occasion, but never served a real sentence. Standing here in this ghostly silence, I suddenly wondered if I'd be man enough to handle it. I hoped never to find out.

Louie returned with another man, this one in an official uniform. "Good morning, Captain Argo," the newcomer said. "I hadn't heard you were coming."

"There wasn't time to send a message ahead. Hope that's okay."

"Well, we do have protocols for visiting the prisoners, especially *him*."

"I know. I came up with them, remember?"

"I do, but it puts me in an awkward position."

Jane leaned casually on the iron bars. "Warden, really. You think I'm here to bust him out?"

"I think we have rules for a reason, Captain."

"She's not a captain anymore, sir," Louie said helpfully.

"That's true," Jane agreed. "I'm just here to visit a friend."

The warden smiled a little. "So he's your friend now, is he?"

Jane laughed. "Warden, in some ways I'm closer to Rody Hawk than to just about anybody else in the world."

The warden nodded at me. "Including him?"

I stepped forward. "Eddie LaCrosse. I'm a business associate of ex-Captain Argo."

"Warden Jim Delvie," he said as we shook hands through the bars. It was firm enough, but the skin was smooth. The warden had been pushing a quill so long that any sword calluses had faded.

"Warden, either let us in or send us on our way," Jane said

impatiently. "Which in my case will be straight to the court of Queen Remy to get permission to visit the Hawk. You know she'll give it to me. And you know what she'll say when I explain why I have to bother her with it."

The warden thought this over, then turned to Louie. "Open up."

"Yes, sir," Louie said.

Through the gate there was nothing but more open space around the main jail building and celebrity tower. The ground was hard and cracked, with no grass anywhere. The building rose only one floor above the ground, well below the top edge of the outer walls. Most of its cells were deep under the hard-packed earth.

Jane turned to me. "So who talks to him, me or you?"

"We can't both do it?"

"No. Only one of us. Less risk that way."

"Risk of what?"

"He has this knack of turning people against each other."

I looked up at the tower, or at least the part of it not hidden in the mist. "I suppose I should do it. It's my case, after all."

"Are you sure? I know him."

"I'm sure."

She grinned. "You want to be able to tell Liz that you met Rody Hawk, is that it?"

I ignored the dig and looked at Delvie. The warden asked, "So who's it going to be?"

"Me," I said.

Delvie and Jane exchanged a look I couldn't interpret. He asked her, "Are you all right with this?"

She shrugged. "He's paying me, so he's the boss."

The warden turned to me. "Have you had any prior dealings with Captain Hawk?"

"No."

That seemed to satisfy him, if barely. "Follow me, please."

He led us to the base of the tower. As we crossed the courtyard, a door opened in the main building and six pale, grimy men chained together at the neck were marched out by an equal number of guards. The prisoners were naked, but their bodies were so filthy, I first thought they wore black pajamas. Their smell stayed behind long after they'd disappeared around the corner.

"Monthly cell block washdown," the warden explained. "They get rinsed off, then they clean their own cells."

One of the prisoners turned and looked at us. His face was long and thin, and one eye socket was puckered shut. There seemed very little humanity left in his gaze, just the numb survival instinct of a clever animal.

When we reached the base of the tower, Delvie gestured at something on the ground. "Well, here we are. Your chariot to the clouds."

A wooden basket about three feet across rested there, attached by a rope to a pulley mounted, I assumed, at the edge of the tower's roof. I looked at it, then at the warden, then at Jane. She bit her lip and looked down to keep from laughing.

"This is how we get his food up to him," the warden said. "If you want to talk to him, it's the only way up." He turned to Louie. "Go get some men to help lift this. A dozen would be good. Check the break room."

"Yes, sir," Louie said, and went into the main building.

I continued to look at Jane. "You've got to be kidding. It's a picnic basket."

With mock camaraderie, Jane punched me in the arm and said, "Come on, Eddie, you're not afraid of heights, are you?"

"No, but I'm a lot bigger than a loaf of bread."

"It'll hold you."

"Says you."

"No, she's right," Delvie assured me. "The balance is a little tricky, but it should bear your weight just fine."

"Do I sit in it?"

"You're better off standing."

"Fine," I said, making no effort to hide my annoyance. Jane could've mentioned this earlier.

"You sure you don't want me to do it?" she said.

"No, damn it," I muttered.

"I'll need your sword," the warden said. "And all your other weapons. And anything that might remotely be used as a weapon."

"I'm not going to hurt him," I said.

Delvie stepped close. I could smell his morning tea on his breath. He said, "We used to send a guard up with the food, in case he cracked and started blabbering. This was back when we seriously thought he might tell us where his treasure was hidden. For a year, nothing happened. Then one day Hawk yanked him out of the basket and held him against the window bars. He threw the guard's sword down, impaling another guard, then killed another with the first guard's crossbow. One-handed, mind you, while still supporting the guard's weight with the other arm. Then he dropped the man to his death." He pointed at a spot on the hard-packed ground that was darker than the surrounding dirt. "He landed right there. You can see that the stain still hasn't worn off."

"The point is, he could've done it at any time," Jane added. "He just picked that day, and that guard. He never said why. So now no one ever sees him. They just send up his food."

"Then how do you know he's even still up there?"

"The basket always comes down empty." He paused, stepped even closer to me, and said in a grim whisper, "Hawk's been called many things over the years, but you know what captures him best, in my opinion? That he's simply a shiver looking for a spine to run up. If you still wish to see him, then I won't stop you."

I looked into the mist. I wondered if Hawk could hear us discussing his exploits. More important, how would I convince him to help me if he didn't want to? What could I possibly offer him? I hadn't put any thought into that.

"You could keep a bigger basket around, you know," I pointed out as I unbuckled my sword belt. "For special occasions."

"I'll mention that at the next budget meeting," the warden said. Louie returned with the requested men, all of whom looked at me with a mix of respect and suspicion. They were big men, with the scars of former battles on their bare arms and faces. I suspected they were also one moral slip away from becoming inmates themselves. Luckily, all I needed them to do was have firm grips and strong backs.

"Yank the rope twice when you're ready to come down," the warden said.

As I started to step into the basket, Jane said, "The knife in your boot, too."

I glared at her. That knife had saved my life more than any other weapon I owned. But as I withdrew it, I suddenly knew what I could offer Hawk that might make him cooperate.

"Ow!" Jane cried. "What was that for?"

"Something to keep my courage up," I said. She took my knife and tucked it into her belt. I enjoyed her annoyed scowl.

I put one foot in the basket, then the other. The ropes from each corner joined at a waist-high iron ring, and above that a single rope led to the top of the tower. I grabbed that rope for dear life, the guards pulled, and I began to rise.

Immediately, I nearly fell back and the whole contraption spun as I fought to regain my balance. Jane laughed uproariously.

I rose into the mist. Jane and the guards disappeared below me, and for a few moments I was isolated in the haze, nothing visible above or below. There was absolutely no wind, and the faceless side of the tower made it hard to mark my progress. Only the squeak of the pulley above me, growing louder, assured me I was rising.

I passed a chink in the stonework where a huge black crow, the one I must've heard earlier, sat preening her feathers. She cawed once and regarded me with the same vague suspicion as the guard below. Even the wildlife knew I was doing something stupid.

Eventually the pulley stopped, and I hung in place outside a wide rectangular window. Vertical bars blocked it, and a heavy fishing net hung just inside them, making a double barrier. The room was painted bright white, even down to the window bars. Nothing moved, and of course in a round room, there were no corners to hide in. The combined net and mist made it difficult to see the dim interior, but I stared until I made out a cot, a chamber pot, and something on the floor.

I risked one hand on the bars to steady myself and called out, "Hey! Rody Hawk!"

There was no reply.

I pulled myself closer to the bars. The basket creaked and tilted as my weight shifted.

The sun chose that moment to flicker through the mist and flood the cell with light. The shape on the floor instantly resolved itself.

It was a body.

The man was sprawled on his back. He was tall and slender, with long dark hair, a long beard, and a black eyepatch. He wore white trousers and a loose tunic, with no shoes.

The sun glinted off his exposed eye. It was wide open, and stared at nothing. I'd seen enough lifeless eyes to recognize this one at once.

"Son of a bitch," I muttered. Rody Hawk was dead.

Then a sepulchral voice commanded, "Don't talk about my mother."

I was so startled that I lost my balance and pivoted wildly in the basket. I saw hazy sky, the barred window, then hazy sky again. I grabbed another bar and steadied myself. I looked around the room carefully, but saw no one except the corpse on the floor. There was also no place for anyone to hide. Where the hell had that voice come from?

I risked a look up into the clearing sky. Was someone on the roof? Had it been a ghost? A *god*? At that moment, as the chill sweat ran down my back, anything seemed plausible.

Then the corpse of Rody Hawk sat up and looked right at me with its dead, milk-white eye.

Before I could do anything undignified like scream, the corpse shifted the eyepatch to the other side, uncovering a perfectly good eye and reseating the patch over the useless one. Then he yawned.

I looked down. Thankfully, the mist was still thick enough to hide me from view. If Jane had seen this, I'd never have lived it down.

Rody Hawk shifted into a cross-legged position and looked straight at me. Even with only one eye, it was like he saw right through to the back of my skull. The hairs on my neck tingled. He said, "I don't know you."

"No," I agreed, trying to steady the basket with my trembling legs.

His voice had no identifiable accent. "You're too scruffy to be a new guard. Warden Delvie is a stickler for appearance. And it's not time for my lunch." His eye narrowed and he cocked his head. Hawk was a small, neat man; even his untrimmed hair and beard looked tended. "Are you from the Society of Scribes, then? No, you've brought nothing with which to write. So who are you, my man?"

"Eddie LaCrosse."

"Doesn't ring a bell."

"No reason it should."

"So you must want something."

"I want a lot of things." I managed to find a balanced position with one hand on a bar and the other gripping the rope for dear life. As long as I kept my knees locked, I stayed reasonably still. It did not, however, convey nonchalance. "Not falling out of this basket is at the top of the list."

Hawk smiled. He had small white teeth. "You're not afraid of me."

"Sure I am. You're Rody Hawk. I'd be stupid not to be afraid of you."

He arched his back and threaded his fingers together behind

his head. "I apologize for the fright," he said as he stretched. "Sleeping on that saggy cot has begun to trouble my back. I find alternating with the floor minimizes the discomfort. So what is it that brings you up this high?"

"I'm looking for a pirate."

"You found one. The best, or worst, depending on your perspective. And if my current accommodations are any indication, perhaps I'm both."

"I'm looking for a particular pirate."

"I've been known to be very particular."

"Not to burst your bubble, but I'm looking for one named Black Edward Tew. An old girlfriend wants to know what happened to him."

"And why are you the one doing the looking?"

"I've been hired to."

"A sword jockey?"

I nodded.

"He hasn't been around for years. I've heard he was dead. Why does your client wish to find him now?"

"She's waited as long as she can."

"That's a woman's reason, all right." Hawk closed his eye in apparent thought. At last he said, "I assume you know the story."

"Not really. I've just heard contradictory hints."

"And so you thought of me?"

I shrugged. I didn't want to mention Jane, or my bribe for him, unless I had to. "You're the first guy lots of people think of when they hear the word *pirate*."

"How flattering. Well, I get so few visitors, I suppose it would be rude of me to send you packing. So you want the story of

Black Edward Tew, eh? Here's the tale as I know it. Edward Tew was a common sailor on merchant vessels, content with his lot, until one day he met a girl in a tavern. I don't know the particulars, and I've heard it told both ways: either she turned him pirate to keep her in jewels, or he turned pirate on his own to impress her. I suppose ultimately only the two of them know what really passed between them. At any rate, shortly thereafter, he signed onto a new ship, and while it was at sea, he led a mutiny. The captain was killed, the loyalists set adrift, and the ship rechristened the *Bloody Angel*. Always liked that name. And young Edward Tew became Black Edward, novice scourge of the waterways."

I was aware of Hawk's horrible deeds, his fearsome reputation, and the fact that if he really applied himself, he could probably kill me before I saw it coming. Yet it was hard not to smile. He had an easygoing air that implied his prison stay was little more than a weekend inconvenience. *Don't forget what he is, LaCrosse,* I told myself, *or what he's capable of.*

"Up to that point, it could have been the story of a thousand pirates, including myself," Hawk continued. "But now comes the miraculous part. King Clovis of Witigan built a new castle far from his old one, and the quickest way to move his treasure to it was by sea. Only the good king outsmarted himself. He put together an intimidating fleet, all right: a dozen Witiganian warships guarded the single massive vessel on which everyone assumed he'd put his treasure. But in reality, he put it on a plain merchant ship leaving three days later, which is what Black Edward unknowingly captured as his first victim. Imagine his surprise when he saw the biggest single treasure in recorded history lying before him."

"I bet he smiled."

"I'd have pissed myself. So Edward immediately headed back for his woman. But a storm came up and sank his ship within sight of his destination. All hands lost, save one to tell the tale. As luck would have it, there's a huge trench there, far too deep for any diver, and there lies Black Edward's treasure, intact but untouchable. They say."

"In my experience, 'they' aren't always that reliable. Convenient there was one survivor. Who was he?"

"The quartermaster. A thoroughly unscrupulous worm of a man."

"You knew him?"

"He tried to sign aboard the *Poison,* but he was more trouble than he was worth. He told me that the tale of Black Edward's demise was a lie, that in fact the treasure was hidden on an island and the whole sinking of the *Bloody Angel* was a ruse."

"You didn't believe him?"

"I wouldn't believe him if he said the sun rose in the east."

"So you never checked his story."

"No."

"What was his name?"

He smiled. "You're the kind of man I could drink with, Mr. LaCrosse. If they let me have drinks here, that is. You assume that since I'm sitting up here desperate for company, that I might break my oath to the Brotherhood of the Surf. Grand Article Number Four: 'No brother will ever betray another to the forces of law and order.'"

"No, I don't think you're desperate. And I'd never ask for information without offering to pay."

Now he laughed. "Mr. LaCrosse, look around. Even if you

were planning to share Black Edward's lost treasure, it would do me no good. So what can you possibly have to trade that I could use?"

Before I could reply, Hawk looked up sharply. He said, "Wait a moment. You didn't know that the *Bloody Angel*'s quartermaster crossed my path, did you? No, you didn't. So why did you come to me, Mr. LaCrosse? Not just because I'm old enough that I might remember." I could almost hear the gears in his brain clicking as he puzzled it through. "You came to see me because . . ." His smile grew broad. "Jane. You're here with Jane."

He stood, a liquid motion that seemed almost inhumanly swift. I jumped. He came toward me, and despite the net and bars between us, I said, "Like I said, Hawk, I'm scared of you. Stay right there or I'll leave."

He stopped and held up his hands. "Of course. So is Jane down below? Hiding beneath the fog?"

"Jane doesn't do much hiding. She's working for me on this, so I wanted to do the asking."

"And now you want the name. But there's still the question about why I would do that. Money doesn't do me much good here." He scratched at his beard. "So what can you possibly have to trade to make me betray a fellow brother of the surf?"

I reached into my pocket, careful to make no sudden moves; I didn't want to startle Hawk, or send myself into another uncontrolled spin. I removed the thing I had claimed below, just before I handed over my boot knife.

He made no move to take it, but his eye never left it. "Is that—?"

"It is."

He extended his hand.

I pulled mine back. "First the name."

He was silent for a long moment. I felt the first stirrings of wind, and the crow below me cawed as if to welcome it. "All right. His name was Marteen, I believe. Wendell Marteen. The last I heard of him, he tried to captain a ship of his own off the Fussell Islands, but he was considered bad luck for surviving the *Bloody Angel*'s sinking."

The initials, at least, matched those of the sole survivor mentioned in the official Watchorn records. "Bad luck for surviving?"

"Sailors are a superstitious lot, and their superstitions don't always make sense. I assumed that was why he made up the tale that the *Bloody Angel* had been deliberately scuttled. Time, I think, has given the lie to that story. After all, if Black Edward were still alive, could he truly sit on a treasure of that magnitude for twenty years?"

"Where can I find Marteen?"

He shrugged. "I'm not in the loop, as they say. No doubt many things have changed since my incarceration. For all I know, he rots in one of the cells below us. That would be ironic, wouldn't it? If that's not the case, I would look in the Southern Ocean, where the pirates are common. He never struck me as the type to explore new horizons."

"All right. Thanks." Then I held out the treasure that had made him cooperate: a lock of Jane Argo's hair.

The net caught his fingers as he slowly reached through the bars. He took the curl from my outstretched hand. He stepped back, carefully maneuvered the lock through the netting, and held it close to his good eye. "Well, I'll be damned. Thank you, Mr. LaCrosse."

"My pleasure. And actually, I do have one more question."

He continued to gaze at the lock of hair. "And it is—?"

"They say you killed a guard for no reason. Is that true?"

He broke his attention away from the curl. "What? No, not at all. I had a reason."

"What was it?"

"He talked about my mother." Then he smiled.

I had to fight surprisingly hard not to as well. "Any message for Jane?"

He looked at me with that one crystal-clear eye, and for an instant I glimpsed the ice-cold consciousness behind it. I was really glad I didn't have to face him across swords. I wondered how Jane had managed to do it.

"Yes," he said at last. "Tell her . . . 'Someday.'"

"'Someday.' A threat?"

"A date."

I nodded, and yanked the rope twice. Hawk said, "Fair wind and following seas to you," and turned away from the window before I lowered out of sight.

DESCENDING through the mist was like leaving some alien place where evil gods lived and returning to the normal world. I stepped out of the basket and leaned against the wall. My heart felt like it was searching for a space between my ribs big enough to jump through.

Jane said, "So did he tell us—?"

Without looking, I held up my hand. I wasn't up to the challenge of Jane's jocularity.

"Sorry," she said. "When you're ready."

At last my brain stopped swimming, and the clammy feeling faded. I took a deep breath and blew it out slowly, then faced everyone. The guards who'd been on basket-lifting detail didn't meet my eyes. The warden's expression was unreadable, but Jane gave me a surprisingly sympathetic smile. "You look like you've seen a ghost."

"No," I said, "just a monster."

"So did he help you?"

"Yeah. We have a name. Wendell Marteen. Hawk says he was Edward Tew's quartermaster, and survived the sinking of the *Bloody Angel*," I said. "If he's still around—"

"He is," the warden said.

"Don't tell me he's here," I said.

"No, but it's funny you should mention that. He just returned to the active list about a year ago."

"Queen Remy has a list of wanted pirates," Jane explained. "They consider it a badge of honor to be on it. Probably not the effect Remy had in mind."

"Probably not." I turned to the warden. "You said he's 'just returned'?"

"Yes. Nobody had heard a peep out of him for over a decade, and now suddenly he's back. Took at least three cargo ships in the Southern Ocean off Fussell."

The watery feeling finally left my legs, and I could breathe normally. "Then I guess we'll have to go find him, right?"

"You're the boss, boss," Jane said.

We thanked the warden, and I retrieved my sword and boot knife. We untied our horses outside the prison gate and re-mounted them. The sun and breeze had eliminated the mist, and I could see the white window bars at the top of Rody Hawk's tower. I wondered if he was watching. Just the possi-bility made the hairs on my neck rise again.

As we rode I said, "I want a drink. I don't care what kind. Just as long as there's a lot of it."

"Wow, I've never seen you like this," Jane said. "Was it re-ally that bad?"

I desperately wanted to ask her how she'd managed to catch him, let alone take him alive. I suspected, though, that I didn't really want to hear the answer. The way he'd taken the lock of her hair told me a lot of vague things I didn't want made into specifics. "Nah," I said with forced levity. "It was mainly the height."

"I'm a little pissed at you giving him a lock of my hair with-out asking me. I suppose you traded that for information?"

"It was a spur-of-the-moment thing."

"Uh-huh." She looked off into the distance. "Did he have any message for me?"

I recalled his single word for her. I imagined how, if such a word was aimed at me, it would ride in the back of my head for the rest of my life, until it either came true or I died. I said, "No."

"That smug bastard," Jane muttered. "After all we went through together. So what now, boss?"

"I think there's no avoiding it this time," I said. "It's time to raise sail. You go over the mountains to Mosinee and round us up a ship. I'm going to Neceda to give Angelina a progress report. I'll be back in a week."

"You going to stop and see that redhead of yours?"

"If she's there. She might be off working."

Jane grinned. "And you trust her to do that?"

"She ain't Miles," I said as I turned my horse and rode away. I didn't look back to see if she was smiling or not, but as I reached the road, I heard her high laugh on the wind.

I made good time back to Neceda and got there a week later, in the late afternoon.

The tavern was crowded. Both Angelina and Callie worked the floor. Occasionally Angie had hired other girls, but none of them lasted very long; she was not, as you can imagine, an easy woman to work for. She demanded almost superhuman stamina and had no patience with mistakes. Callie succeeded, I always thought, because she never took Angie seriously.

I stood in the door until my eyes adjusted and waited for Angelina to notice me. When she did, she nearly dropped the tray of empty tankards she carried. She quickly regrouped and said, "You're back already?" as if my appearance were worth no more than a raised eyebrow.

"It's an update, not a final report. I need to talk to you alone."

She waved at the full tables. "I'm busy right now."

"Then *take a break*," I said through my teeth. Normally, I wouldn't have been so brusque, but I'd had the whole ride back to stew over the fact that she neglected to mention her son, and who knew what else. I was, to put it mildly, peeved.

She saw it, too. "Okay," she said, and stepped over to catch Callie as she headed out with a fresh round of drinks. The younger waitress listened to Angie, then glared at me.

Upstairs, I closed both doors and gestured for Angelina to have a seat. As she did, I opened the windows to let in some fresh air. I said, "Looks like you need to get Callie some more help."

"She's the only girl in this town who comes in to work, not to snag a new boyfriend."

"What about Minnow Shavers?"

"Are you kidding? She'll be out of town as soon as her father looks away long enough. She can't stand Neceda."

I paused, took a deep breath, and tried to remain calm. Starting off with a rant seemed counterproductive. "Just so we're clear on definitions, Angie, leaving out something really important counts as lying. So you lied to me."

"About what?"

"Your son."

Her expression didn't change, and she said nothing.

"I met him," I added.

She had to lick her lips before speaking. "And . . . how is he?"

"Grown up. And a little bitter," I added wryly.

She continued to look steadily at me. "I didn't realize he'd still be around Watchorn, or I would've mentioned him. I wonder who finally took him in when I left?"

I didn't answer. If she truly didn't know, that tankard of parental worms could wait for another day. "I have to tell you, Angie, I'm awfully close to giving you back your gold and dropping this right now. What else have you left out that might be important?"

"He's the only thing. I really didn't think he'd still be there. Will you think less of me if I say he hardly ever crosses my mind?"

"I'm in no position to judge anyone. That's between you and your conscience."

She said nothing for a long moment. "I can't fix what I did to him. And it was still the best choice out of a pile of bad ones. For him, and for me. I'm sorry he's upset about it, but life's tough for everyone."

Her blithe answer annoyed me, so I pulled out the big sword. "He's a better parent than you, at least."

That took a moment to sink in. "I . . . what?"

"You're a grandmother."

She blinked a few times, then looked down at her hands in her lap. At last she said, "A boy or a girl?"

"One boy. Not sure what the other one is."

"Two?"

"Not much else to do where he is."

She nodded slowly, the way you do when all the implications of something haven't quite registered. "Then I suppose I should—"

"No. Don't do anything. He doesn't want to see you, and his life is chaotic enough. Just file it away under 'Things I should've told Eddie before I sent him off on that wild goose chase.'"

"So are you giving up?"

"You know I'm not. I've already spent enough of your money to feel obligated. And believe it or not, I've got a lead. But I'm telling you now: If I come across any other big secrets like that, I'm packing it in. I won't work for someone who doesn't level with me."

She nodded slowly. "Understandable," she said blankly.

"Goddammit, Angie!" I slapped my desk and she jumped. She stared up at me as if she'd just noticed I was in the room. I'd never seen her like this, all flat and numb. Then again, I'd never imagined her as a mother and a grandmother.

Finally she said, "I'm sorry, Eddie. I've kept things to myself a long time; it goes from being a habit to a lifestyle. So what *have* you found out about Edward?"

"That he was known as Black Edward Tew, and that the *Bloody Angel* sank in a storm off Watchorn Harbor with only one survivor. Supposedly it was loaded with treasure, and he was coming back for you."

She nodded. "I've heard that story, too. But I never met this so-called survivor, and I don't know anyone else who has, either. So there's no proof that his ship sank there, or anywhere."

"No, but he's my sole lead, so I'm going after him. His name's Wendell Marteen. Mean anything to you?"

"I never heard the story told with the same name twice."

"It came from a reliable source."

"Who?"

I shook my head. I didn't want to mention Rody Hawk. He was like a demon you summoned by saying his name out loud, and I didn't want to invoke him here.

"I'm your client," Angelina pressed.

"That means you pay me to do my job, not tell me *how* to

do it. Now, let me ask you again: Is there anything else I need to know before I go back out to look for this guy?"

"No."

"Are you sure?"

She nodded.

I sat heavily in the chair behind my desk. "All right. I'll be heading out again in the morning. I'll be in touch again when I have something to report."

"Do you need any more money?"

"No. If I do, I'll let you know."

She stood. I did not. I said, "People remember you. They said you were a witch."

She smiled. It was the kind of smile that made swords rise on their own. "I was. My spell was that I liked doing things other women didn't. Like being with their men. If those proper ladies had said yes instead of no more often, I'd have been powerless." Then she left without another word.

I sat listening to the muffled sounds of the tavern for a long time, wondering about Angelina's effect on Edward Tew. Had he turned pirate because of her, or had she turned him in spite of himself? And did that really matter, if he was lying dead on the bottom of the ocean?

AFTER Liz showed me how glad she was to see me, we lay in bed and I told her about my adventures so far, once again leaving out Rody Hawk. If I didn't want him manifesting in my office, I sure didn't want him here.

When I finished, she said, "Wow. Angelina's a grandmother. Hell, even picturing her as a mother is hard. Or a cranky aunt. She hates kids."

"Maybe that's why. If every kid reminds you of the one you abandoned, you probably wouldn't want to be around them."

"What about you?"

"Oh, I think she likes me okay."

She tugged on my beard. "No, kids. What about you and kids?"

"They're all right." I hadn't been around many, but they didn't make me nervous like they did some men. I'd found that if you were honest with them, they were pretty much like anyone else, except smaller and with shorter attention spans.

"You ever thought about having any?" Liz asked.

"Who says I don't? I was a wild blade for a long time before I met you."

She chuckled. "If you had kids and knew about it, I'd know, too. You'd be sending them money and making sure they stayed out of trouble."

"Maybe."

She was silent for a moment, then said, "Think we're too old to have any of our own?"

"Yes."

"You're probably right. Tough to squeeze 'em in between my deliveries and your saving the damsels."

I turned on my side to look at her. "Have you been thinking about this much?"

"No, not really. I mean, the time for this was when we were both twenty years younger, right?"

"Yes. Nobody wants their dad to be so old, he could be their grandpa."

"Yeah." She snuggled close, and I kissed the top of her head. I felt her breathing change as she settled in to sleep, but I stayed awake staring at the ceiling. If I found him alive, I wondered how Edward Tew would react when I told him he was a grandfather.

When I finally fell asleep, I dreamed I was on a ship. Two men stood at the wheel: Rody Hawk, and a man with Duncan Tew's jet-black hair whose face I couldn't see. Hawk smiled, pointed at me, and gestured that I should join them. I was terrified down to my toenails and screamed, *"Son of—"*

chapter EIGHT

"—a bitch!"

I snapped wide awake, finishing the curse I'd begun in my sleep. I looked around, momentarily disoriented, then remembered I was on a pirate-hunter ship headed for the Southern Ocean, and had been for two weeks. I tossed the light blanket aside, sat up, and shook my head to clear it.

In my half-awake state I'd just realized something that should have been obvious, and I was astounded at my own idiocy. How had I missed that? It was right in front of me, plain as day, and hadn't registered.

I swung my bare feet off the bed. The wooden deck was damp with condensation, as was my skin. The tiny master's cabin—a closet-sized space located between the much more spacious captain's quarters and the equally claustrophobic one belonging to the purser—had one round window that was essentially useless unless the door was open to allow a cross breeze. Seated on the edge of the bunk, I could touch my forehead to the opposite wall if I leaned far enough. My saddlebags lay beside the door, and my sword rested under my bunk.

I stood, wiped the sweat from my face, and looked around for my tunic. I'd cut the sleeves off my second day at sea; now my face and arms were deep brown, and the crisscross marks of old sword battles stood out pink and white against my new tan. I could've gone shirtless like most of the crew, but I'd discovered over the years that the big scar on my chest, and its matching one on my back, led to lots of questions I'd rather not answer.

I pulled on my trousers and boots, then opened the door. I was still furious. The little cabin boy who generally slept right outside jumped to his feet when he saw me. "Yes, sir!" he exclaimed with a rigid salute.

"At ease," I said as I tied a bandanna around my sweat-matted hair. "Dorsal, is Captain Argo in her cabin?" She'd been given the purser's cabin next to mine.

"No, sir, she went on deck about an hour ago." He had the serious face of a child for whom childhood was not an option. I guessed he was about nine or ten, barefoot and dressed in adult clothes cut down and cinched up to fit him. "I think she's talking to Captain Clift."

"Thanks," I said, and he jumped aside as I went out into the dim hold. A good number of men still slept in the hammocks, as the ship carried a crew twice what was required to operate on a day-to-day basis. Since I was paying for this charter, I was also subsidizing their apparent laziness. I was assured, though, that in battle every man would earn his keep.

The heat was just as oppressive in the hold, but the smells were worse. This was the odor of pirates, all right, and even if they now worked on the right side of the law, they hadn't substantially changed their ways, certainly not their personal hygiene routines. I'd let myself slip a bit, too, but I still managed to wash in vital places every day.

I stopped at the piss barrel. Apparently stale urine did a great job getting blood out of clothes, so everyone contributed; well, except the female crew members, although I wouldn't put it past Jane. I added my allotment, marveling again at how the human nose can eventually get used to any smell. I wondered if I'd ever be able to appreciate a rose or good cooking again.

"Hey, sword jockey," a man said sleepily. One leg dangled off the edge of his cot, and was long enough to rest his bare foot flat on the ground. This was Suhonen, the biggest man aboard, a towering piece of muscle who, I suspected, played dumber than he was. "What's the hurry? We won't hit the Southern Ocean for another two days."

"I just thought of something," I said honestly. I left out *that I should've caught a damn month ago*. No need to advertise my shortcomings.

"Must be some thought to have you busting out like a moray eel," he said. Other heads popped up from hammocks, aroused by the voices and any break in routine.

"Nah, nothing important," I said. I went up the stairs to the main hatch and stood halfway out as I waited for my eyes to adjust to the blinding sun. I heard a voice below me murmur, "Cap'n Jane says he's the most vicious swordsman in Muscodia."

"That's not saying much," someone replied, and I fought not to laugh.

"She also says he took a sword to the heart and lived."

"And *that's* just impossible."

"Did you ever know Cap'n Jane to lie?"

"I never sailed with her before. All I know is what you moony-eyed schoolboys tell me about her."

"Well, call her a liar, wake up a eunuch, so say those of us who *did* sail with her."

I climbed through the main hatch and emerged on deck before I laughed out loud. Instantly the breeze hit me, a rush of clean salt air that felt especially wonderful after passing through the hold. The morning sun was about a hand's-width above the horizon, and the heat had not reached the egg-boiling proportions it would by midday. If this was what it was like at this latitude, I really wasn't looking forward to the heat of the Southern Ocean.

But at the moment, the heat I was most concerned with was my own temper. I looked around the ship that had been my home for the last two weeks, seeking Jane Argo.

Our ship bore the unlikely name *Red Cow*. She was a two-masted schooner eighty feet long and weighing in at about 220 tons. The crew complement was around a hundred. I knew very little about ships, but I did notice that the *Red Cow* sported an extra-long bowsprit, the purpose of which I had yet to discover.

She was a twenty-gunner as well, with five ballistae mounted on either side of the deck, and five more set to fire through ports below. The bolts might not pierce the hull of another ship, but they pierced the crew just fine. They could also grab fast to the other ship's wood and allow the *Red Cow* to winch the two ships together, which was how pirates often secured their prey. Using their own tactic against them was just one of the ironies about the whole pirate-hunter enterprise.

The *Red Cow* was one of the fleet supported by the international coalition known as the Anti-Freebootery Guild, formed forty years ago in an attempt to stop the rampant criminal activity in and around the Southern Ocean ports. At first the various countries that signed the Guild charter used their navies to enforce it, but there were too many language barriers, cross purposes, and old grudges. In the first three years, twice as many naval vessels as pirates were sunk, often at the hands of so-called allies.

Finally someone clever suggested the creation of a special fleet of fast, heavily armed ships designed for the sole purpose of catching, capturing, and returning for trial any and all pirates. Someone even more clever—our old friend Queen Remy—realized that the best ones for the job were former pirates themselves.

So, for the last twenty-five years, the Anti-Freebootery Guild had done an adequate job keeping piracy confined to very specific, well-known areas of the ocean. Why had they not wiped it out entirely? For two reasons: One, pirates were as renewable a resource as corn or whores, and second, if they did wipe it out, the pirate hunters would be unemployed and might return to their old ways.

We'd been at sea for two weeks without encountering any pirates, but no one seemed too concerned. Certainly not the *Red Cow*'s captain; in fact, I had yet to see him concerned about anything.

As my eyes finished adjusting, a new voice said, "Good morning, Captain."

I turned to see Quartermaster Seaton clinging to the port mainsail shrouds. He was like many seconds-in-command I'd known, competent but happy to stay in the background. He had a goatee decorated with little bits of seabird bone, and a fringe of sun-lightened hair around his head. His otherwise bald pate was tanned dark and spotted in places with big moles. His arms sported muscles that looked like leather cords, and were covered with elaborate tattoos from ports all over the world. The captain led the crew, but Seaton made sure they followed his orders. He continued, "How'd you sleep?"

"Mostly on my back," I deadpanned. "Still getting used to the heat. Have you seen Captain Argo?"

He nodded forward. "She's down there jawing with Captain Clift."

I followed his gaze. Jane, clad in billowing trousers and a sleeveless tunic tight enough to let everyone know when she got a chill, stood at the port bow rail. Beside her was our captain, Dylan Clift.

Clift was taller than Jane, slender, and deeply tanned, with a thin mustache along his upper lip. He was as likely to leap into the crow's nest himself as send one of the crew to do it, and much like Jane, he tended to laugh a lot. He knew every crewman's name, usually his background, and instinctively handled them in the most efficient way, goading with some, no-nonsense with others. He was the reason we—well, really Jane—had chosen the *Red Cow*. He'd served as Jane's quartermaster during her pirate days, and followed her into pirate hunting. Several of the crew had also put in time under "Cap'n

Jane" on both sides of the law. The rest had heard enough about her to be properly respectful, and they treated me well because I was with her. Jane's exaggerated hints about my past helped, too.

"Interesting to see the two of them together again," Seaton said.

"Did you serve under Jane?"

He nodded. "Aye, on her last two voyages."

"When she captured Rody Hawk?"

Seaton's expression hardened. "We don't mention that name, Mr. LaCrosse. He's bad luck. And no, that was before my time. In fact, no one who was on that voyage, except Cap'n Clift, still follows the sea."

"My apologies," I said. At least I wasn't the only one leery of saying Hawk's name aloud. "Lots of new rules to remember."

He smiled. "Aye, it's true. But as the man who's paying our way, I suppose you can follow or not any rules you please."

"I'll still try to be less disruptive."

Seaton saluted me. "Aye, sir, it'd be much appreciated."

The conversation had caused a lot of my anger to burn away, but it grew hot again when I heard Jane's laugh on the wind. I went along the rail past the windlass and joined the two captains at the bowsprit.

Clift turned to greet me. "Good morning, Mr. LaCrosse," he said. His dark tan made his white teeth startling.

"Morning, Captain Clift. Any imminent action?"

"Not yet. Possibly tomorrow at the earliest. We're still not in the real shipping lanes, so unless we come across a pirate skulking out of his hiding place, we have the luxury of peace and quiet."

"I guess I can stand the wait."

"You seem to be able to stand anything that's necessary, Mr. LaCrosse."

"I imagine my job is kind of like yours. Days of boredom punctuated by moments of total panic."

He threw back his head and laughed. "That's it exactly."

I turned to Jane. Smiling, I said, "May I speak with you for a moment? In private?"

"Sure," she said. "Excuse us, Dylan."

"Certainly," Clift said. And once again, I caught the moment that I'd seen now at least once a day since we left port. Clift smiled at Jane, then looked quickly away. He seemed to be changing clothes internally, putting on a different face for Jane than for everyone else. The "Jane face" wasn't that different from his regular demeanor, and if I hadn't caught on to the moment he switched, I might never have noticed. I had asked neither of them about it, because I could interpret it for myself: Captain Clift had it bad for ex-Captain Argo.

I pulled Jane across the deck to the starboard bow rail. She twisted out of my grip and said, "Hey, what's the matter with you?"

I said quietly, "It took me a while, but I finally realized you lied to me."

She looked outraged. "The hell I did."

"You knew *exactly* who Black Edward Tew was the first time I mentioned his name."

She started to protest some more, but bit it back. She knew I had her.

"When I asked you if you'd heard of him, you deliberately

said something like, 'There's a lot of pirates in the world,' which is *not* an answer. You were hiding that you knew about him without having to actually lie about it. And it was only *after* that that you started asking about his treasure. I thought you were just joking, but you *knew* there might be a treasure involved. At that point, even I didn't know that."

She said nothing.

"Now tell me why you did it," I finished.

She started to speak, then stopped, then looked out at the water. I waited. A few sailors passed us, regarded us oddly, but said nothing.

At last Jane said softly, "Okay, you got me. I knew about Edward Tew. I should've told you. But I didn't lie to you."

"Don't split hairs with me. Tell me why."

"Why do you think? Miles. That stupid son of a bitch. Ever since I've known him, he's been after the big score. I thought about telling you, but I know how good you are at this kind of thing, Eddie; if you started looking from scratch, without any hints from me, you might turn up a clue everyone else missed, and we might actually find Black Edward's treasure. Even if I only got a cut of it, it'd be a fortune. Maybe then . . ."

She trailed off and looked away, but I heard the words anyway. *Maybe then Miles will stop gambling and whoring.*

"I'm not interested in Black Edward's treasure, Jane. I'm really not."

"I know that. I didn't believe it at first, but I do now." She looked contritely down, and then slowly her smile returned and she cut her eyes up at me. "Still, if we happen to, you know, stumble across it . . ."

I threw up my hands. "If we come across it, I don't care who takes it. To be honest with you, the last thing I want is a pile of ill-gotten blood money."

She grinned knowingly. "You're piling it on thick, Eddie. I'm starting to not believe you again."

I poked her in the hollow of her throat. "This is your warning shot, Jane. If you lie to me again—and just so we're clear, just like I told Angelina, keeping things from me counts as lying—I'm leaving you at the next port we come to."

"Okay," she said seriously. "I'm sorry, Eddie. I should've trusted you."

"Yeah," I said.

"But I didn't lie to you. I wouldn't." She poked me in the chest. "And you know damn well if you'd been really paying attention, you'd have caught me. So it's really your fault for being sloppy."

She said this playfully, but the seriousness beneath it was clear. And damn it, she was right. She smiled, which was bearable; if she'd laughed, we might've fought right there on the deck. But she didn't.

I turned and walked away. As I did, I spotted Clift watching with the same mixture of curiosity and faint jealousy I'd noticed before.

The *Red Cow* was not a big ship to begin with. I wondered just how much smaller it would get before this trip was over.

chapter
N I N E

The lookout, a gangly girl named Estella who stood on the foremast crosstree, called, "Sail ho! Right ahead."

It was the first change in routine since we left port, and I expected a major reaction. What I got was a collective, ship-wide shrug. The crew did not rush; they *sauntered* into action. Half the men continued to lounge around the deck, while the other half waited to see if this was anything more than a passing vessel minding its own business.

You couldn't miss one change, though. Suhonen emerged from the hold, clad only in knee-length pants and a sword belt holding a cutlass. Around his thick neck stretched a tattooed line of dancing human skeletons. Men scrambled to get out of his way as he went to the rail and stood casually, as if waiting for a carriage. But his eyes never left the horizon directly ahead, where the mysterious ship now appeared as an unmistakable silhouette.

Clift yelled to a man halfway up the mainmast shrouds. "Greaves, you old seagull, what do you see from your perch up there?"

Greaves, the sailing master, was a solid man in every sense: thickly muscled, unflappable, and with a manner that ensured he never had to give an order twice. He kept a short unlit pipe perpetually clamped between his teeth. "It appears t'be a Langlade merchant vessel," he said. "But she's flying the flags in the right order."

Murmurs traveled through the crew around me. More men stopped what they were doing and came to the rails to watch. Clift said, "Verify that with the lookout."

"Verify!" Greaves called up.

"Confirmin' the mate's statement!" Estella called down.

Jane and I joined Clift at the port bow. The ship ahead flew several flags and banners, so I wasn't sure which ones conveyed the information they all recognized. "This is damned peculiar," Clift said, wiping sweat from his chin. "A Langlade *merchant* ship."

"Maybe she was taken before the pirates could refurbish her," Jane said. To me she added, "Pirates don't build their own ships, they just take existing ones and modify them. Usually they pick something with a little more muscle, though. A Langlade merchant ship is just a raft with ambition."

"Why would a Langlade merchant ship be flying the pirate-hunter safety signals, then?" I asked. "For that matter, what exactly *are* the pirate-hunter safety signals?"

"It's a way to let other pirate hunters know a ship has already been taken," Clift said. "There's a code in the way the flags are flown, which masts they're attached to, which ones are higher or lower. Otherwise, we might start fighting before either side recognized the other."

"Could it be a trick to lure us in close?" I asked. I felt tingles of excitement at the thought of a break in the monotony, even if that break might mean bloodshed.

"Maybe," Clift said thoughtfully. "If someone bought the code, which gets changed every six months, and used it correctly. It's not a simple thing. Still, that doesn't explain why a ship like that would be sailing under such a banner." He looked back at the quartermaster and called, "Call the watch below, Mr. Seaton. The men can use the practice."

"Aye, Cap'n," he said, then repeated the order in a roar that rippled the canvas.

Turns out "call the watch below" meant, essentially, what we were already doing: watching as the new ship grew closer. Jane's description of it was accurate. It had a single mast, a low waterline, and a deck that was flush from bow to stern. The big, crude tiller seemed wholly inadequate to open ocean travel. In the middle of the deck, just forward of the lone mast, stood a pyramid of wooden crates held in place by a net and ropes.

There seemed to be about half a dozen men aboard her, no more frantic than our own. At last Greaves bellowed, "That's Fernelli, first mate on the *Randagore*. They're for real."

"The *Randagore* is another pirate hunter," Jane explained to me.

"So everything makes sense now?"

"Fuck no. Not a lick."

The man Greaves had indicated waved from the other ship's deck. "Hello, *Red Cow*! Do I smell rum from your ship?"

"You smell it from your own foul breath!" Clift yelled back good-naturedly. "But come aboard anyway!"

The ships pulled abreast, and a boat lowered from the other ship. A few minutes later, Fernelli, bald and with a bushy beard decorated with ribbons and little bells, leaped aboard the *Red Cow*. His two oarsmen followed with much less flair.

He gave Clift a hearty kiss on each cheek, then froze when he saw Jane. "By the giant stingrays of Bola Bola, it's Jane Argo!" he cried. He wrapped her in a hug and spun her around as if she weighed nothing. Jane laughed with delight and, when he put her down, kissed him on the mouth.

"Fernelli, I'm glad to see you saw the light and joined the right side," she said.

"The light had nothing to do with it. I got tired of lice in my beard and no gold in my pocket. At my age, regular wages plus bonuses sounds mighty good." To Clift, he added, "What are you doing in the *Randagore*'s part of the ocean? She's only a day behind us. Did they redraw the patrol districts again?"

"We're chartered," Clift said.

Fernelli's eyebrows rose. "A private charter? You got permission for that?"

"Of course not. It's easier to ask for forgiveness than permission," Clift said with a grin. "We're looking for Black Edward Tew's old quartermaster."

"Marteen?"

"Aye. He's back on the account."

"So I've heard." He looked at Jane. "You back hopping waves as well?"

She shook her head and nodded at me. "I'm hired muscle. He's the gold."

Fernelli gave me a once-over. "And why would a land-bound gentleman such as yourself be wanting to find Wendell Marteen?"

"I just want to talk to him," I said.

"About Black Edward's lost treasure?"

"Just about Black Edward."

"Right," he said with a knowing wink. "Find the man, find the money. I never put no stock in the tales of his sinking, either. Always assumed he changed his name and retired, like old Captain Lowther. They hung him when he was eighty-five, did you know that? After forty years as a law-abiding citizen. All because of a few massacres when he was a young man. I guess Marteen didn't want to sit around waiting for the hangman to catch up to him."

"I'll ask him when I see him," I said noncommittally.

"Well, you should also ask him if he knows anything about these damned ghost ships, because no one else does."

"Ghost ships?" Clift repeated.

Fernelli jerked his thumb at the ship he'd just left. "Found this one five days ago. Still under full sail, just like you saw her now. A few odds and ends gone, but most everything still there. Certainly all the cargo crates are still full. No sign of anyone aboard her, or where they might've gone. And you can save your lips the effort, we've looked into every possibility, and there's nothing. It's like they just vanished right off the ship in the middle of whatever they were doing."

I looked at Jane. "Does that happen a lot?"

"No. I mean, sometimes, sure, but usually if you look hard enough, there's an explanation."

"You said 'ships,'" I pointed out to Fernelli. "Plural."

Fernelli scowled. "What's that word mean?"

"More than one," Jane said.

"Oh, aye, this is the fourth one I know of. The *Vile Howl* found one; the *Sea Dagger* found two. Might be more. They're all locked up in Blefuscola, which is where we're heading with this beauty. It's not a prize if it ain't officially tallied, now, is it?"

Clift noticed that the crew were all looking at us, hanging on Fernelli's every word. Their growing apprehension at this talk of "ghost ships" was palpable. I recalled Rody Hawk's comment about their superstitious nature and wondered if Hawk had gained such a fearsome reputation in part because he'd learned to exploit this gullibility. He lost a lot of his mystique with that realization.

"Gentlemen," Clift said, "I think we should adjourn to my cabin and discuss this in private." More loudly he added, "Because we wouldn't any *gossip* to get started before we knew any of the *facts*, would we? That would make us a bunch of cowardly harbor hogs, and we sure ain't that, are we, lads?"

The crew's halfhearted murmurs of assent were not reassuring.

"Not sure I'd trust Fernelli's word on this," a new voice boomed.

Suhonen strode through the crew, which moved aside quickly. His bare chest gleamed with sweat, and he looked down on the little bald man with contempt. Suddenly we could hear the creaking of the yardarms above us.

Fernelli wasn't intimidated. "Aye, if it ain't the walking sword arm. Still wearing short pants, I see."

"And you're still blaming everyone else for your own misdeeds. Ghosts now, is it?"

"I've told the plain truth, you festering tar stain. And anything I did before was wiped clean by my pardon. Ain't that right, Captain Clift?"

"That's the law," Clift agreed neutrally.

"And what about you, you overgrown canvas crab?" Fernelli stepped right up to Suhonen as if he might strike him. "You were the parson's daughter, I assume? So sweet, bees looked for pollen in your arse?"

"What I did, I did looking right at them," Suhonen said. "No man had to fear turning his back on me."

Finally Clift stepped in. "Stand down, sailors. We have a common enemy out hiding in the wave troughs, not striding the decks beside us. Come on, Fernelli." He gestured toward the hatch. Fernelli and Suhonen kept their gazes locked for a moment longer; then the smaller man walked past Clift and took the steps down into the darkness, his back straight and shoulders back. As we followed, Clift said, "They're cousins. Sometimes it's a small ocean."

We followed Clift down the steps into the hold. As we did, Dorsal the cabin boy jumped aside to let us pass. I winked at him and he grinned shyly back at me, hands clasped behind him in a childish approximation of military at-ease. The others paid him no mind.

Below the deck, everyone was on their feet, and while they didn't salute the way a naval crew would, there was a sense of respect in their casual nods toward Clift. With ex-pirates,

I suppose you take what you get. We went through the crew space into the captain's dayroom, where he closed the door. With his open cabin to port, there was a nice cross breeze through the portholes. RHIP was all a matter of what you compared it to.

In the cabin we sat on the benches on either side of the short table. Clift retrieved a jug and a handful of heavy wooden tankards, the kind that wouldn't slide at the slightest swell or shatter if they hit the floor. He poured us each a large portion, then put the jug back in its padded cloth box.

He raised his tankard. "To justice on the high seas," he said, the official motto of the Anti-Freebootery Guild. We touched our drinks together and repeated the phrase. Clift said, "All right, Fernelli, tell me more about these abandoned ships."

"I only know firsthand about the one over there," he said. "We found her adrift off Swedborg Reef, near the great trench where the ocean is fathomless."

"Who is she?" Jane asked.

"The *Mellow Wine,* a cargo ship out of Langlade."

"What's her cargo?" I asked.

Fernelli looked at Clift, who nodded that it was okay to answer me. Fernelli said, "Bolts of cloth, mostly. Some personal items being shipped. Nothing easily sold."

"You said some things were missing," I said.

Fernelli looked at me with unmasked suspicion. "I'm sorry, but I'm still not clear on exactly who you are. Are you a captain?"

"The name's Eddie LaCrosse," I said. "I'm a private sword on a case."

Fernelli looked at me as if I'd suddenly grown feathers. Apparently even ex-pirates looked down on sword jockeys. "What the devil could Wendell Marteen know that anyone could want?"

I smiled. "I'll ask him when I see him."

"You don't seriously think he knows anything about Black Edward's treasure, do you?" Fernelli looked at Jane. "And this guy's with you?"

"No, I'm with him. You can talk to him just like you would me, Fernelli. But be more honest." She winked at me. "He can tell when you're lying. Eventually."

Fernelli didn't seem to like that idea too well, but he accepted it. "All right. The only thing for certain that was missing was the ship's medicine chest. For all we know, the crew took it with them when they left. And if this had been a lone fluke, we'd have simply taken ourselves as lucky to have the clean salvage. But as I said, there's been three others that we know of."

"All missing the same thing?" Jane asked.

"Don't know."

"And there's no sign of who did it?" I said.

"Oh, there's a sign. A double *X* carved into the door of the captain's cabin. But no one knows what it means."

"When you say 'no one,'" I said, "exactly who do you mean?"

He looked at me now with undisguised contempt. "I mean, me and everyone I know."

Clift and Jane exchanged a look. Clift said, "I suppose we'll keep an eye out ourselves, then. See if we can't get as lucky as you."

"Not sure if it's lucky or not. Damn well creepy, that's for sure. Be more'n happy to get this wreck back to port and my boots back onto an honest ship with no shadows, that I tell you."

AS we watched Fernelli row back to the *Mellow Wine,* I said, "What happens if we do run across one of those ghost ships?"

"We do the same thing the *Randagore* did," Clift said. "I'll assign some men to sail her to port and claim the salvage prize. Although I'd hope that, with two trained investigators aboard, we might get closer to the bottom of things."

"Only if you pay us," Jane said. "Right, Eddie?"

"Twenty-five gold pieces a day," I agreed. "Plus expenses."

"Each," Jane added.

Clift laughed. I looked at the *Mellow Wine* bobbing ungracefully in the waves and was secretly glad her mystery wasn't mine to solve. The one I had was complex enough.

And of course, even a blind man could've seen where this was leading.

hen I came on deck the next morning, the sky was cloudless, and the sunlight reflected off every ripple. The heat was already intense, and the ship's distinctive odors felt renewed and strengthened. Even the breeze that filled the sails seemed muggy and rancid. As my eyes adjusted to the glare, I saw Quartermaster Seaton before me.

"Good morning, Captain," he said with a jaunty salute.

"I'm not a captain," I said in what had become our usual morning exchange.

"Any man who pays the bills is a captain," Seaton replied with his standard half smile.

"Any ships pass our way?"

"A small galleon from Boscobel. Two Ilyrian warships going in for repairs."

"Repairs? Is Ilyria at war again?"

"Didn't stop to chat, so I don't know. But it's been six months, which is about all the peace they can stand."

"No pirates or ghost ships?"

"Alas, no. But starting today, we'll be following prime shipping routes. We could see action at any moment." He gestured around him. "That's why we're putting on our best civilian frock."

I'd wondered how such an obvious vessel could possibly catch an experienced pirate unawares. Now I saw: wooden boxes were strapped to the deck in a pile ten feet high, just as seen on the *Mellow Wine*. Since they were empty, though, they did little to slow us down and could be quickly cast overboard. Instead of the banner of the Anti-Freebootery Guild, we flew the flag of Klarbrunn, and beneath it the banner of the International Cargo Federation. Most significant, the deck ballistae were gone from their sockets, arranged in a neat row on the wooden deck. The ones below remained in place, though, and I knew the gunnery crew could have the deck crossbows remounted and ready to fire in minutes. I used disguises myself on occasion, and could appreciate the scale and effectiveness of this one.

Sweat trickled down my spine and forehead; I'd probably melted off ten pounds on this trip already. I excused myself, walked to the starboard bow rail, and looked down at the bow waves. The spray, at least, was cool on my face. Big fish leaped gracefully out of the ship's path, only to circle back and repeat the move.

A man hung over the side, strapped in a harness, removing the brass letters that spelled the ship's name. He saw me, smiled, and waved.

On one of my first days at sea, I'd asked Seaton the origin of the ship's strange name. Far too loudly, he said, "Ah, so you be wanting to know why she's called the *Red Cow*. She's not always borne that moniker, though."

He waited. So did every man on deck, grinning in anticipation. At last I played along. "What was she called before?"

"The *Impatient Cow*. Come on, lad, ask me why."

"Why was she called the *Impatie*—?"

"*Moo!*" bellowed every sailor from the open hatchways to the foremast crosstrees.

I sighed and shook my head. I was on a ship crewed by twelve-year-olds.

The actual explanation was much more mundane. Originally she was known as the *Red Crow,* but a letter had fallen off during battle. The crew believed this to be a sign that the ship had chosen her own name, and so *Red Cow* it had remained ever since. Her reputation ensured that no one familiar with the sea laughed when she was mentioned.

"Morning to you, Mr. LaCrosse!" cried a voice from above, bringing me back to the moment. Celia Zandry, the boatswain—which of course came out "bos'n" whenever anyone referred to her by rank—hung from the mainmast shrouds and directed adjustments to the rigging. She was almost as tall as Suhonen, although she weighed considerably less. She reminded me of a stick insect; rumor said that when the wind was strong enough, she could raise one bare arm and it would whistle.

"Morning, Celia. How's the wind today?"

"Strong and damp. Makes the canvas sluggish."

"Does the same to me," I said.

I greeted several other crewmen with whom I'd become

friendly. They were, on the whole, a good-natured lot, content with their jobs and glad not to be in Queen Remy's prison, or worse. Some diligently scrubbed the decks, while the crossbow crew, under the direction of Mr. Dancer, the gunnery master, disassembled and cleaned the ballistae before storing them below. With such a large crew, shifts were short and we had an adequate, if strictly controlled, supply of rum. Sometimes I got so bored, I almost volunteered to help, but I sensed that these professionals wouldn't welcome a dilettante like me. Besides, they sang while they worked, and no one needed to hear me sing.

Then I saw something new. Three men emerged from the hold carrying barrels on their shoulders. They had to be empty, given the ease with which the men handled them. They went to the stern and handed them over the rail to waiting hands below, where more men evidently hung in harnesses.

"What's in those barrels?" I asked Captain Clift when he joined me.

"Why, nothing at all."

"So you just dump your empties over the side?"

"Oh, no. They have a very specific function."

When he said nothing else, I prompted, "And?"

He laughed. "Should we need them . . . Well, you'll see."

"Good morning, gentlemen," Jane called. Today she wore an even skimpier outfit; I never knew she had a tattoo below her navel. She leaned on the rail between Clift and me, looked out at the sea, and said, "We're in the shipping lanes, if I'm reading it right."

The ocean looked the same to me as it had every day before this, but Clift nodded. "Aye. And we're now the totally defenseless merchant vessel *Crimson Heifer.*" He looked at her while she gazed over the water, and again I saw that little shift in his demeanor. "If you'll both excuse me, I'm sure there's something more productive I can be doing." He touched his knuckles to his forehead in a casual salute.

When he was out of earshot, I said to Jane, "Are you deliberately trying to torture that poor guy?"

She looked blank. "What?"

"What?" I repeated, imitating her. "I've seen less skin on a Selian bride." Selian women wore only ankle bells during the ceremony; the men wore bells in a much less discreet location.

"Hey, this is just how I dress at sea. When I was a captain, I wore the same sort of thing. And you know what?" She winked. "I never had to give an order twice."

"I bet. What about when you went into battle? A getup like that seems to leave a lot of things . . . unsupported."

"Maybe, but half the bad guys surrendered with a smile before the first blow was even struck."

She laughed, and it was so wide open and joyous that I smiled, too. I'd seen Jane in action on land, of course, her cape aswirl and her fur-edged boots sliding into a battle stance, but I realized that *this* was actually her element. It wasn't just her lack of self-consciousness; it was clear that she felt so at home here that she knew she could always turn any situation to her advantage. I envied that, especially since I couldn't imagine *ever* feeling that way. For her to give that up for Miles Argo must have taken an awful lot of willpower.

I noticed that the sailors scrubbing the nearby deck watched her very closely, hoping the wind would blow her blouse tight against her body. I'm sure she noticed it, too; she just didn't care.

The first time I saw her dressed like this, I commented, "Where's your cape?"

"Cape's aren't real practical at sea."

I nodded at her ensemble. "And this is?"

"Were you looking at my sword arm?" When I didn't reply, she said with a grin, "I rest my case."

Now I said, "So why are they putting empty barrels on the stern?"

"You'll see."

"I'm paying for this trip. I don't think it's polite to keep secrets."

"It's not a secret; it's a surprise. Trust me, you'll love it." She mussed my hair again, and I remembered my earlier promise, but punching a woman so gleefully flashing her boobs to a bunch of sailors seemed both ill-advised and rude. Still, I promised one day to even the score.

I opened my cabin door. The boy Dorsal stood beside my bunk. He jumped and backed up to the far wall, eyes down, clearly guilty of something. "What are you doing in here?" I asked.

He scuffed one bare foot against the floor. "Nothin'."

He wore the same often-patched shirt and pants that were too big. I wondered if he even had a change of clothes. His hair was cut raggedly short, the mark of a knife instead of scissors. I noticed his rope belt had a series of loops tied into it at regular intervals. I grunted in disapproval and said, "Whatever it was, it ain't as bad as lying. Let's try that again. What are you doing in here?"

He chewed his lower lip, then nodded at my bunk. "Lookin'."

"At what?"

"Your sword."

It didn't appear that he'd moved it; it was still in the scabbard, on the floor beneath my bunk. I closed the door and said, "I appreciate you telling me the truth."

He rolled his shoulders.

"Is your name really Dorsal?"

"No, it's Finn. Finn Calder. But that's what they call me."

Dorsal Finn: more pirate humor. "Do you have a job, or are you someone's son?"

"I have a job," he said almost defiantly. "I'm a bolt runner when we're fighting."

That explained the loops on his rope belt. He carried crossbow bolts from the ship's carpenter to the men during battle. "Important job."

He nodded, and his little chest puffed up. "Yes, sir, indeed."

I sat on the bunk. He quickly scooted around me toward the door. "You don't have to run off," I said. I pulled the sword from its scabbard and held it so the light from the porthole shone on the blade. It needed cleaning, especially in this salt air, but it was in good enough shape to impress a barefoot cabin boy: His eyes widened in delight, and light from the blade sparkled in them.

"What kind is it?" he asked reverently.

"It's called a Point Major. It's made in Estepia by a family of swordsmiths named Tomatt. They do a special kind of metal folding that makes the blade stronger than it looks. The downside is, it doesn't hold a razor edge like some other swords, so you have to stab instead of slice after you've used it for a while."

"Is it heavy?"

"Not so bad. Want to hold it?"

He shook his head.

"You sure? It's all right."

He shook his head again.

"Okay. I don't mind you asking to see it, but I don't want to catch you going through my stuff again. Am I going to find anything missing?"

He shook his head once more.

"Thanks. I hope I can trust you. By the way, do you *like* being called Dorsal? I don't want to use a nickname you don't like."

"I don't mind. Could be worse."

"That's true." I took my eyes off him momentarily to put away my sword, and when I looked back he was gone. I hadn't even heard the door open.

I went through my bags just to be sure. Nothing was missing. It appeared that "Dorsal" Finn Calder was a man of his word.

WHEN the sun was high enough it didn't shine directly in anyone's eyes, I took my sword on deck. The *Red Cow* now looked like any other cargo-carrying vessel, with no visible sign of her true identity. Even the men on deck wore the drab clothing of sailors used to numbing drudgery, not the bright colors of pirates, current or ex-.

A different sailor hung over the side, painting the name *Crimson Heifer* where the brass letters had proclaimed *Red Cow*.

"That's not much of a disguise," I pointed out to Seaton.

"Aye, perhaps. But it's bad luck to change a ship's name in mid-voyage. And you're assuming that most pirates can read."

"Everyone here seems to be able to."

"Aye, it's part of their pardoning. They have to learn to read to ensure they understand the consequences of returning to the Brotherhood of the Surf."

"Queen Remy's idea?"

He nodded. "She's a tough old buzzard, but she plays fair."

"Could you read before you were pardoned?"

He laughed. "Yes, Captain Argo required it as well. Said she wouldn't command a bunch of ignorant lampreys." He nodded at my sword. "And where might you be off to?"

"Teaching the lampreys," I said, and indicated the pile of phony cargo crates. A half-dozen men lounged on them, looking at me with decidedly skeptical expressions.

After hearing Jane's embroidered tales of my exploits ("I swear, you'd think he'd been trained by some royal fighting master," she'd said, not realizing she was exactly right), Captain Clift had asked me to show the members of his boarding crew some advanced sword-fighting tactics; to combat the ennui, and because Clift made sure I'd had plenty to drink first, I agreed. I understood his concern: his men were tough, brave, and eager, but their skills were the result of chance and experience rather than any actual training. They were certainly the equal of any pirate crew they faced, but he wanted them to be better. He picked six of his best for my first class, intending for them to subsequently instruct the others. If I was able to teach them anything.

I'd suggested having the ship's carpenter turn out wooden practice swords, but Jane assured me the men would not take them seriously. So we were practicing with live blades on a constantly shifting surface, something that went against all my common sense.

Jane and Clift watched discreetly from the stern. If I saw Jane laugh, I might toss her over the side, so I did my best to ignore them. "Hello, gentlemen," I said. "Who have we got there?"

They lined up, faced me, and tersely introduced themselves. There were six of them, but only one registered: Suhonen. He folded his arms across his chest, but just barely, and his whole demeanor said, *Impress me.*

By now, the crewmen not engaged in actual work had also gathered to watch, some hanging from the shrouds or sitting on the spars. It would be tricky not to embarrass the men who'd been volunteered for this; it might also be tricky to avoid getting skewered myself. I said, "I'm not here to change how you fight. You're all pros, and the fact that you're alive means you're already pretty good. But I've been a soldier and a mercenary all over the world, and I've learned some stuff you might find useful."

I drew my sword and pointed it, not at Suhonen, but at a smaller man named Hansing. "Show me how you attack someone."

He had a huge mustache that covered the lower part of his face down past his chin. "What, for real?"

"Close to real. I'd rather you didn't actually kill me. Come on, show me."

He shrugged, stepped forward, and raised his sword. He shook it menacingly, then swung down at my head. I had no trouble dodging it.

He took a deep breath, tried a side slash that was no better.

Our blades clanged together, and his bounced aside to stick point-first in one of the empty crates.

The watchers laughed.

He turned red beneath his tan, and when he blew out a sharp breath, his mustache billowed like a curtain. He wrenched his weapon free, stood with his shoulders hunched in defeat, then said, "Can I yell?"

"What?" I said.

"Yell. Shout. Do you mind?"

"No."

With a bloodcurdling shriek that startled everyone on deck, Hansing sprang at me. I didn't exactly parry his blow so much as turn it slightly off course at the last moment, and his backhand slash could've disemboweled me if I'd been a hair slower dodging it.

But he was so sure that this last blow would end the fight that he left himself wide open. I slapped him across the neck with the flat of my own blade, then kicked him in the knee. He sprawled back into two of the other would-be students, and when they pushed him back to his feet, he came up swinging. But I put the tip of my sword against the center of his chest and said, "Whoa, remember, this is just practice."

For an instant the rage remained; then it faded. He nodded and sheathed his sword. I kept mine out. No one was laughing.

"I thought I had you," he said, shaking his head.

"The only mistake you made was assuming that," I said. "In most cases you'd be right, but the minute you get someone with a cool head and fast reflexes, you've left yourself wide open. How many of you have killed a man with the first blow when he saw you coming?"

One raised his hand, then added sheepishly, "He still managed to stab me, though."

"Exactly. You have to disconnect your emotions from your brain. It's okay to scream or yell or do anything to try to startle the other guy. But it's got to be an act, and you've got to be above it watching."

They looked grudgingly impressed. Or rather, most of them did. I said, "Now, who wants to try me next?" I pointed my sword at Suhonen. No sense putting off the inevitable any longer. "You?"

The big man stepped away from the group and drew his huge, curved cutlass. His bare muscular body gleamed like a well-polished wooden idol. Only the sound of the ship creaking broke the silence.

I had little experience with cutlasses, either wielding or avoiding, but a sword was a sword and a man was a man. If I couldn't take him, I had no business in this job. Or so I told myself as he towered over me.

"It's practice, Suhonen," Clift warned from the stern.

"I won't hurt him much," Suhonen said. He smiled as if taking me down wouldn't make him muss his hair. When he flexed, the skeletons around his neck seemed to dance.

I didn't even raise my sword. I just waited. It was one of my best talents. I could outwait a rock until it turned to gravel.

Suhonen couldn't. He suddenly slashed at me, which was the only real way to use a cutlass. He did it all with his arm, which was bad because it was weak and left him off balance. I knocked the stroke aside, impressed with the casual strength behind it, and put everything I had into a blow that would've decapitated him had we been fighting for real. As it was, my sword flat rang his bell and he dropped at my feet, his blade skittering across the deck until it knocked over a bucket of soapy water. He didn't go all the way out, but it was a near thing.

I belatedly felt the sheer force of the blow I'd blocked in my arm, shoulder, and back. Fuck me—if he'd been really trying, I'd have been in trouble.

"He had reach and size on me," I said to the others, "but he—"

Suhonen, dizzy and pissed off, tried to tackle me when he thought I wasn't looking. I tossed my sword to Jane, who'd appeared at the front of the crowd; then I stepped aside and snatched Suhonen's wrist as he stumbled across the spot I'd just occupied. I bent it back hard and he fell to his knees, his superior size and strength useless. "Ow, stop, I give!" he cried.

I wasn't quite ready to believe him. "He's younger, bigger, and stronger, yet he hasn't laid a hand on me," I said, and wrenched his arm so that he cried out again. "That's because he's angry and embarrassed, and I'm not emotionally involved in this. Now I'm going to let him go, and if he tries anything else, I'll put him down just as easily."

That was the kind of thing I *had* to say. Truthfully, I had no idea if I could catch him off guard again.

I released him and he jumped to his feet, eyes blazing, cradling his wrist against his chest. I stood with my hands at my sides and kept my gaze locked on his. I saw the rage fade, replaced by uncertainty, fear, then respect. He rubbed his temple where my sword had smacked him. At last he said, "This is stupid. I know how to fight. I'm outta here."

He stomped down into the hold. The other five watched him go, then looked back at me.

I glanced over at Jane, who just smiled and shook her head. Clift watched as if he'd seen it all before. And Dorsal the cabin boy perched atop a barrel, knees drawn up to his chin and his little brow furrowed in concentration.

Jane tossed my sword back to me. I caught it, twirled it end over end, and said, "Next?"

chapter

ELEVEN

S undown again found me on the forecastle staring out
at the water. I noticed many of the crew, when not actually working, did the same. There was something about the
ocean's vastness, and that unbroken horizon always out of reach,
that encouraged introspection at both sunrise and sunset.
Still, I tried very hard to keep my mind pointed forward, and
not back; I was in no hurry to revisit my past. But after a
while, it grew harder and harder to avoid. I sure hoped we
found some real pirates soon.

Avencrole, the ship's cook, came up from the hold with a
basket of assorted chicken heads, feathers, and feet. He was
the palest person on board because he hardly ever emerged
during the full light of day. He went to the rail and dumped
his refuse, saying, "Good-bye, Leon. Farewell, Mr. Allen Sr.

Give my regards to the sharks, Harry." He rattled off a dozen other names and good-byes before all the pieces were gone.

I had to ask. "You *name* the chickens?"

"Of course I do," he said cheerfully as he shook the last of the feathers from the basket. "Name them after every enemy I have. That way it's a tremendous joy chopping off their squawking little heads."

"I hope you're careful not to name them after any current shipmates. They might take it the wrong way."

"Everyone on this ship is a darlin'. Well, except for a couple of the new men, who haven't learned their sea manners yet. There's one lad who keeps bothering me for lemons to bleach his hair, of all things. As if we should all get scurvy just to preserve his vanity. A few more weeks should get rid of that particular defect of personality." Whistling, he carried the basket belowdecks.

That left me alone with my thoughts again. Thankfully Jane joined me at the rail, handed me a tankard and poured me some rum. We touched rims and she said, "That was some show you put on today. Where'd you learn to do that?"

"Fight?"

"No, teach."

"I was a mercenary for a long time. Someone had to train the new recruits."

"I thought you didn't become a mercenary until you'd already had training."

"Not always. Sometimes you have to pack the ranks with whoever you can find."

"Arrow fodder?"

"Hopefully not. Hence the training." I raised my tankard

in salute, hoping it would end that thread of conversation. Just to be certain, I asked, "So what's it like being back at sea?"

"It's okay. Parts of it are nice. But it'll never be what it was, will it?"

"Most things aren't."

She looked out at the glorious sunset. "And as much as I hate to admit it, I miss Miles. Do you miss Liz?"

"Sure."

"You trust her while you're gone?"

"I do."

"That must be a good feeling." She took a long drink and emitted a dainty burp. "Speaking of good feelings, that big guy you took down at swordplay practice is muttering about how he's going to pay you back the first chance he gets."

"Suhonen?"

"His first name is Sue?"

"Don't be a jackass."

"You're no fun. Yes, Suhonen."

"Well, I'm not hard to find."

"I imagine he'll wait until our first boarding action, figuring in all the confusion no one will know who actually stabs you."

"Is that right?" I took another drink. I'd half suspected this would happen, and knew what I had to do. "Doesn't he realize *you'd* know?"

"He doesn't know me." She batted her eyelashes dramatically. "I'm sure he thinks I'm just a big ol' helpless girl."

I handed her the mug. "Where is he?"

She nodded toward the foremast. A handful of men stood together talking, and Suhonen towered above them. "Do you want to go get your sword first?"

"Nah. I don't want to kill him."

"I was thinking maybe you didn't want *him* to kill *you*. But it's your life."

I walked over to the group. Suhonen stood with his back to me. His friends saw me and fell silent. I said, "Suhonen."

He turned slowly, first his head and then those enormous shoulders. If you could awaken a mountain, I suspected it would move like that. He said nothing, but his right hand went to the cutlass at his waist. In the light from the sunset, he was already the color of blood. Great omen.

I kept my hands loose at my sides. Beneath my feet, the deck rolled in a steady rhythm. My stomach trembled a little at the movement; must've been a touch of seasickness.

"What do you want?" he said.

"I hear you've been talking about me. I'd like to hear what you have to say."

"Why?"

"I'm paid to be curious, so sometimes I do it just to stay in practice."

His expression grew dark. "Where's your sword?" he rumbled. "My cutlass does my talking."

"I don't need it. I'm not here to fight with you."

His friends backed away.

"What if I'm here to fight with you?" he challenged.

"Then you'll die," I said as simply as I could.

"That's big talk for an old man with no weapon."

"Yes," I agreed. "You should think really hard about what kind of weaponless old man would say that kind of thing."

I wasn't as tough as I implied, but I was better than Suhonen thought. As he pondered my comment, though, I did begin to wish I'd brought my sword. Still, I was betting that under the bluster and hurt pride, he really didn't want to fight me, he just felt like he had to. I needed him to realize he didn't.

"What's going on here?" Quartermaster Seaton said, barging in between us. "Suhonen, are you causing trouble?"

"No trouble," I said, never taking my eyes off the big man. "I was correcting some of his misconceptions."

Seaton showed no fear of the larger, stronger man. "Is this about this afternoon? Grow the hell up, Suhonen. No matter how good you are, there's always somebody better. Fact of life, on land or sea. Even for you."

"I've got no fight with you, Suhonen," I added. "If you have one with me, let's settle it now."

The moment hung there long enough for the last edge of the sun to drop below the horizon. In the fading glow Suhonen said at last, "Nah. I just . . . I don't lose many fights. I don't have much practice at it."

That was fair, and honest. I extended my hand, and he shook it. With a little extra effort, he could've shaken all of me. But if I read him right, we were back on the same side.

Seaton *hmph*ed in annoyance. "Well, unless you two are going to get married as well, I'm going back to finish my dinner."

I felt Jane behind me, nudging me with the jug of rum. I took it and poured a round for Suhonen and his friends. When I returned the jug to Jane, she felt its weight, scowled, and said, "That'll be on my expense report, you know."

JUST after solid nightfall, a cry of "All hands on deck!" rang out. I left my cabin and followed Jane through the hold, where we joined the line of crewmen going up the steps. On deck I saw no immediate reason for the order, but seeing the entire crew mustered in one place drove home again how crowded the little ship really was. I thought how ironic claustrophobia was in the middle of the wide ocean.

"What's going on?" I asked Dawson, the ship's carpenter.

"Time for the show," he said, then added proudly, "I built the props, you know."

"Show?" I repeated to Jane.

"A ship's crew has to entertain themselves at sea," she said. "I always made sure we had three good musicians aboard. Without it, all that downtime can be deadly."

A row of lanterns were lit along the front edge of the quarterdeck, and a curtain made of old sailcloth was strung across on a frame. The men sat or stood, some climbed the shrouds, and a few perched on the fake cargo crates. A spot was reserved for Jane and me right up front, with Captain Clift. I sat between them like a chaperone.

Seaton stepped out in front of the curtain. He clutched the lapels of an officer's jacket and puffed out his chest. He said, "We have a surprise for our employers tonight. In honor of their quest, and ours, we'd like to present a short production of *The Wake of the Bloody Angel,* composed by—" He bowed. "—yours truly."

The men clapped enthusiastically, and some chanted, "Black Edward! Black Edward!" Several men raised their knives above their heads and tapped the blades together in a chorus of metal clacks. One man, a red-faced sailor with a cap and voluminous sideburns, was already so drunk, he didn't even notice he'd dropped his knife, which stuck point-first into the deck between his feet. He still waved his hand among the knives, and miraculously avoided any slashed knuckles.

Seaton held up his hand for silence. He cleared his throat and in a booming orator's voice said, "Oh, for a spark of lightning, that would inspire the highest heaven of creation. The wide ocean for a stage, admirals to act, and captains to cheer the rolling scene! Then would the great Black Edward stand before us for true, and at his feet, snapping like sharks, should slaughter, heartbreak, and avarice crouch in readiness."

He paused, and the crowd cheered and clicked knives again.

Impressed, I leaned close to Jane and asked, "He really wrote this?"

"Shh," she replied.

He gestured behind him. "Now, lads, let us claim your imaginations. Envision on this tiny deck the great *Bloody Angel,* and its legendary captain, Black Edward Tew, sailing his very first course as captain."

He stepped aside, and the sail curtain drew back to reveal an actor dressed, presumably, as Black Edward. He wore a black wig that lagged behind whenever he turned his head, and so needed constant adjusting. He stood at a makeshift prop wheel and gazed dramatically into the distance.

"Tew" said, "Here I stand on the deck of the *Bloody Angel,* master of my fate. Somewhere on the sea before me lies the first ship I will conquer as a member of the Brotherhood of the Surf—" Here a few cheers made him pause. "—and the first step on the path that will take me back to my beloved as a wealthy man worthy of her. Then, by heaven and ocean, we shall claim an island and live like royalty!"

I looked around. My shipmates were rapt.

"Captain Tew!" a sailor playing a sailor cried as he rushed onstage. "We have sighted a simple cargo ship. Shall we raise the black flag?"

Tew turned his profile to the audience and pointed his chin. "We shall, but make certain no member of our crew strikes the first blow. If they do not resist us, we will not harm them. We are after plunder, not blood."

"Plunder not blood, aye," said the sailor before rushing off.

Tew paced before the prop wheel and struck a pose, fists on hips. "I crave plunder only, for back ashore awaits a girl who has claimed my heart as sure as I will claim this ship's gold. Even now she strides the desolate dunes as I do this quarter-deck, hoping to glimpse my sail, and whether it be now or doomsday, I *will* return to her a rich man."

This soliloquy was followed by the sailor's return. "Captain Tew, the ship's crew dares to fight back! What shall we do?"

Again more to the audience than to his fellow actor, Tew said, "If they dare to draw steel, then steel they shall draw! Arm every man, and tell them it shall be—"

He drew his sword, raised it aloft, and cried, "Gold, glory, or the cold embrace of the sea!"

The audience, including Jane and Clift, shouted the line along with him. Many shook their fists or waved weapons in the air. At that moment, I wondered how many really considered themselves *ex*-pirates.

The sailor followed Tew offstage, and the curtain closed to end the scene.

Men rustled behind the curtain, and when it rose again, it

showed a captain's cabin. Tew sat in a chair, while another actor, hands bound, stood between two "guards."

Tew said, "So, Captain. You have fought, and you have lost. Now we will take what we wish, and send your ship to the bottom of the ocean."

"Pirate dog!" snarled the actor playing the other captain; he was a much better performer. "You do not know from whom you steal!"

Tew leaped to his feet and again stood with his hands on his hips. "I do not care from whom I steal! The ocean is mine, mine and my fellows', and its bounty is ours for the taking!" He paused elaborately. "I am sorry you must lose your ship, for I hate to do unnecessary mischief, but you fought when you should have surrendered. And *you* are the dog here, and so are all those who put themselves under the laws wealthy men have made for their own security. Would it not be better for you and your crew to join us, rather than sneak after these villains for employment?"

The other captain said, "I took an oath to be loyal to my king and my country."

Tew spun with flouncy, theatrical outrage. "An oath! It is not what you swear, Captain, but to whom you swear it! I am a free man, and I have as much right to make war on the whole world as he who has a hundred ships and a thousand men in the field!"

This speech drew another cheer.

Just then the sailor returned and cried, "Captain, you won't believe it! This is no mere merchant vessel, but a treasure ship!"

In gigantic, exaggerated surprise, Tew cried, "What?"

"King Clovis's well-guarded treasure fleet was a decoy." He held up a small wooden chest filled with fake gold coins. "*This* ship carries the crown jewels and treasury of Witigan!"

"No!" cried the defeated captain. "You'll not touch my king's treasure!" Suddenly free, he leaped toward Tew with an extra-large stage knife.

"Watch out!" someone screamed from the audience.

The same drunken sailor who'd earlier dropped his knife stood up and threw the blade at the stage combatants. "I'll save ye, Cap'n Tew!" he cried before falling across the men seated in front of him. The knife struck the enemy captain in the behind.

"Ow! Fuck!" cried the unfortunate actor. He pulled the knife from his ass and glared out at the crowd, squinting against the lantern light. "Who threw that? By thunder, I'll feed you to the seagulls! Who was it!"

Clift stood and gestured at the knife thrower, who was now sprawled on the deck. "Get him out of here. Lash him to something until he sobers up."

Two seamen jumped to obey. The knife thrower struggled, mumbling, "I'm not drunk, they ain't made the liquor that can unsober me. . . ."

Onstage, the captain's guards led the actor away as blood spread on his trousers. I'd finally get to see if piss really got out the stain.

When the audience settled back down, Tew stepped to the edge of the stage and raised a single gold coin to the sky. "I am now rich," he declared, "and at last I can return to my beloved! Set course for Watchorn Harbor, men, with as much canvas as she'll take!"

The curtain drew across the scene, and there was restrained applause; no one wanted to inspire a repeat of the knife-throwing. When the curtain opened again, the props were gone. A single figure stood onstage: a girl, wearing a wig of thick wavy hair and the dress of a tavern wench. I got chills as I realized who she was supposed to be.

"There is no sign of my beloved," she said. By her Kenoshan accent I recognized her as one of Celia Zandry's rigging crew, a girl named Linda Shoji who navigated the spars and lines with the agility of a spider. But she was a much better actor than Tew, and no one spoke or moved around as she performed. She'd never met Angelina, and looked nothing like her, but the plaintive desperation in her voice matched that in Angelina's the day she told me her story.

"I have waited so long for him," she said. "I know he would return to me if he could, and since he does not, it must mean that he has met his end on the great waters. Therefore I have no choice but to join him. The land holds nothing for me but heartbreak and loneliness; I shall try my luck with the sea."

And then, to the collective gasp of us all, she ran to the rail and jumped off the ship. The real ship, not the pretend one. Several men started up to go after her, but other hands pulled them back down, assuring them it was part of the act.

The curtain closed yet again, and Seaton stepped back onstage. He said grimly, "Thus far, with ragged quill in hand, your humble author—" He indicated himself. "—has pursued the story. On a little ship sailed by lusty men, seeking and finding the true course of their glory. Black Edward Tew never reached his destination, and now sleeps with his gold in the icy depths, while the girl from Watchorn Harbor pines for his embrace." He shrugged, self-deprecating and yet somehow dignified. "And so, for their sake, in your fair minds let this acceptance take."

The curtain opened, and Tew stood there, head down. When he looked up, the audience gasped. His skin was painted white, with big crude circles of black turning his eyes into the deep sockets of a skull. It was surprisingly eerie. When he spoke, his singsongy cadence changed to an ethereal monotone.

"I lie in the deep now, with my treasure, safe from all. And yet my spirit does not rest, will not rest, *can* not rest. Not until the day my true love joins me in this cold, dark kingdom for all eternity. . . ."

He lowered his head and backed out of the light. In the darkness, a stringed instrument began to play and a plaintive voice sang,

The sea refuses no soul
All are welcome in its waves
To wait in the deep and cold
Curled up in watery graves.

Suddenly someone behind me screamed. The real kind. We followed his pointing finger to where a lone lantern illuminated a feminine figure standing far behind the stage near the stern. Battling impulses of relief that the girl hadn't really jumped overboard and goose bumps at her creepy appearance left me speechless. Like Tew's, her skin was painted white and black encircled her eyes. She looked like a genuine apparition.

The footlights began to go out one at a time. Squinting, I

saw a black-clad figure crawling along the stage, snuffing the lamps as he went. The singer continued:

When love binds two as one
The trough as well as crest
Embrace them for all time
And that's no lover's caress.

At last, only the girl's lamp remained. Tew appeared beside her, they embraced, and then everything went dark.

There was a moment of total silence. Only the creaking ship and cresting waves made any sound. In the distance, the plaintive cry of a whale seemed to provide the perfect coda for what we'd just seen.

Then the crew burst into genuine, rapturous applause. The cast took their bows, and the loudest response was saved for Seaton. He absorbed it with the graciousness of a man who knows exactly how good his work is.

chapter

TWELVE

Everyone stayed on deck murmuring about the play, not wanting to break the mood. The actor who played Tew came from behind the curtain minus his black wig and accepted congratulations and swigs of rum. Someone threw a bucket of water on the knife-throwing drunk and he sat up sputtering, fighting the ropes that lashed him to the mast.

Linda Shoji appeared, still wiping the white paint from her face. Instead of the applause Tew got, though, the men stepped back and stared as if she were really the ghost she'd pretended to be. She stopped, stared, and chuckled.

"There was a ladder hanging over the side," she said. "It wasn't that hard to grab. Ya bunch of babies."

After a moment's pause, they applauded. She grinned, shook her head, and accepted a mug of rum from one of them.

Jane took my arm and pulled me aside. "I just had a thought," she said softly.

"And you need me to rub your temples until the pain goes away?"

"Now who's being the smart-ass? Just listen. Only one person survived the sinking of the *Bloody Angel*, right? Wendell Marteen, the first mate."

"That's the assumption."

"But what if it wasn't Marteen? What if it was someone who just used his name?"

It took a moment for me to process this. "You think Marteen is really Tew?"

"I think it's possible. I mean, he was a pirate for exactly one attack, so it's not like a lot of people would recognize him. All the stories about him grew up after he supposedly died. Hell, if I'm right, maybe he started all the stories himself, creating his own myth." She paused. "And if he deliberately sank the ship, then he had a motive for pretending to be someone else."

"Why would he do that? It was loaded with treasure."

"Was it?" I couldn't see her face, but nevertheless I knew she was smiling. "How do we know? If he sank an empty ship in water too deep to recover it, he could say anything had been on board."

"But didn't the whole crew die, too?"

Again, I could feel her sarcastic half smile even though I couldn't see it. "He was a pirate, Eddie. He might have regretted it, but it wouldn't stop him. Ever hear of Captain Beardsley, the Grim Teacher? They called him that because he could always show people a new way to die. Anyway, his crew had gotten so big, the shares were tiny, so one night he deliberately ran his ship aground where he had a launch waiting. He escaped; his crew either drowned or were captured."

I nodded. Then a problem hit me. "If he did hide his treasure somewhere else before he sank the *Bloody Angel,* then why has he come back to being a pirate now?"

"Who knows? Maybe he spent all his money. Maybe he got bored. Maybe he got married and his goddamn wife won't stop gambling and whoring. We'll ask him when we see him." She lightly punched my shoulder. "So? What do you think?"

"I think I'm going to bed. It's late, and I'm tired. We'll talk about it tomorrow." I punched her back, turned, and headed for the main hatch.

"If I'm right, I still get the treasure, right?" she whisper-called after me.

"All yours, Jane," I assured her as I descended into the hold.

In the dark outside my cabin, I noticed something in the corner. I squinted until I could make out the curled-up shape of the cabin boy. "Dorsal?"

"Aye," the boy said, and got to his feet.

"What are you doing there?"

He put a finger to his lips. "I'm keeping an eye on Cap'n Clift," he whispered. "He's in his cabin drinking."

I whispered as well. "I just saw him on deck. He didn't look drunk."

"He's got no head for it. One drink and he's off."

"Why do you have to keep an eye on him?"

Dorsal nodded toward my cabin door. I opened it and he preceded me inside. When the door was closed again, he said, "I have to watch him so he doesn't come out and hurt himself or someone else. He's okay when he's inside, but he tries to pick fights if he goes on deck. Mr. Seaton usually stops him, but I figure if I can keep him inside, it's better for everyone."

"What does he pick fights about?"

Dorsal chewed his lip, then said, "Can I ask you something?"

"Sure."

"Is Captain Jane really the queen of the whores?"

I was glad *I* wasn't drinking at that moment, because I would've spit the length of my cabin. "I beg your pardon?"

"Captain Clift talks about her a lot, especially when he's drinking and he thinks no one is around. He says she's queen of the whores. I knew she was a captain, but not a queen. So do the whores in port have to bow to her and stuff?"

I tried to think of a good response to this. As I did, I heard the door to Jane's cabin open and shut; guess she'd made an early night of it as well. Finally I said, "Dorsal, I don't think you should take anything the captain says when he drinks too seriously."

"Oh, it's not just when he drinks. It's when he's mad about things, too. He tends to blame her for everything, even the weather."

"He's probably just making a joke."

The boy shrugged.

"And I'm sure he wouldn't want you telling total strangers about it. He's the captain, he has to command respect."

"That's what Mr. Seaton says, too. That's why I'm standing watch."

He took this task so seriously, I could only smile. "Well, you're doing a good job. If you need any help, let me know."

He saluted. "Yes, sir. Keep this between us, then?"

"Definitely."

I opened the door for him and he went back into the hall. I sat down, took off my boots, and stretched out on the bunk. I tried to relax into the ship's motion, but I had too many thoughts bouncing around in my head. Jane's new theory just added to the confusion.

Either Tew was a sailor turned pirate due to Angelina's influence, or he was a pirate determined to score big to impress Angelina, or he was a pirate who'd dallied with Angelina but was mainly concerned with his own career and riches. He was either dead at the bottom of the sea, or . . . not, I guess. If he'd escaped as Wendell Marteen after murdering everyone on his ship, he was now back on the water but keeping a mighty low profile. Did he know they'd written plays about him?

I closed my eyes. All these possibilities made my head hurt, and the interminable waiting on the *Red Cow* didn't help.

Someone knocked softly at my door.

I sighed, sat up, and opened it, expecting either Dorsal or Jane. Instead Dylan Clift stood there, or rather leaned there, using the frame for support. He was shirtless, shoeless, and without his ever-present bandanna. His hair was noticeably thin on top, and stood out from his skull like wispy weeds. Dorsal hadn't exaggerated his intolerance for liquor: in the brief time since the play ended, Captain Clift had gotten hammered.

"Can I talk to you?" he rasped in a drunk's idea of a whisper. His breath reeked of rum, and his words ran together. Behind him, Dorsal—back at his post in the corner—looked imploringly at me.

"Sure," I said. "You're the captain." He stumbled in and

closed the door. I lit the lamp so we wouldn't be sitting in the dark.

He did that drunk thing where they get way too close before speaking. "I have to whisper," he said, and pointed at the wall between Jane's cabin and mine. "I don't want her to hear."

I tried to breathe through my mouth. "Yeah."

"She's a whore, you know that?"

"I respectfully disagree."

"Well, you don't know her like I do, do you? You see her now, all professional and serious."

"I don't know about serious."

He continued as if I hadn't spoken. "I've seen her kill men for looking at her cross-eyed. I've seen her kill women for doing it. Ask her sometime about the handmaiden. Just ask. That's the Jane Argo I know."

"Why are you telling me?"

"To *save* you!" he cried, and grabbed me by the shoulders. "So you don't turn into me. So you don't waste your life waiting for a whore who'll take everything and then walk away laughing!" He released me and sat heavily on my bunk. "I stood back to back, shoulder to shoulder with that woman. Our blood mingled on the deck at our feet. That should count for something. But would she give me anything? Hell, no. I mean, it's one thing if she preferred women; that's understandable. But no, she was stuck on some guy who was such a loser that she ran away to sea to get away from him! And then she went back to him!"

By now he was shouting, and unless Jane had poured wax in her ears, she had to hear. I said, "She gave her word. She takes that seriously."

"That's not what counts! It's who you give it to!"

I wondered if Clift realized he was quoting the play. "She doesn't see it that way."

"Then you're a fucking fool," he slurred, and stood to leave. Then, his hand on the door, he began to sob. They were big man-sized sobs, the bellow of a wounded animal. No one who heard them would ever doubt how he felt about Jane, and I could only marvel at the composure that allowed him to be near her all the time without letting on more than he did. Unfortunately, he was now loud enough that nearby sea lions might think he was making a pass at them. I had to do something to salvage his dignity, and mine.

I kicked his legs out from under him.

He slammed face-first against the wall, then hit the floor hard. I knelt beside him and said, "Wow, are you okay? You got your feet tangled up there. Maybe you better sit down."

"Maybe I better sit down," he said.

"Good idea," I agreed. He sat on the bunk, and then with no encouragement lay on his side, rolled onto his stomach, and passed out. In moments, he was snoring.

I looked down at him. Between his bare, sweaty shoulders was the final indignity: a tattooed representation of Jane Argo, scantily clad and bearing a sword in one hand and a jug in the other. She literally rode his back all the time.

I eased away from the bunk and opened the door. Dorsal stood there. He said, "Is Captain Clift all right?"

"He'll have a headache tomorrow, but he'll be okay. I'm going to go find somewhere on deck to sleep."

"I'll watch the captain for you, if you want."

"Okay."

I started to give him a coin, but he said, "No, thanks. I get a share of every prize, just like the captain."

I nodded, mimicking his sincerity. He went in, and I closed the door behind him. I took a moment to compose myself, then knocked on Jane's door. There was no response, but I heard her moving around. I quietly snarled, "Jane Argo, open this goddamned door right now or I'll throw you overboard."

She opened it a crack. "Don't insult the alligator until you've crossed the river, Eddie."

"Bite me. I assume you heard all that?"

"His voice does carry. That's one reason he's a good captain."

"Did you know he felt that way about you?"

She opened the door some more and looked around to see if anyone was in the passageway. Then she gestured for me to enter. I did and she closed the door.

"Yes, I knew it." She'd changed into a shift for sleeping that was so sheer, it might've given Clift a heart attack. "I thought by now he would've gotten over it. Who the hell carries a torch for five years?"

I thought of Janet and Cathy, the torches that still burned me after far longer than five years. "Some things you don't get over."

She sat heavily on her bunk. "Fuck you, LaCrosse. His crush is not my goddamn fault. Now, is there anything else you'd like to criticize? Because I'm tired."

"What about the handmaiden?"

She looked up sharply. "Did he tell you about that?"

"He said to ask you about it."

"Yeah, well, you can just ask the door as it smacks your ass on the way out." She crossed her arms and turned deliberately away.

"All right, but I need both you and the captain focused on the job that I'm paying you for."

"You know damn well I'm focused."

"And Clift?"

"He only drinks when there's no danger. Trust me, when we catch up with Marteen, he'll be on top of his game. I taught him, after all."

I could think of nothing to say to that, so I left and went on deck. The men on watch nodded at me, then resumed whatever they were doing. I'd lost my novelty, apparently. I looked aft at the ship's wake, glowing as it stirred up luminescent creatures floating on the waves. I missed Liz so much, the scar over my heart ached.

chapter THIRTEEN

There was no sleeping on deck, though; the buzz from the play was too strong, and men clustered in groups talking about it as they drank. They weren't discussing the dramatic presentation so much as sharing stories about Black Edward that hadn't made it into the show.

"I heard he disappeared in front of the whole crew just before they ran aground. Just rose up into the rigging and vanished."

"A mate of mine once swore he saw the *Bloody Angel* off Blefuscola. Jet black she was now, with bloodred sails. A flock of red ravens followed her, cawing for the souls of drowned men."

"I saw him once ashore. No, really, I did. He ran a tavern called Watchorn's Folly. His hair was still jet black, but he'd throw you out if you mentioned the *Bloody Angel*."

"They say that he appears to the captain of a ship about to sink, warning him of what's coming. But his curse is that no captain ever believes him."

I wandered around looking for a spot to settle, and finally crawled into a sheltered corner on the pile of fake cargo crates. A man sat at the very top, strumming some stringed instrument, and it was actually relaxing. When he began to softly sing, I realized he was the same performer who'd sung during the play. His voice quickly had my eyelids gratefully drooping.

Until a voice I recognized, one that most definitely should *not* be here, began to curse not five feet from me.

I sat up, completely alert. The shadow of my little nook hid me from view. The voice came from a young sailor trying to untangle a coil of uncooperative rope. I waited until he spoke again, cursing the rope and kicking the tangle at his feet.

In an instant, I'd leaped from my hiding place and grabbed him by the back of his tunic. "What the *hell* are you doing here?"

Duncan Tew had grown a scraggly beard and somehow lightened his long jet-black hair. He glared at me with the same insolence he'd shown on our visit to his farm. How had I missed him this long on this tiny little ship? Instantly I knew the answer: I hadn't been looking for him. I *was* getting old.

"I'm working, what are you doing?" he said defensively, and wrenched out of my grasp. "Get the fuck off me. I'm not bothering you."

I pushed him toward the nearest rail. "Can you swim?" I said when I held him halfway over the water.

"No!" he shrieked, grabbing frantically at me.

Heads turned toward us and conversations fell silent.

"Then you better start talking." I let him up, and he didn't let go of my arms until his feet were flat on the deck.

A shadow fell over us. Suhonen stared down through narrowed eyes. "Problem here, Mr. LaCrosse?"

At first I wasn't sure whose side he was on, but he fixed Duncan with a stare that might slay a man at twenty yards. I said, "No, just needed to impress on my friend here the importance of being honest."

"It's real important," Suhonen said to Duncan.

"All right," the boy said resentfully.

"I'll be around," Suhonen said, and drifted back into the darkness. For such a big man, he moved like a wisp of smoke. When did he and I become pals?

I returned my attention to Duncan. "So talk. What are you doing here? How did you *get* here?"

"I trailed you to the Mosinee Prison, and when you left, I followed that woman. She hired a boat, and when she wasn't looking, I signed aboard."

Part of me couldn't wait to hold that little bit of obliviousness over Jane's head. *Pot/kettle, ex-Captain Argo?* But then I'd have to admit my own obliviousness. "And why haven't I seen you before now?"

"I fucking volunteered to work middle watch. The rest of the time I helped the cook."

He got points for subtlety. Middle watch started at midnight, and of course the cook did all his work belowdecks. I bet I knew who asked Avencrole for those lemons now. "That doesn't answer why."

"Why do you think? You're looking for my father, and I want to find him, too. I want to look the son of a bitch in the eye and tell him I'm his son."

"He's probably dead," I said. "And if he's not, he doesn't even know you exist. Your mother never told him."

"My mother's dead, t—" He stopped. "Wait. Is she—?"

"She's alive. She hired me."

He paused, nervously straightened his clothes. Even in the dark, I saw the emotions warring in his expression. At last he asked, "What's she like?"

"She's just . . . a woman. I don't think I should be any more specific."

With a voice like a sad little boy, he said, "She's my *mom*."

"She's also my client," I snapped, painfully aware of how cruel it sounded. This was something they didn't teach you about in sword-jockey school. The anger had drained from Tew's face and he looked only sad and lost. Annoyed, I said, "Tell you what, if we find your dad alive, and he wants to see her, you can tag along. That's the best I can do right now."

He wanted to make more of it, to go all tough-guy and intimidate me into telling him about Angelina. I could see his muscles tense, but his head at least knew better. "All right. But you better be straight with me."

"Understood. By the way, did you use your real name when you signed up?" Having a Tew on board might lead to difficulty.

He shook his head. "The name's Duncan Smith."

I nodded. "Probably a good idea."

At that moment, Seaton emerged from the hold and gazed at us with a slow, measuring eye. "Heard a storm was brewing on deck. Everything all right here, lads?"

"Yes, sir," Tew said, ducking his head and scuttling around me to return to his work. I didn't try to stop him.

Seaton nodded. I tried to nonchalantly walk away, but Seaton said, "A word, Mr. LaCrosse. Would you join me on the fore-deck?"

I followed him, aware that everyone but Duncan Tew watched us. Ahead, the horizon was just visible, a line between the deep black of the sea and the starry mass of the sky. Here the noise of the ship's passage through the water made sure we wouldn't be overheard.

"What can I do for you?" I said, expecting to be chewed out for picking a fight with a crewman.

Instead he gazed out at the night and said, "Tell me, do ye know about the history between Captains Clift and Argo?"

"Just bits and pieces. I know it's why she picked this ship. Why?"

"Captain Clift was Captain Argo's quartermaster for seven years on both sides of the law, before she left the sea to pursue other interests. In case you don't know the chain of command, the quartermaster's main job is to keep the captain honest. Clift did a good job. He would've covered himself in sorghum and crawled through a hell of ants had she asked him."

"Yeah, I've seen how he looks at her when he thinks no one's watching."

"Aye, I could tell you were a perceptive gentleman. Alas, she did not return his affection, or at least refused to act on it. He very nearly ended himself after she left. At my sugges-tion, he took the pledge, and stayed cold sober until the day she again appeared before him."

I waited while he turned his back to the wind, lit his pipe, and took a few deep puffs. "He's drunk in his cabin right now, Mr. LaCrosse."

"Good. Not long ago, he was drunk in *my* cabin."

"He's at the edge of the whirlpool and about to spiral down to the monster at the bottom. He'll be useless to the ship in a week at this rate."

"I wish I could help."

Seaton smiled. "Do ye know how pirates choose their captains? It's by a vote. Every man has a voice, and the captain can be replaced at any time. Usually by the quartermaster."

"Too bad you're on the other side now."

"That's true. But as I'm sure you've sussed out, we're all still pirates inside. We just channel it in a different way. We get to make our own rules, fight our own battles, live how we like. We just don't have to fear ending up as a warning dangling from a gibbet at the tide line."

"That's how I ended up in my line of work, too."

Seaton laughed. "Then I can ask you a favor?"

"Sure."

"Convince Captain Jane to at least treat him kindly, not with that mockery she presents to everyone else."

I didn't mention my little chat with Jane. "I don't think I should get in the middle of things."

"Aye, that's a sensible course. But as the man who's paying for this voyage, you have more than the usual interest in its outcome. If we don't find Wendell Marteen soon, I fear the captain won't be up to leading the fight to capture him. And while the crew might follow Captain Argo, there's a fair number here who know nothing of her, and see only a woman out of her place."

He had a sure grasp of his crew's psychology. "I'll say something to her if I can figure out a way to do it gracefully. How's that?"

He nodded in appreciation. Then he looked back out at the water. "It's been a quiet voyage so far, hasn't it, Mr. LaCrosse?"

"I don't have many to compare it to, but it has been pretty uneventful."

"We've sighted hardly a ship. Not that you'd know, but we've been crossing shipping lanes for a day and a night, and we've encountered no one. That's odd." He paused. "I think I'll suggest to the captain that we put in at Blefuscola tomorrow."

"Where is that?"

"She's an open safe harbor for all shipping. Neutral ground. We can sniff around, see what pirates are working in the area, and maybe hear some scuttlebutt about Wendell Marteen."

I grinned at him. "How come you're *not* a captain, Mr. Seaton?"

He gestured modestly with his pipe. "It's not in my nature to carry so much worry."

THE boy Dorsal was asleep in front of the door to Clift's dayroom. I started to wake him up, but he looked so peaceful, I left him alone.

I looked at Jane's closed door as well. Seaton was right: Jane was driving Clift incrementally mad, and since this whole trip was on my money bag, I did have an interest in stopping things before they got out of hand. But what could I say? It wasn't her fault he was lovesick. No one implied she'd led him on dishonestly. And Seaton was also right that she treated Clift the same way she did everyone else.

I slipped quietly into my cabin and shut the door. It still reeked of Clift's ale, so I opened the porthole. It didn't help much.

I stretched out on the bunk and stared at the unlit lamp dangling from its ceiling chain. It swayed with the ship's movement. I felt that weird tightness that comes from impatience and isolation, and spent a few moments taking deep breaths to calm myself. If something didn't happen soon to break this monotony, I'd go crazy.

The next day, I got my wish.

Blefuscola rose from the horizon long before we reached it, thanks to a towering dead volcano located in the center of the island. From a distance it looked lush and tropical, but it was deceptive: the green clinging to the volcano's slopes was mostly moss. It was uninhabited except for the allegedly neutral port on its northern side.

The *Red Cow* had doffed her disguise and was now back to her old identity. The false cargo crates collapsed into thin flat piles that could easily be stacked below, and the ship's real name replaced her alias *Crimson Heifer*. The empty barrels stayed lashed to the stern, though. I still didn't know what purpose they served.

If Captain Clift was the worse for wear after the previous night, it didn't show. He was on deck before me, calmly issuing orders for Mr. Seaton to then repeat very loudly. Jane stayed below; I don't know if it was from boredom, sleepiness, or our confrontation. I also saw no sign of Duncan Tew, but if he worked the night watch, he was probably sleeping as well.

The *Red Cow* circled Blefuscola until we reached the north side. The coastline seemed to be all high rock cliffs, with no apparent entrance. I wondered where this supposedly safe harbor was, until suddenly Seaton called for more canvas and the *Cow* began to pick up speed directly toward those same high cliffs.

I stood at the bow, trying to stay out of the way and trusting that Clift, Seaton, and the rest of the crew knew what the hell they were doing. We shot toward the island; waves crashed into the base of the rocks, sending up great white plumes. I began to get a little nervous.

Seaton, standing at the ship's wheel, continued bellowing Clift's orders to the crew. They were all in nautical-ese, and none of them seemed to be *Slow down*. I gripped the nearest rail and tried to look nonchalant. They *had* to know what they were doing, didn't they?

Then, at the last minute, the ship's undulation separated one rock wall from the other. There was an opening, but you could see it only from an angle because the ends of the two rock walls overlapped. I also saw the reason for the straight approach: rocks just under the surface on either side of the ship's course.

"A bit flabbergasting at first, isn't it?" Mr. Greaves said beside me.

"It does make you question the navigator's sanity," I admitted.

He gestured at the rocks on either side of us. "Steeple rocks.

If the tide's right, they're hidden just below the waterline, and they'll gut a ship the way Avencrole does a pig. Only safe course through them is straight in."

"How many ships did it take to figure that out?"

He laughed. "I'm sure the bones of quite a few rest at the bases of those things, impaled like a knight on a lance. But I've not known any sailor who didn't know about them, so the word's well and truly out by now."

"But you don't tell the passengers."

He clapped me on the shoulder. "Ah, Mr. LaCrosse, a seaman's life is filled with so few moments of delight, it'd be a shame to deprive them of the look on your face."

I glanced around in time to catch several men quickly look away. How could I not laugh, too? "Glad to help the morale."

Greaves saluted me. "You're a good sport, Mr. LaCrosse."

The ship sailed gracefully through the opening. For a moment, the huge cliffs blocked any view of the sea behind us or the harbor ahead. Birds nested in crevices, and in places strange nautical images and hieroglyphs were carved into the rock. This passage had been used for quite some time, maybe hundreds of years. I'd have to ask how it was established as a neutral port, since a neutral anything was, in my experience, a rarity.

Then we reached the end of the inner wall, turned to port, and entered the harbor itself.

It was quite a sight. The harbor was an almost perfect circle, and the dark blue water hinted at extreme depth. Directly across from the entrance, a small city stood along the beach, with that tangled, warrenlike appearance of places that grew haphazardly over time. And except for the beach where this city stood, there were only rock walls going straight down into the water.

And suddenly we knew where all the other ships were.

The harbor was a jungle of masts, spars, and shrouds. The packed docks of Watchorn were nothing compared to this. It looked like every type of vessel in the whole Southern Ocean had decided to hide here.

But why?

Once inside the harbor, the wind died to a whisper, and the water was so still that the cliff walls reflected as clearly as they would in a mirror. Clift ordered, "Ease your helm, Mr. Seaton."

"Aye, sir," came the quartermaster's reply from the wheel.

Our momentum carried us forward. We slowed so that by the time we got close enough to anchor near the back of this ad hoc fleet, we were barely moving.

"Bloody golden starfish," Clift muttered as he surveyed the ships. All had their sails furled away, and many had gangways crossing from one vessel to another, forming a complex web. "Looks like they've settled in for good."

"It'll take us a day just to get to shore from here," Seaton grumbled.

"What the hell?" Jane said from behind me. I turned, and was surprised to see she was dressed more demurely than before; a vest covered her, ahem, points of interest, and she'd procured knee-high boots from somewhere.

If Clift noticed, he gave no sign. Instead he said, "This must be why we haven't seen any ships in the cargo lanes."

"No kidding," Jane agreed. "There's no weather in the sky, and it's the wrong time of year for the big storms, anyway. What could have driven them here?"

"We'll never know till we ask," Clift said. "Mr. Seaton, ready the wherry. We're going ashore."

"The wherry, sir? Will you not be taking a few men for security?"

"This is a friendly port, and with our two guests along, I'm sure I'll be safe."

"I'll pack you a picnic," Seaton muttered, then began shouting orders.

"I take it this is unusual," I said to Jane when we were alone.

"Yeah, I didn't even know the ship *had* a wherry. I thought all the boats were launches."

"I meant about this," I said, and gestured at the harbor.

"Oh. Yeah, this is absolutely nuts," she agreed. "Look at all the flags, too. This isn't just one kingdom's fleet; this is everyone. It's a total shutdown of trade. Nobody's getting anything."

Clift, Jane, and I boarded the wherry, rowed by two young sailors. Navigating among the big ships was a bit like canoeing down a canyon, with only a narrow band of sky visible above us. Although the vessels were anchored, there was still plenty of slow movement, and we had to push ourselves away from shifting hulls more than once. It was a sunny day, but the shadows between ships felt isolated and spooky.

As we passed one ship, Clift said, "I know this ship's captain." He stood, cupped his hands around his mouth, and called, "Ahoy, sloop *Raccoon*! Is Captain Freisner aboard?"

A face appeared over the rail. "And who might you be?"

"Clift, of the *Red Cow*."

"Well, Clift of the *Red Cow*, that coward Freisner went ashore three days ago and we haven't seen him since! If you run across him, tell him his crew no longer requires his presence!" The face withdrew without waiting for a reply.

Clift sat back down. Jane said, "Do you suppose all these vessels are captainless?"

"I don't know what the fuck they are," Clift snapped. "Any insights from the great investigators?"

Jane said, "Dylan, that's not fair—"

"What are ships like this afraid of?" I asked.

Clift turned slowly and looked at me, but his anger had already dissipated. "Only war, weather, or pirates could stop a merchant ship from delivering her cargo. There's no war big enough to account for all this, the weather's perfect, and we haven't seen any pirates, either."

"But look at that," Jane said, and pointed. "A Rafelian navy frigate."

"So it's not just commercial ships," I said.

"Apparently not."

It took a long time, but eventually we reached the end of a dock where we could tie up alongside the launches from several other vessels. The town beyond the docks swarmed with people, but they weren't moving much; they stood in groups talking, or listening to speakers pontificating from storefronts, or just numbly standing around.

Clift turned to our pair of rowers. "Men, stay with the wherry. If we're not back by nightfall, return to the ship and tell Mr. Seaton he's in charge, and that my advice is to get the hell out of here."

"Aye, sir," they said.

He kept looking at them. "I'm serious, lads. I'm trusting you. I don't know what's going on yet, but I see plenty of vessels who seem content to molder here. The *Cow* is not one of them. Am I clear?"

The two sat up a little straighter, and their simultaneous "Aye, aye, sir," was more emphatic.

"Good. I always knew I had the best crew in the fleet."

As we strode down the dock toward solid land, I noticed something and asked, "What's that?"

A dozen ships were blocked off from the rest of the harbor by red buoys connected by stout chains. Armed men stood along the waterfront, isolating these vessels from land. None had any visible damage, or crew.

"There's the *Mellow Wine*," Jane said, pointing.

I recognized the abandoned ship we'd encountered before. "Are all those ghost ships, then?"

"Maybe that's what everyone is—" Suddenly Clift stopped, staring at one of the ships behind the quarantine line.

Jane said, "What is it?"

"The *Indigo Ray*," Clift said in disbelief. "She's one of ours. A pirate hunter."

The ship he indicated had the same general lines as the *Red Cow*, but was painted dark colors to better suit her name. Clift headed toward her, only to have one of the guards move to block his way.

"Sorry, Cap'n Clift," the guard said. "Nobody goes aboard. Harbormaster's orders."

"Who brought in the *Indigo Ray*?"

"I can't really say. You'll have to talk to the harbormaster."

"Was she one of the ghost ships?"

The guard looked at his fellows, then leaned closer. "D'you remember me, Cap'n? Ah, well, no matter. You gave me a fair shake once when you didn't have to, and I remember it. The *Copper Lance* brought in the *Ray*. She was found empty and adrift, just like the others. 'Tis one thing to have a cargo vessel overtook, but first naval warships, then one of the pirate hunters . . ." He shook his head. "Now no one will leave the harbor."

"Anyone mention a strange mark left on them?" I interjected.

He looked at me suspiciously. "What sort of a mark?"

"A double *X*," Clift said.

The guard turned his attention back to the captain. "Aye, I've heard rumors of that. Haven't seen it myself. On the door to the captain's cabin, they say."

"Where's the captain of the *Lance*?"

"No idea, Cap'n. Try the harbormaster, if you can get through the crowd."

"Thanks, Mr.—?"

"Weston, sir."

"Weston. Sorry, I don't recall when we met."

"Only one of us has to, sir."

"We'll not get answers here," Clift said to us. He marched down the dock with such purpose that people instinctively stepped aside. We almost ran to keep up.

At the end of the dock stood a huge sign welcoming people to Blefuscola in a dozen different languages. The town's motto was also repeated multiple times: "A safe place for all ships in need."

That noble sentiment was balanced by the most godawful smell I've ever encountered outside a privy. I'd acclimated to the ship's odors, to the point that the piss barrel didn't even register on me anymore, but this was about a million times worse. Unwashed bodies, mud, urine, and rotting garbage contributed to a wave of aroma that made my stomach roil. Even Jane wrinkled her nose.

"Overcrowding," she said. "There's usually only about a tenth this many people here."

"What do they want?" I asked.

"Safety. Protection. Answers."

"I want answers, too," Clift snapped in annoyance. "And we won't find them cowering here, put off by a little stink."

Those ashore who noticed us did not look happy to see us, and turned away as soon as we made eye contact. Our progress was significantly slowed by a crowd gathered in front of one of the little buildings to hear a wild-voiced man pontificate on something. We couldn't avoid his harangue as we worked our way around.

"It was a cable's length long, from maw to tail tip. And it came roaring out of the dark, with one big baleful eye. *Whoosh!* We're smashed in to starboard. *Wham!* We're crushed to port. And then, it come up amidships, tore away our masts, and sunk us. Thirty good and true sailor men, drowned and dead."

The crowd murmured.

"And whatever is behind these ghost ships is part of the same vile family! I tell ye, it probably flies down and snatches the folks off the deck before they even know what's coming! Flies out of the sun, I bet ye, like an eagle snaring a field mouse."

"Flying monsters," Clift said disdainfully, then added loudly, "Flies out of your goddamn liquor jug, maybe!"

"And who might you be?" the old man demanded.

"Someone who has sense enough to know there's no flying one-eyed monsters out there. If your ship sank, friend, I'd be looking at the captain first; maybe he just can't read a map, and decided a monster was a better cause than a reef he didn't spot in time."

I said nothing, but recalled vividly a cave in the hills above Neceda where I faced the last of the fire-breathing dragons. So I wasn't so quick to reject the idea out of hand.

"You!" someone else cried. We looked around. A peg-legged sailor hobbled through the mud toward us, using the shoulders of others in the crowd for balance. When he reached us, the one-legged man said, "You're from the bloody Anti-Freebooters, aren't you?"

"Yes," Clift said guardedly.

"Then why are you here? Why aren't you out there finding the villains who did this?"

"And who are you?" Clift challenged. "Doesn't look like any of you are in a position to call another man coward."

This raised some hackles in the crowd. I leaned close to Jane and said, "Should we expect a fight?" She shrugged, but surreptitiously moved away to guard the captain's other blind spot. I folded my arms, which put my hand near my sword hilt.

"We're not fighting men, you cur," peg leg said. "We pay taxes and tariffs so your kind will do that dirty work. So why aren't you out there?"

We were now the focus of the crowd's ire, and they closed in around us. The fight would be long, and we'd take a lot of them with us, but eventually they'd have us by sheer numbers. I saw the muscles in Jane's shoulders flex as she got ready.

Clift walked up to peg leg, looked him up and down, and then slapped him so hard, he fell to the mud.

"You stinking, bilge-sucking son of a bitch!" he yelled.

"You want to pick a fight with me, get up and do it! I won't stand for your slander." He looked at the crowd. "What about the rest of you? Any of you feel lucky?"

When no one responded, he looked down at peg leg. "I just arrived in this stink-hole. I don't have a clue what's happening with these ghost ships, but by heaven, I'll make a ghost of the next man who calls me a coward." He yanked peg leg to his feet . . . well, foot. "Go sign aboard my ship, the *Red Cow*. Tell them Captain Dylan Clift sent you personally. Then when we find the source of these attacks, you can be right there to see for yourself. If your balls hang low enough for the job, that is."

Peg leg wrenched free and disappeared back into the crowd. Clift glared around us, his gaze hot enough to make the crowd retreat wherever it fell. In moments, no one looked our way at all.

He turned to us and said, "That was fun." I think he meant it.

People got out of our way even faster as we continued into town, the muddy street sucking at our boots. We reached a small building with a sign out front that announced, again in a dozen languages, that the man inside was both the town magistrate and the harbormaster. A crowd waited outside, while within, a dozen other captains shouted at one another. Clift pushed through them to the desk, where an old man with long white hair sat, a quill and inkwell before him.

"I'm Captain Dylan Clift of the *Red Cow*," he announced. "I need to see the harbormaster."

The old man barely looked up. "Take a seat, wait your turn."

"I'm a pirate hunter, I get priority," Clift said.

"Not today, you don't. All those ships in the harbor? The captain of every one of them is ahead of you."

Clift leaned down. "I don't think you heard me. We get priority."

The man's weathered face drew into a grimace as if a string tightened it from within his skull. "I don't think you heard *me*, youngster. Not today, you don't." He dipped his pen in the inkwell to tell Clift he was dismissed. "Take a seat, wait your turn, and stop bothering me."

I stepped up to the desk and deliberately jingled the coins in my money bag. "I think we can reach an agreement."

The old man's face tightened even more. "Oh, a bribe. With a harbor full of uncouth and barbaric sailors, no one's thought to try that yet. My God, you're brilliant." He snorted in disgust.

Jane said, "I guess we've got no choice." She turned and went toward the door marked PRIVATE in the same list of tongues. A guard I hadn't noticed stepped in front to stop her. I didn't see exactly what she did to him, but it was fast and silent. She caught his unconscious body and lowered him to the floor.

Heads turned toward us. As the old man rose to protest, I tossed a gold coin on his desk. The *clink* got the attention of just about everyone in the room. I said, "Thanks, pops." I could imagine how happy the others would be to think the old man let us in ahead of them.

There was a man seated before the harbormaster's desk, and he jumped up when we appeared. "Dylan!" he cried, and shook the captain's hand enthusiastically. "At least one other of us has made it to safety."

"Captain Shaw of the *Copper Lance,* this is Eddie LaCrosse and Jane Argo," Clift said.

Shaw stared at Jane. "*The* Jane Argo?"

"Definitely *a* Jane Argo," she said with a grin.

"It's an honor to meet you." He blatantly looked her up and down. "You certainly live up to the tales about you."

"Ahem," the harbormaster said. He was a little round man, with leathery skin and a gold hoop in one earlobe. The wooden placard on his desk read HENSE MOLEWORTH, HARBORMAS-TER. A man whose name and job had the same initials must've found the right career. "I hate to interrupt this nautical good fellow society, but may I ask what you people are doing here? You have to wait your turn and—"

"Why are all these ships hiding here?" Clift interrupted.

Moleworth rubbed the bridge of his nose in annoyance. "We have a harbor full of unpaid, unwelcome guests who re-fuse to leave because they believe something supernatural is out there swallowing up ships' crews. And for all I know, they may be right."

Clift turned to Shaw. "Is that what you think?"

"I wouldn't be so dramatic about it, but it's the damndest thing. These empty ships started turning up six months ago. We found two passenger vessels abandoned, and brought them in. Then five days ago, we came across the *Indigo Ray.* Totally empty, not a thing out of place. There was even a kettle with a fire still under it."

"And no indication of what happened?" I asked.

Shaw looked at me. "You're not a sailor."

"He's my charter," Clift said.

"You're chartering now?" Shaw asked.

"Only this once. And only for—" He nodded at Jane. "—special circumstances."

"Well, if you want to get out of here, you better do it before your crew hears about the *Ray*. Once mine did, they flat-out refused to leave. Even talked about going back on the account if I try to force them. The bunch of yellow flying fish."

"They're that scared?" I asked Shaw.

"The *Ray* was no pussy willow," he said.

"No," Clift agreed. "It wasn't. They had more captures than anyone else last year." He turned to us. "Come on. Shaw's right—we're leaving."

WE left the harbormaster's office, but we didn't head back to our wherry. Instead we returned to the quarantined ships and Weston the guard.

"I want to go aboard the *Indigo Ray*," Clift said, softly so that the other guards wouldn't hear.

"I can't allow that, Cap'n," Weston whispered back. "Nothing personal."

"You said I once gave you a fair shake. That's all I'm asking from you. We need to go aboard and look around. The authority that told you to keep people off the ship would understand, and would grant me permission, but that would take time we don't have. We won't move things around or take anything off. We just need to look."

"I'm sorry, sir."

Clift reached into his pocket. Weston said stiffly, "I don't bribe, sir."

"I'm not going to bribe you. I'm going to show you a piece of parchment. Only you and I will know what it says. If I say it's permission to investigate the *Indigo Ray* signed by Queen Remy herself, and you don't contradict me, who's to say either of us is lying?"

Clift produced a small rolled parchment, untied it, and held it for Weston's perusal. The guard looked at it, then at Clift, his face impassive. At last he said, "Very well, Captain Clift." He turned to his nearest coworker. "Cap'n Clift and his party have permission to go aboard the *Indigo Ray*. Pass them through."

"Aye," said the other guard.

Weston said, "There's some launches tied at the end of the pier. You'll have to row yourselves, I'm afraid."

"I remember how," Clift said. "Thank you, Mr. Weston. If you ever want to return to the sea, there's fair work and wage for you on the *Red Cow*."

"Much obliged, Cap'n. It might just happen."

THE *Indigo Ray* was essentially the same ship as the *Red Cow*, and searching it did not take long. It was hard to know what to think about it, since it was obvious others had been here before us: chalk outlines showed where various items had rested before being removed. The captain's cabin was closed off with the yellow ribbon of authority, but we slipped under it and went inside.

The double *X* was carved on the door, just as Fernelli had described on the *Mellow Wine*. As the others poked about, I stared at this symbol, struck by something I couldn't quite pull forward from the back of my mind. It made sense that a criminal would mark the scene of his crime, especially if his future success depended as much on reputation as it did actual prowess. That was why so many pirates had their own flag designs. They *wanted* potential victims to know who they were.

"The medical box is gone," Jane said. "Just like on that merchant ship."

"The logbook's gone, too," Clift said. "I'd love to know their last noted position."

"If there was a pattern, don't you think the harbormaster would've mentioned it?" Jane said.

"You're getting soft," Clift said. "You trust quill-pushers now?"

Jane ignored him and joined me to stare at the door. "What do you see?"

"Something," I said. "Just not sure what yet."

She leaned close to my ear. "This isn't our enigma, Eddie. Maybe we should try to find another ship. I know Dylan: he's going to go after this. He takes any insult to the guild personally, and it's hard to be more insulting than to leave one of their own ships in this condition."

"I heard that," Clift said.

"Stop eavesdropping," Jane shot back.

"You're across the room, it's impossible not to," Clift replied.

Suddenly the *XX* image resolved itself. I said, "I'm not so sure this isn't our mystery, too. Give me your knife."

Jane took the blade from her belt, and I held it horizontally across the middle of the two *X*'s. I asked, "Now what do you see?"

She got it at once. "Ha!" she bellowed in delight.

Clift joined us. "What? I don't see anything but two *X*'s."

"No," I said. "With a line dividing them, it becomes a *W* on top of an *M*."

"For Wendell Marteen," Jane added, still grinning.

Clift stared at the symbol. "Is this," he said at last, "what you'd consider a 'clue'?"

"It is. I can't say for certain that it does stand for Wendell Marteen, but it's a coincidence if it doesn't."

"Are you willing to start searching for the source of these ghost ships under the belief that it will lead to Marteen? Because I can't continue the charter otherwise. This is too serious, and the *Cow* needs to get back to her real job."

"Yeah, I'll go along with it."

He smiled. "Then let's get to work."

WHEN we climbed back onto the dock from the launch, I felt eyes on me at once. It took me a moment to spot my watcher, but there he was: a man in a faded jacket and patched trousers, with a black handkerchief around his neck. His pox-scarred face resembled the cracked bed of a river after the waters had dried up. He was just beyond the docks, staring at us—at me—as if I owed him money. People gave him a wide berth.

Jane saw him, too. "Friend of yours?" she said softly.

I shook my head. "Never saw him before."

The man pointed at me. I did as well, raising my eyebrows in a question: *Me?* He nodded.

"I'll meet you at the boat," I said.

"I'll come with you," Jane said.

"No," I said, and my voice sounded strange even to me. "I want to talk to him alone."

"Why?"

I wasn't sure myself. "I just do. I'll tell you what he says."

"Okay," Jane said, although she clearly thought I was bonkers. I went through the cordon of guards, down the steps, and onto the muddy shore, where the man awaited me.

"You wanted to see me?" I asked when I was face-to-face. He smelled of mud and fish.

"You be the man with the hole in his heart?"

I assumed he meant my scar, although I couldn't imagine how he knew about it. "Maybe. Who wants to know?"

"My name isn't important. Just that I hear things before they happen."

I smiled wryly. "And you heard something about me, right? How much will it cost me to find out?"

"I don't want your money," he said with a twitch. "I just want to tell you that you will find the man you seek. The man with black hair."

I felt goose bumps on my back. I tried to stay nonchalant. "Oh. Well . . . thanks."

"And you will find him alive."

"That's good, too."

"But don't seek after his gold. It's got too much blood on it."

"I'm not interested in his gold."

He laughed. "A man may say that, until the gold's before him."

"And a man may mean it."

He shrugged. "As you say. This is my claim, my threatening, and my message."

"You do your office fairly," I said in court-speak, and pressed a coin in his hand.

He jumped back as if scalded, and the money landed in the

mud at my feet. "I told you, I don't want your money!" He rushed away toward town and disappeared back into the crowd.

I bent and picked up the coin. I wasn't a superstitious man, but I'd seen enough to convince myself that I had little knowledge of how the universe truly worked. I took his warning under advisement. Very serious advisement.

BACK at the dock, the two sailors who rowed us from the *Cow* rushed to meet us. "Did you hear, Captain?" one said. "The *Indigo Ray* was found as a ghost ship. They took down a pirate hunter!"

I knew the sailors had no idea who "they" were, which made the concept even scarier. If they got back to the *Cow*, we might be as marooned as the *Copper Lance*. I pulled out my money bag and handed each man a gold coin. "You're to stay here," I said. "Learn as much as you can. When we get back, I'll want a full report." I looked at Clift. "Right?"

Clift understood. "Right."

Jane and I rowed while Clift navigated the boat back among the anchored ships. When we got to the *Red Cow*, Clift called for all sails, and in the faint wind, we eased toward the harbor opening. Finally we emerged, the real wind caught us, and we shot forward into the ocean, toward our rendezvous with a nightmare.

We found the *Vile Howl* the next day.

The sunrise revealed an ocean as empty as you could imagine. Somehow knowing every ship was huddled back at Blefuscola added to the effect. It seemed like the only things out here were us and whoever had been raiding the ships. There was a breeze, and the waves had little whitecaps that made the ride rougher than normal.

I stood with Seaton at the starboard bow rail. Jane had watched for a while, but left when it became clear nothing was going to happen quickly. Clift slouched with his arms draped over the wheel without an apparent care in the world; he received reports every few minutes from the foremast crosstrees. So far, they'd been variations of "all clear."

Suhonen appeared over me. "May I have a word with you,

Mr. LaCrosse?" He looked at Seaton. "If you don't mind, Mr. Seaton."

The quartermaster did not even look at Suhonen, but he said, "Any trouble, you'll wake up on the bottom of the sea with lobster claws around your pecker, got me?"

"No trouble, sir," the big man assured him.

I followed him across the forecastle to the port rail, where a seaman quickly scampered away to give us privacy. "Must be handy to intimidate everyone," I said.

"Sometimes," he agreed. "Sometimes it's just a pisser, though."

"So what can I do for you?"

"I'd like to ask a favor," the big man said respectfully. "I'd like to be included in whatever you and Cap'n Jane are doing."

"Why is that?"

"I want to see how you work. A man can't stay on the sea his whole life. I want to live to an old age, like you."

He said this with a straight face, and I was really glad Jane wasn't there to hear it. I suppose, for him, I did seem old; he was maybe twenty-five. I said, "Well, okay, but isn't Jane a better role model? She was a pirate and a pirate hunter, too, just like you."

With a completely straight face, he said, "She's a little scarier than you. I wouldn't know how to talk to her."

Now I did smile. "She scares me sometimes, too. All right, you can tag along, but there's no extra pay in it, just so we're clear. No treasure."

"Aye," he agreed with no hesitation.

When I returned to Seaton, he asked, "Suhonen give you

more trouble? I thought you two had settled things. Want me to have a word with him?"

"No, he just wanted some career advice," I said.

Seaton's eyebrows rose, but he did not comment.

The lookout standing on the foremast crosstrees cried out, "Ship right ahead!"

Everyone on deck rushed to the rail, the opposite of their casual interest when we sighted the *Mellow Wine*. Blefuscola had them all on edge, even though they hadn't left the ship.

"Battle stations, Mr. Seaton," Clift called nonchalantly.

Seaton repeated the order, and men rushed to the rails, glad to have a task. They snapped the ballistae into place, cranked the strings tight, and loaded the first bolts. Mr. Dancer, the gunnery master, strode behind them checking their preparations.

Now I could make out the approaching vessel well enough to see it veer, tack, and plunge with no apparent purpose. It pitched fitfully over the waves, riding the swells and then falling off. "Searching for a man overboard, perhaps," Seaton muttered, but he didn't sound like he believed it.

"Not enough sail for this wind," he added a few moments later. That was true—the *Cow* had many sails set to capitalize on the light breeze, but this stranger showed only a few hung from its rigging.

"It's the *Vile Howl*," Seaton said at last. His words were picked up by a seaman passing close behind us, and moments later the whole crew seemed to know. The rest of the men came on deck, some of them armed. I spotted Duncan Tew among them. I had that tingly urge to have my own sword close at hand, but there was no graceful way to scamper back to my cabin for it.

At last, the *Howl* was close enough to truly observe. She was about the same size as the *Cow*, but with a slightly larger stern and without the mysterious extra-long bowsprit. Only a jib was flying, and a foresail that was still partly tied up on one end. She rolled from starboard to port with the motion of the waves that passed beneath her.

"Signal flags, Mr. Seaton," Clift said. Seaton relayed the command, and a young sailor with a pair of flags made an elaborate dance to get the other ship's attention. There was no response. There was no one visible on deck at all.

"Mirror signals," Clift said, and these were duly used to reflect sunlight at the other ship, concentrating on the portholes. Again, there was no response.

"I seen a ghost ship off Kolantar Head," I heard one seaman tell another. "Came out of the fog on a moonlit night—so close, I could see the blind eyes of the skull-faced crew."

"More like the blind eyes of a shit-faced sailor," his friend mocked.

"Say what you will, I know what transpired."

"Well, whatever this ship be, she's no ghost," his friend said.

Jane appeared beside me. "I'm going to get my sword," she said quietly. "Want yours?"

I glanced at her, expecting mockery, but her expression was dead serious. I nodded. If something rattled Jane Argo, I definitely wanted to be armed.

Clift steered us parallel to the *Vile Howl*, staying well out of ballista range, although no gunners were visible on her deck. In the whole time we watched, there was no sign of life or movement. There appeared to be no overt damage, only what might have occurred from neglect or abandonment.

At last, Clift turned the wheel over to Greaves and joined us at the bow. "Opinions?"

"Seems we won't learn much by watching," I said.

"Are you volunteering to go aboard her?" Clift asked.

"Sure. It's my area of expertise, after all."

"Seems ill-advised to let the man with the gold go into danger." Clift turned to Jane, who had returned with our weapons. "I suppose you'll want to go as well?"

"Try to keep me from it."

"We all know the futility of that," he said without making eye contact with her. "Mr. Seaton, can we grapple up to her?"

"Yes, sir. The wind isn't too bad and she's not showing much canvas. We can hook up."

"Then do it."

"I think Suhonen will want to go, too," I said.

"Oh, he's going whether he wants to or not," Clift assured me. "He's going to watch you like a wandering babe."

I looked at the other ship. Its dark portholes and open hatches seem to beckon us to an unspecific but nonetheless serious doom.

SEATON, now at the wheel, nudged the *Red Cow* closer to the *Vile Howl*. The crew had trimmed sail until we ran under no more canvas than the other ship, and we began to bounce in the waves at the same rate.

As we neared, we saw that the hull was intact. A few lines and bits of sail hung over the rail and dragged in the water, but it wasn't enough to affect its course. There was still no sign of the crew.

"Ahoy, *Vile Howl*!" Clift yelled through a megaphone. "It's

Dylan Clift and the *Red Cow*!" The only reply was the snap of the sail tatters.

Suhonen stood behind me. I wondered if this new master–apprentice relationship meant I'd have to get used to his looming presence at the periphery of my vision. I asked him, "Do you see anything that looks like deliberate damage?"

He shook his head. "Nothing that neglect wouldn't cause."

Clift hailed them again, then passed the megaphone to Greaves. "Won't learn anything listening to ourselves talk," the captain said. "Mr. Dancer, hook us up."

Dancer shouted out commands, and three men shot bolts attached to lines across to the other ship. The bolts had grappling hooks for heads, and men on the *Cow* yanked the lines tight. Each shouted, "Hooked!" when the grapple attached itself to the *Vile Howl*'s rail. Crews at winches took up the slack and hauled the two ships together. The vessels struck with a solid bump, and the hulls squealed when they rubbed against each other.

Instead of steadying the *Howl*, though, the maneuver made the *Cow* pitch in unison with it. It was the first time I'd truly had to struggle to keep my feet under me. "Turn us into the swells, Mr. Seaton," Clift ordered. Slowly the *Cow* swung around, dragging the *Howl* with it, until we were cutting through the wave crests instead of riding limply over them.

"We'll have silence while the boarding party is over there, Mr. Seaton," Clift said. "If they holler for help, I want to be sure to hear it."

"Aye, sir," the quartermaster said, then bellowed, "All hands will be silent!"

"Does he appreciate the irony of yelling for silence?" I whispered to Jane.

"Well, he could use a whistle, but I think he likes the personal touch."

Jane, Suhonen, and I swung over on ropes. It was something I hadn't done since childhood, and I realized it when my shoulders protested the move. We all crouched, letting our legs absorb the deck's movement while we listened for anything unusual. Except for the creak of the rigging and the shiver as the two hulls slid together, there was nothing. The crew of the *Cow* crowded the rails, watching us, armed and ready for any eventuality. They hoped.

"Damn my bloodshot eyes," Suhonen said softly. "It's a ghost ship for sure."

"I'll change your diaper later," Jane said in annoyance. "Spread out and search the deck. Don't go below."

I wasn't sure what I was looking for, or at, since I didn't know ships well enough to spot something out of place. Just like the *Indigo Ray,* the *Howl* looked abandoned but not damaged— there were plenty of old scars in the wood, but no sign of recent battle action. The others found nothing as well.

"We're going to check below," Jane called to the *Cow*.

Belowdecks, the *Vile Howl* mirrored the *Red Cow* in general outline. We found no evidence of anyone, alive or dead. The sleeping hammocks were all in place, and all empty. Some items had been knocked askew, but it looked more like the result of the ship's uncertain motion than any struggle or fight.

"Pipes," Jane said, pointing at a table. Four of them lay there, a pouch of dried leaves on the floor where it had fallen. "Sailors don't go anywhere without their pipes."

"These did," I said, and nodded at two empty scabbards hanging from wall pegs. "But they did take their swords."

"Is that a clue?" Suhonen asked.

"It sure as hell is," Jane said. She knelt by the hanging sword belts, examining them minutely without touching them. A quick search found a dozen more empty scabbards. "They snatched their weapons without taking time to strap on their belts." She looked back at Suhonen. "What does that tell you?"

The big man pondered this. "Something came up suddenly?"

Jane smiled, and I nodded. I said, "They grabbed them and ran. But to where?"

"And to do what?" Jane said. "It's not like another ship could just slip up on them. These were ex-pirates."

"Wherever the fight was, it must've come up in a hurry," I said. "But it doesn't look like it happened here."

"The crew didn't vanish," Suhonen said succinctly. "They just . . . left."

We proceeded to the officers' quarters, which were in the same condition. The captain's door was marked with the same double *X*—or rather *W* above an *M*—that we'd seen on the *Indigo Ray*. Jane went immediately to the desk and sought out the logbook. She opened it, turned to the last completed page, and muttered, "Damn."

I looked idly over the captain's bunk and belongings. Sometimes not looking for something specific helped you find it, especially when you didn't know what it was. To Jane, I said, "No clues in the log?"

"'Quartering Tendecca Shoals per orders,'" she read. "'No sign of any pirate activity or abandoned ships.' That's the last entry, and it was dated a week ago."

"Does that tally up with the ship's condition?"

"Untended for a week? Yeah."

Suddenly I stopped, backed up, and looked at the bunk again. The hairs stood up on my neck. "Jane," I said casually, "look at this."

She joined me, puzzled, and then it registered. She whispered, "No fucking way."

Suhonen came over and looked at the black yarn hair sticking out from under a pillow. Using her knife, Jane lifted the pillow to reveal button eyes, a hand-sewn dress, and the wear and tear of a favorite toy.

"Would the captain of this ship really have brought his child along?" I asked.

She shrugged. "He might."

"On a ship that was sure to see combat?"

"These guys are tough," Suhonen said. "Served with a Captain Lyvers once who brought his twin teenage daughters along. Apparently he hadn't noticed that they weren't six years old anymore, but the rest of us did."

"I don't follow," I said.

"The idea that there's something he can't handle might not even occur to a man like the *Howl*'s captain," Suhonen said. "Sure didn't occur to Captain Lyvers."

Jane shook her head. "Bloody hell," she whispered, speaking for us all. "Where *are* they?"

WE found one thing missing—the medicine chest, just like the *Ray* and the *Mellow Wine*. We brought the charts and logbook back on board the *Red Cow*. Seaton was given the unenviable task of reconstructing the *Vile Howl*'s previous course using her present locale, the last position noted in the log, and the weather as best he could estimate it. Meanwhile Jane, Suhonen, and I gave Clift a detailed report in his cabin. Jane did most of the talking, and covered everything succinctly.

"You'd make a good first mate," Clift said with the hint of a smile.

"The best in any damn navy," Jane shot back.

He chuckled, but it passed quickly. He said, "So what are we dealing with here? Mutiny?"

I shook my head. "No sign of violence. And way too many personal effects lying around. If the crew left, they did it very damn calmly, and they didn't take their pipes, which tells me they thought they were coming back."

"Or they were so surprised, all they had time to grab were their blades," Suhonen added. I nodded in agreement.

"Another ship, then?" Clift mused. "But what kind? That whole 'no sign of violence' seems to rule out an actual pirate attack." He paused thoughtfully. "I suppose we have no choice except to assume that whatever happened here is the same thing that happened to those other ships back at Blefuscola."

"Seems silly not to," I agreed.

"Very well: once we get an approximate course from Mr. Seaton, we'll proceed to backtrack. If the wave gods are with us, we will find the solution to everyone's mysteries at the other end."

"Or just more mysteries," Suhonen said. He learned fast.

chapter

SIXTEEN

The tug of the two mysteries—what happened to the ships, and whether Marteen was involved—kept me antsy and ill-tempered. The ship's routine became even more maddening since I had no real part in it. The one bright spot was the ongoing sword-fighting lessons, now attended by everyone not actively on duty. The deck was almost too small for all who wanted to participate. Suhonen quickly became a second teacher, absorbing what I demonstrated and tweaking it for ship-to-ship combat. I started to learn as much as I taught.

The men were tough enough as a group, but they had no individual discipline. They counted on intimidating their opponents as much as they did outfighting them, which was a holdover from their piracy days. What I tried to show them was that when they waved their swords overhead and screamed curses, they left their entire torsos wide open to a simple thrust to the heart. If we'd been in combat against a trained force, they'd have been massacred. It took a lot of drilling to break those old habits, but they began to operate more quietly, and with more lethal efficiency, as every day passed.

The night after we sent the *Vile Howl* back to Blefuscola, I was on deck with Suhonen and his friends. We'd passed the rum around, and I'd gotten more talkative than usual, telling them about some of my adventures. I chalked it up to the drink, but truthfully, I was growing to really like these guys. They were men who'd voluntarily changed their lives, yet still found a way to operate largely on their own terms. I admired that.

"How'd ye meet Cap'n Jane?" one of them asked. The others eagerly repeated the question.

"We crossed paths professionally," I said, and tried to leave it at that, but they insisted on more, so I relented. "I was handling security at a conference of lords and ministers trying to hash out a border dispute. Jane was bodyguarding one of the lords, whom somebody knifed during a formal dance. She took it personally. We did some questioning, figured out who was telling the biggest lie in a castle full of professional liars, and ended up fighting it out with the personal guard of one of the other lords. Turns out, his wife was behind it all. She was hanged, and I split my bonus with Jane. We've been friends ever since."

That was the story, all right, but the truth was in the details. We'd caught two groomsmen who were in on the plot but refused to say who was behind it. After we tied them to chairs, Jane produced a snake whip and said, "I'm going to use this on you both until one of you tells me what I want to know. That means one of you will take a whipping for nothing." It took only three lashes before one of them cracked.

Then, as the woman behind the murder tried to escape under the protection of her guards, Jane fell from a parapet and broke her leg, but still managed to hobble to the drawbridge and stop the vicious bitch from escaping. Think about that—one severely injured woman took down five professional soldiers single-handedly before I could make it down to join her. I watched her fight the fever for a week that resulted from her injury. When she came out of it, the first thing she asked was about the case. I gave her half my bonus because the family of the murdered man wasn't going to pay her at all. I'd never doubted her toughness or her commitment to her job since.

Suddenly there was a commotion from the hatch. Jane climbed on deck, dragging a struggling figure behind her. She looked around, spotted me, and came over. "Look who I found skulking about like a bilge rat." She tossed Duncan Tew at my feet. He sat up and wiped his bloody nose.

Damn. I'd forgotten to tell her.

"Claimed he followed us from Watchorn and signed on here when I wasn't looking," she continued. "And he's been hiding ever since."

"Uhm, actually—" I began.

Duncan roared to his feet and put all his weight and strength into a punch to Jane's chin. It was an uppercut that would've broken a normal person's jaw, and it rocked Jane back a step, but she didn't go down. Her eyes blazed with full-on battle fury and she reached for Tew, but I stepped between them. "No, wait, settle down, both of you."

Duncan tried to get past me, so enraged, he didn't realize Jane was truly mad enough to kill him. Suhonen grabbed him by the hair and held him. "The man said settle down."

"You, too, Jane," I said warningly, in a tone I wouldn't use on her unless it was life or death. Given the murderous look in her eye, I was pretty certain it was. She stopped, the cords in her neck straining, then settled down. "What?" she snarled.

"I knew he was here. He came up to me and told me. I just forgot to tell you."

She glared at Duncan. "Really?"

Suhonen still had him by the hair, so he just said, "Yeah."

Jane took a deep breath, and the rage faded. She held up one hand; her bejeweled fingers trembled with the fury she would've poured into Duncan. "You're a lucky man. That's how close it came." Then she smiled, laughed, and walked away to the stern.

"Let him go," I said to Suhonen. Duncan spent a moment shrugging his clothes back into place, then said, "If that bitch thinks she can—"

"That bitch knows she can," I said. "And you know she can, too. So shut up. This was my fault, and I want her mad at me, not you. Understand?"

Like her, he took a deep breath, but his anger didn't entirely fade. "Whatever," he said. "Just keep her away from me, okay?"

"She's not on a leash," I said. "You'll have to do some of that yourself."

When Duncan had gone back belowdecks, Suhonen asked quietly, "How do you know him?"

I figured this was as good a way as any to test his honesty. "Just between us?"

Suhonen nodded.

"He's the son of Black Edward Tew."

Suhonen's expression didn't change. "Really."

"Yes. His mother's the one who hired me. He never knew either of them, but everyone where he was raised knew who his father was, and held it against Duncan all his life."

"That might put you in a permanently bad mood," Suhonen agreed.

I was impressed with his empathy. It wasn't a quality I associated with my idea of giant ex-pirates. "That's what I figure, too." Then we rejoined his friends and resumed telling lies about how tough we were. I knew if word got around about Duncan's parentage, there would be only one source. I truly hoped Suhonen proved trustworthy.

THE next day, Duncan Tew showed up at swordfighting class. I didn't know if Suhonen or Jane had said something to him, or if he'd simply decided he needed to know more than he did. I quickly realized that wouldn't be hard—he had virtually no sense of how to handle a weapon. After class, as the half-dozen novices walked away rubbing their sore wrists, I motioned for Duncan to step aside.

He looked at me suspiciously. "I know, I'm not very good at this. Killing people isn't something I'm really looking forward to."

"You shouldn't, but that's not what I wanted to say." I paused to get the right words together. "I'm sorry for being so rough on you."

"I have to learn it, don't I?"

"No, I don't mean today. I mean since we met. I tend to see the worst reasons for people doing things, and usually I'm right. But not always."

The insolent defensiveness in his glare slowly faded.

"Well . . . thanks. I appreciate it. Does that mean you and your lady friend won't smack me around anymore?"

"I can't speak for her, but I don't think she'll need to." Again I paused. "Who's taking care of your children while you're gone?"

"April moved back in with her parents. They'll be fine."

"Why *are* you here? Really."

He looked out at the sea. "You saw my sons, right? They're more important to me than I can explain using words. I need to know who I am, so I can make sure I don't turn into the man my father was. Then maybe they won't turn into me."

"Your father never knew about you."

"You say. I want to hear it from his own lips. Tell a man you're his son, he either takes it as good news or bad news. That'll tell me all I need to know."

"What does your wife think?"

"She doesn't think I'm coming back, but I'll show her."

"You know, she's not the enemy."

"You haven't lived with her."

"No, but . . ." I stopped. I was about to offer relationship advice, and I had no business doing that. I managed what I hoped was a friendly smile. "You know, you're right. I don't know your situation."

"What were you going to say?" He added earnestly, "Really, I'd like to know."

"Just that you and she are supposed to be on the same side. The enemy is anyone else who comes after either one of you."

"Is that how you and your wife are?"

It seemed pointless to explain that no, I wasn't married, but yes, I was committed. So I nodded.

"I miss her, you know," he said quietly. "We may fight all the time, but to tell you the truth, I like the way she fights."

"You've got time. If she really doesn't think you'll come back, then showing her that she's wrong will go a long way toward fixing things."

"What if she's found somebody else by then?"

"Well, that's always a chance. And if it happens, you'll have to deal with it. But remember, what those boys see you do is what they'll think a man is supposed to do. Make sure they see the right things."

He sat up a little straighter when I called him a man. Raised without a real father, by people who never let him forget his origin, he'd probably never been called that. I patted his shoulder and left him there, afraid that if I kept going like this, I'd soon be giving him fashion tips.

As I headed toward the hatch, I met Jane emerging. She acted as if yesterday's altercation had never happened. "How'd the babysitting class go?"

"You could help, you know. Especially with the beginners."

"Me? I'm the worst teacher imaginable."

"But they need a good opponent. Right now they're just clacking swords together like kids. They don't seem to realize they're supposed to try to hit the other guy, not just his weapon."

She laughed. "Maybe when I'm too old to swing a blade myself, I'll paint a bull's-eye on my back and rent myself out as a target." She looked out at the sea. "Man, I just spent an hour helping Seaton work out our course. It's really hard to tell where that ship came from. I couldn't do that much math if you put a crossbow to my head."

Quietly I asked, "And how are things with the captain?"

She shrugged. "As well as can be expected, I suppose."

"Have you talked to him?"

"No. But I've tried to . . . not provoke him."

"I noticed. Thanks."

"He's not a bad guy, you know."

"I know. You could do worse."

"I have done worse. Last time I saw worse, he was chained to a rock, whining that his ankle was chafed."

"But your word is your word." It wasn't a question.

She nodded. "If it's not, what have I got left?"

I started to quote the play myself, but knew better. In Jane's case, as in mine, who you give your word to is irrelevant. Your word is your word.

I excused myself to go clean up after class. Dorsal sat in the corner outside my door, and jumped up as soon as he saw me.

"How are you today, sir?" he asked brightly.

"I'm okay," I said. I wondered where he slept when he wasn't huddled here. "And how about you?"

He beamed. "Shipshape and wagon tough, sir!"

I laughed. "That's a good one." I went into my cabin, shut the door, and sat down on my bunk. It was hot, still, and quiet as the ship rolled over the waves, and my eyelids grew heavy. I lay back, stared at the waving lamp hanging from the ceiling, and tried to focus on my case. That was usually helpful, but now it simply made me too frustrated to sleep. There was absolutely nothing I could do to speed the process along, and if we didn't find something or someone soon, I might slaughter my beginner's class just to keep from going mad.

Or worse, I might keep giving people advice.

chapter

SEVENTEEN

Seaton gave us a heading based on the *Vile Howl*'s log-book, and we followed it. I mean, I guess we did. We sighted no land, the sea looked the same, and I could never navigate by the stars the way sailors could. It appeared, by the sun, that we headed southwest. It certainly got no cooler.

Clift kept two men posted atop the foremast crosstrees at all times. No one was going to slip up on the *Red Cow*. I wondered if perhaps we were overlooking the obvious reason for our villain's actions, whoever he was: maybe clearing the sea of traffic *was* the point. But again, we were brought back to the why. What good is a pirate without ships to attack? The more I thought about it, the more I was certain some crucial bit of information eluded us. As it stood, the puzzle made no sense at all.

When I discussed it with Jane, she was just as perplexed.

"You clear things, usually, to make sure you have room for something else. Troops clear a road so an army can travel. But goddamn, the ocean's already mostly empty."

"So is it just someone showing off? 'Look how powerful I am'?"

"Fuck, Eddie, I don't know. But I tell you, I'm about ready to bury a blade in somebody, and if we don't find some bad guys soon, I can't promise it won't be one of the good guys."

I knew what she meant. Even the daily sword practice did little to help my impatience.

One night over dinner, Suhonen—who had been admitted to the captain's table, his huge size making us all feel like kids sitting in the corner while the grown-ups ate in the main hall—demonstrated his innate knack for logical thinking, something he'd previously kept to himself. "The one constant thing they've taken is the ship's medicine chest, right? Maybe someone's sick."

"Maybe, but they've taken an awful lot of medicine, more than enough for a ship's crew," Jane said.

"What if the sick people aren't on the ship?" he said.

"That's an idea," I said. "How well settled is this part of the world?"

"Pretty much every place that can be occupied, is," Jane said. "There are a lot of small uninhabited islands, but even those are well known and used to replenish supplies. Not a lot of surprises left in this part of the ocean."

"Only takes one," Suhonen pointed out.

And there was only one needle in the proverbial haystack, an analogy that grew more apt with each passing day. We thought we were in the right area, but that was as specific as we could get, and now it was a matter of persistence and luck. Only one of those things was under our control.

Finally, just after sunrise, on a day as fine and clear as any, one of the lookouts yelled down, "Ship to port!"

Clift gave orders that Seaton repeated. Men scurried up the shrouds and rushed to the ropes on deck. Jane and I pushed our way through the crowd of unoccupied crew at the bow rail.

We waited for additional information. I'd never heard the *Cow* so silent during the day. Finally the lookout said, "No pennant, no sails. No sign of life!"

"Another one," Greaves said. "Another ghost."

"Don't jump to conclusions," Clift snapped, "especially not where the crew can hear."

"Aye, sir. My indiscretion."

"Bring us alongside, Mr. Seaton. You know the drill."

Sails were adjusted, ropes were pulled and tied, and the *Red Cow* turned to port, heading directly toward the oncoming vessel. Mr. Dancer's gun crew readied themselves, and the rest of the men made sure they were armed with swords, axes, and cutlasses. A few of the men, too nervous to just stand around and watch, went through the exercises I'd been teaching; I only hoped they'd remember them in the thick of battle. Could that be what happened to all the other ships, even the *Vile Howl*—their crews panicked? But what could rattle a bunch of ex-pirates so badly? These were men who knew all the tricks of both sides.

As we closed in on this new vessel, we quickly saw it was not just "another one." For one thing, this ship bore no name or other form of identification. Her hull was worn and faded, and all the deck fixings were stained with rust and corrosion. She was bigger than the *Red Cow*, with three masts to our two. Yet she sat perfectly upright, her empty masts swaying only slightly in the breeze that drove us.

"Where are her sails?" Jane asked softly.

"Is that important?"

"Yeah. I mean, she had to get out here somehow. Her sails aren't furled, they're *gone*. No rigging at all, just masts and spars. Somebody took down all the canvas deliberately."

"Why?"

"So she'd stay put, I imagine. She must be anchored." She shook her head. "What the hell *is* she?"

"Beats me," Clift answered. "I've never seen anything like it. It's just a generic *ship*. She hasn't been fitted out for any particular purpose. She's not a warship, nor a cargo vessel, nor designed to carry passengers."

"Then what's keeping her upright?" one of the sailors inquired. No one answered.

"She must be anchored," Jane repeated.

"This water's far too deep for anchorage," Seaton said.

"Then why the hell isn't she moving?" Jane said.

"Belay that order to come alongside, Mr. Seaton," Clift said. "Keep us at a distance."

"Aye, sir," Seaton said, then shouted to the crew. We slowed and turned to starboard, then back to port until we were parallel to the strange ship but with fifty yards of water between us.

"You ever hunt geese, Mr. LaCrosse?" Suhonen said, so quietly only I heard.

"When I was a kid," I said.

"Then you'll know what this ship reminds me of." He paused. "A decoy."

His insight sent cold chills through me. But if he was right, where were the hunters? The sea was empty in all directions; where could they have put their blind? Unless, of course, they waited out of sight in the ghost ship's belly.

"We're putting off the inevitable," Jane said. "We have to go over there."

"Someone on the *Vile* may have thought the same thing," Clift said.

"You don't know that this ship has anything to do with the *Vile*," Jane said.

"No, I don't. But I do know we found it by backtracking the *Vile*, and that's a big honking coincidence. I'm not in a hurry to lose my crew the way those other vessels did."

"Then Jane and I will go," I said. "We're not part of the crew."

"Why are you so eager?" Clift asked.

"Because he hates mysteries," Jane said with a grin.

"Shut up," I said, annoyed.

She grinned wider. "Am I right?"

"You'll take one of the boats," Clift said. "I don't want to get the ship any closer."

"Are you scared?" Jane teased.

"I'm properly cautious." To me, he asked, "Do you want Suhonen?"

I looked up at the big man. He nodded.

"And a couple more," Clift said. He scanned the men on deck and said, "Kaven and Veasley, you're volunteering."

Veasely said, "Do I have to, Cap'n? I had my stars read, and they say I shouldn't take on any special work assignments right now while Mercury is aspected by Uranus."

"My foot's going to impact your anus if you keep whining," Clift said. "Yes, you have to go."

Kaven, with a long braid that I knew included a strip of thorny vine to prevent enemies from grabbing it during battle, *hmph*ed and said, "We get a hazard bonus?"

"You'll need a hazard bonus if you talk back again," Clift snapped. "What's wrong with you people—when did you start trying to get out of fights? If we *were* still on the other side of the line, I'd send you swimming home."

"Not afraid of a fight with any *living* man," Veasely said.

Duncan Tew suddenly appeared before Clift. "Can I go along, too?" he said, his voice shaking. He added, "Sir."

"Who are you again?" Clift said.

"He's been taking my swordplay class," I said before Duncan blurted out his last name. "He's pretty good. If he wants to go, it's okay with me."

"Yeah," Clift said skeptically. "Well, one more can't matter either way, so sure, go ahead. No hazard bonus, understand?"

Duncan saluted. "Yes, sir."

I watched the other ship as Seaton got the wherry ready to go. Part of me wished for a bigger boat and more men, but surely two experienced sword jockeys and three tough ex-pirates could both avoid whatever traps awaited and watch out for one nervous amateur. If not . . . well, then I hoped we'd at least have time to know what was killing us before it finished.

KAVEN and Veasely rowed, Suhonen steered, and Duncan sat between Jane and me in the bow. The sea was a little rough, and we rode up and down a lot more than I expected, but we quickly approached the strange ship.

Kaven turned his head to look behind us, and Veasely said, "Watch that braid, will you?"

"Sorry," Kaven said. "Sometimes I forget."

"You've got a damn saw blade tangled in your hair, and you forget?"

"It's not a saw blade; it's viper thorn."

Veasely shook his head. "Whatever. Why don't you just cut your hair, then you won't have to worry about it?"

"I promised my mother," Kaven said darkly. It was apparently enough explanation, because Veasely turned to me and said, "So you're a sword jockey, huh?"

"Yeah," I said.

With his hands wrapped around the oar, I saw he had a letter tattooed on each knuckle. Together they spelled CANT SWIM. "My brother ran afoul of one of you. He was dillydallying with all the captains' wives in town while their husbands were at sea. Sword jockey followed him around and gave one captain the list of all the times he'd buried his harpoon into Mrs. Captain, if you take my meaning. He decided it was time to sign aboard another boat. Posthaste." He grinned, revealing several missing teeth. "With a bachelor captain. But before he left port, he made sure that sword jockey wouldn't be bothering any more honest sailors."

I turned to Suhonen. "We don't get a lot of respect."

"Most of us don't deserve it," Jane added.

"A man gets respect, not his job," Suhonen said.

"You're a lot smarter than you let on, aren't you?" Jane said.

He shrugged. "Not every job requires a smart man. But a smart man can do almost every job."

We were close to the other ship now. The hull's wood was aged and sun-bleached. A row of four portholes ran from bow to stern, and when we got closer, I realized they were much larger than the ones on the *Red Cow,* big enough for a man to easily crawl through. That seemed a dangerous invitation to sinking in rough weather. Above us, the rail looked weathered but intact.

"Ahoy!" Jane called. "Anyone aboard? What ship are you? What master? This is Captain Argo with the *Red Cow*! Do you need assistance?"

There was no answer.

"She's riding low in the water," Veasley observed. "Must have a full belly of cargo."

We found no ropes or ladders, so Suhonen and Kaven tossed up grapples and hooked the rail. I hadn't climbed a rope in a long time, and those same muscles still sore from swinging onto the *Vile Howl* protested again. But I made it, much more gracefully than Duncan, who may never have climbed a rope before in his life. Suhonen had to haul him up the last couple of feet.

We paused to get our bearings. The deck was empty. Totally. Of everything. There were no ropes, no lines, no nets, nothing, just bare wood stained with neglect. The only sound came from the creak of the empty masts above us, and the water slapping against the hull. It didn't even smell like a ship: no odors of people, food, or cargo.

"No flies," Jane observed. "So probably no dead bodies or rotted provisions."

"How many people would it take to crew a ship like this?" I asked.

"Six, bare minimum," she said. She went up to the wheel and spun it. It turned easily, and kept going when she released it. "The wheel's not attached to the rudder."

I asked, "So how is this thing staying still?"

"Seaton was right, I can't imagine an anchor chain long enough to reach the bottom here," she said. "Even if it did, it would be so long, the ship would still swing around like a kite on a line."

"Aye, you'd need more than one," Kaven said. "One fore, one aft, to really hold her this still."

"I'm getting a little creeped out," Suhonen observed. His tone was as steady as if he'd been ordering a drink in a tavern.

Jane walked to the starboard rail and looked over it. "She's riding low. Really low. She must be loaded with something heavy, like Weasely said."

"That's Veasely, ma'am," he corrected politely.

"Whatever. That would explain a little of why she doesn't move."

I walked onto the forecastle and looked back toward the quarterdeck. "You know what this reminds me of?" I said to no one in particular.

"A decoy?" Suhonen said. He wasn't about to let someone else take credit for his idea.

I shook my head. "A set for a play. Like the one you guys put together. I mean, it *looks* like a ship, but nothing really functions."

"It floats," Kaven pointed out. He held a short-chained mace in his hand, the kind of weapon you had to wield expertly if you didn't want to smash in your own skull.

We checked the captain's cabin, but it was an empty room.

No bunks, no tables, nothing. No double *X* on the door. Cobwebs sparkled with dried salt in the corners, and the dust on the floor showed only our footprints. Had the *Vile Howl*'s crew not made it this far, or did the dust at sea simply settle faster than on land?

"Let's check below," Jane said. "I'm curious to see what cargo she's carrying."

"Should we split up?" Duncan asked. His voice was higher than normal, and he was sweating buckets that had nothing to do with the heat. "I mean, should somebody stay up here in case Captain Clift tries to signal us?"

"No," I said. "We stay together. If this is a trap, we're walking right into it."

Suhonen put a big hand on the boy's shoulder. "Just stay with me, do what I say, and you'll be all right. I pissed myself on my first boarding, too, and that was a normal one."

Kaven and Veasely lifted off the hatch cover. It was not fastened; it was just a big piece of wood covering the square hole in the deck.

Jane lay flat and peered over the edge. Instead of the pitch-black opening I expected, I saw light inside, probably from those huge portholes. "Well, that's weird," she said as she got to her feet. "I think you're right, Eddie. But if it's a play, where are the actors?"

"Us?" I suggested dolefully.

"Then who the fuck is the audience?"

Jane led the way down the ladder into the hold. I wondered what sort of cargo, one that needed no tending at all, could be weighing down the ship. Treasure? Rocks?

Corpses?

hat we found was . . . unexpected.

On the *Red Cow,* the hold consisted of a big area for the crew, and several smaller rooms for things such as sail locker, galley, and carpenter's cabin. The captain, quarter-master, and sailing master also had quarters there. The ceilings were low and beams crossed them inconveniently. Below the hold was the bilge, where water and rum barrels were stored.

This ship had none of those. Its hold was one big empty room from bow to stern, and from the deck down to the keel. No bulkheads, no bilge.

The four huge portholes let in plenty of light, but there was little to see. Mold grew in places, and the same heavy cobwebs filled the corners and edges. A few mosquitoes rose from the stagnant water that had collected in the very bottom. A raised walkway, perhaps all that was left of the keelson, ran the length of the hold. A round wooden hatch covered something at the walkway's center.

The smell was also odd. There was the odor of stagnant water, damp wood, and mildew, but over all this was something I couldn't quite identify. It was fishy, both literally and metaphorically.

Jane stepped off the ladder and stopped, keeping the rest of us on the steps above her. She muttered, "What the hell?"

"There ain't nothing here," Veasely said.

Jane took a few steps down the walkway and swiped at the mosquitoes swarming to us. If they hadn't fed since the *Vile Howl,* they had to be starving. "Mosquitoes don't cross the ocean. They must've come aboard when this ship was docked somewhere."

"What does that tell us?" I asked.

She chuckled. "Not a damn thing, really."

We followed until we all stood single-file along the walkway. The flat ceiling was as featureless as the walls that curved in toward the keel beneath us.

Jane sheathed her sword and scratched her head. "This doesn't make any sense. With this much open space, the ship should bob up and down like a cork."

"Maybe it *is* anchored," I said.

"Where's the anchor chain, then, smart-ass?" she snarled, then sighed. "Sorry, I just don't understand this at all."

Duncan said, "And what do you figure that hatch is for?"

No one answered. Jane and I looked at each other. She eased along the walkway, falling into rhythm with the ship's slight roll. I looked behind the ladder, where the walkway continued until it dead-ended at the stern. There was nothing.

Duncan looked as pale as the first winter snow. Even Veasely and Kaven were visibly nervous. Only Suhonen seemed entirely unaffected.

"What made those?" Kaven asked. He indicated a series of random, deep scratches in the hull walls.

I examined one. It was about the width of my little finger, and at one end there was a slightly deeper puncture. The wood was gouged away from this hole in one direction, like something had been stuck into the wood, then pulled along. It reminded me of a bear's claw sign in a tree, but none of the other scratches were parallel, or even seemed remotely related. Was it the mark of some weapon? If so, judging from the vast network of similar marks, whoever wielded it hadn't gone down without a fight.

"I'm going to fall back on Jane's standard answer," I said. "Beats the hell out of me."

Jane was nearly to the hatch when she stopped and said, "Uh-oh." We all waited while she knelt, reached into the water, and retrieved a white head scarf stained with water and what looked like blood. She also pulled out a seaman's dagger and a woman's slipper. Then she held up the most disturbing thing of all: a child's doll, clearly the mate of the one we found on the *Vile Howl*. She gently placed it on the walkway beside the shoe.

"That can't be good," Suhonen rumbled.

She continued to the hatch. The lip rose about two feet above the walkway. The hatch itself was round, a yard across and hinged on one side. There was no apparent latch.

"Man, this stinks," she called. "I don't know what's under here, but it must be nasty as all get-out. Come on and help me open it."

Veasely and Kaven exchanged a look. Duncan sat heavily on the lowest stair as if he might pass out. I looked at Suhonen. "I guess she means you and me."

He looked disdainfully at the others. "Someone has to guard the way out, I suppose."

"Exactly!" Kaven almost yelped. "We'll make sure the path to safety stays clear. Right?"

"Let them try to get past us," Veasley agreed. I didn't press him on who he meant by "them."

I scanned the bilgewater as we walked and saw other scraps that spoke of previous visitors. It certainly wasn't enough for the whole crew of the *Vile Howl,* let alone the other ships that had turned up crewless. But someone had been here and met with serious trouble.

Jane was right. The smell grew almost unbearable by the time we joined Jane at the hatch, and I recognized it: *vomit.* The vomit of someone who'd lived on nothing but fish for quite a while. But there was no sign of puke anywhere on the ship.

We stood around it in silence. Kaven called, "Do ye think it's going to open itself, then?"

"You're welcome to help," Jane said.

"Take your time," he replied, extra magnanimously.

Finally I said, "You sure this isn't like a bathtub plug? If we open it, it might sink us."

"I don't think so," Jane said. "It's hinged, but it ain't locked. And that smell ain't pure, sweet seawater. I'm betting the source is under there."

"Garbage?" Suhonen suggested.

"You throw garbage over the side; you don't keep it in the hold," Jane said.

He nodded at the relics she'd recovered. "Dead bodies?"

"Does it smell like dead bodies?" she shot back.

"No," he had to admit.

"Arguing about it isn't going to tell us anything," I said.

Jane lifted the edge, and it rose about an inch before she stopped. "Someone wants this to be easy to open."

"Nobody makes a trap hard to get *in* to," Suhonen said.

She took a deep breath, then lifted the hatch all the way.

The smell that surged forth made us gag. Jane and I stepped back, and even Suhonen stepped off the walkway and into the bilgewater. Except for the smell, though, nothing emerged. Water didn't gush in to send us to the bottom.

Suhonen set the hatch aside, scowled, and said, "That's really unpleasant."

Jane, holding her nose, said, "Nothing gets past you, does it?"

I didn't hold my nose, but I tried to mouth-breathe as I pointed to the hatch. "Look."

On the underside was carved the same double *X*.

"What does that *mean*?" Jane seethed.

"Maybe 'gotcha,'" Suhonen suggested.

Then the three of us peered down into the round chamber the hatch had covered.

For a long moment we were silent. I heard someone down at the ladder vomit into the bilge as the odor hit him, and assumed it was Duncan. Kaven called, "It smells like a vegetarian's outhouse! What the hell is in there?"

That was a good question, because even though I was looking right at it, I couldn't answer.

A round mass of pink, veined flesh was stuffed into the

opening. It was puckered toward the center. The wet surface gleamed. It looked almost as disgusting as it smelled.

Finally Jane said tentatively, "Is that—?"

I shook my head. "It looks like . . . well . . ."

"An arsehole," Suhonen said. "It looks like a giant arsehole."

"I'm married to one of those," Jane said wryly. She drew her sword and gently, tentatively poked the disgusting rippled flesh.

The orifice spit out a stream of thick, chunky liquid. At least two of the chunks were fish heads that sailed past me to splat against the wood. We jumped back as a big, hard disk emerged edge-up, then split in half—it was an enormous, razor-sharp *beak*. It sliced the air with a sound like a pair of gigantic shears.

Then the entire ship rocked to one side, knocking us all off our feet. Something slammed into the hull beneath us, and the huge beak extended up on a fleshy shaft. It bent to the side, snapping toward Jane, who scrambled to stay out of its way.

As I took in all this, the room fell dark. The portholes were now blocked by the tips of gigantic writhing tentacles that slithered in from outside, growing thicker and larger as they extended and showing no sign of stopping before they reached us. Something scraped and rattled along the bottom of the ship, and there was no mistaking its source: the links of a heavy chain. A *very* heavy chain.

I admit, the obvious connection between all these things escaped me until Jane bellowed, *"There's a goddamned sea monster chained to the bottom of the ship!"*

I knew about the octopus, the squid, and the cuttlefish, all disgusting pulpy creatures with long arms laden with suction cups. I'd even seen squids as big as a man attack a horse that had fallen off a troop transport. But whatever lurked below this nameless ship bore about as much resemblance to those creatures as my boot dagger did to a battering ram.

The arms poking through the hatchways were already as big around as I was, and those were just the tips. They reached unerringly for the puckered flesh and enormous beak, seeking the source of the sudden pain. For the moment the path to the deck was clear, and Kaven made a break for it, clattering up the stairs and shrieking like a girl. He'd just reached the top when something knocked him back, and he landed across the walkway with a thud. The ship swayed back and forth, rolling his limp body into the stagnant water. The tentacle that had smacked him now filled the hatch entrance, blocking our escape.

I glanced at Jane. She was flat against the curved wall, slashing madly at the tip of a tentacle. It withdrew with each cut but resumed its attack at once. Suhonen, meanwhile, had pinned the tip of one beneath his boot, and as I watched, he sliced off a good six feet of it. The ship rocked in response, and the stump covered him with a spray of blue-tinted blood.

More tentacles squeezed in alongside the first ones, spreading out along the walls, alert for any movement. I got a good look at the damp, revolting suction cups that lined the undersides. In the middle of each cup was a single hooked claw as long as my index finger, made of the same shiny black material as the beak; now I knew where all those gouged tracks came from.

Veasely slashed at the tentacle coming down from above, but didn't notice the one from the stern porthole that suddenly wrapped around his waist. He screeched, the high cry of agony that I'd heard many times on the battlefield. The arm lifted him as if he weighed nothing and carried him over me toward the beak. The vicious maw strained at the top of its shaft, open wide and ready. I jumped and grabbed one of Veasely's feet, but the creature shook me loose with no effort. I landed in the stagnant water.

"Help!" Veasely shrieked, beating futilely at the tentacle. *"Help me!"*

I risked a look at the stairs. Duncan huddled on the bottom step, knees drawn up to his chin and his eyes scrunched shut. Kaven lay where he'd fallen, and another tentacle was almost upon him. Neither could help. "Suhonen!" I yelled.

He looked up, saw Veasely in trouble, and stepped off the tentacle he'd cut.

This was a mistake, as the stump simply thwacked him across the back and sent him, too, flying toward the thing's mouth. Luckily the creature was still reaching up for Veasely, so that when Suhonen hit the puckered flesh, the beak was five feet above him. He drew back his sword to cut the beak's shaft, and if he'd been able to do it, a lot might have been different.

But the stump hit him again, and another tentacle wrapped around his torso. The pain of those long black claws puncturing his skin made him yell and drop his sword. He, too, was lifted into the air and pushed toward the snapping beak.

Veasely got there first, though, and the tentacle stuffed his shrieking, struggling form down the creature's gullet. The beak snapped shut, and one of the sailor's legs was severed at the knee. It dropped with a thud to the walkway, then bounced into the stagnant water. Immediately, a swarm of pale crabs rushed from beneath the walkway and began devouring the leg's flesh.

All this took about five seconds. During that time, I scrambled toward the mouth's hatch, hoping I could finish what Suhonen had tried to do. The ship careened back and forth, alternately slamming me into the hull and tossing me across to the other side. I was nowhere near close enough when the creature pushed Suhonen toward its ravenous, now-bloody maw.

"Fuck!" Jane yelled. Now it lifted her into the air by one leg, dangling her upside down. She'd lost her sword as well.

The beak opened so wide, it was almost horizontal. At the last second, Suhonen slammed his feet down, one on either half of the beak, and jammed them apart. Red blood spurted from beneath the tentacles as it squeezed his chest, but he held fast, roaring his defiance. Jane hung above him, waiting her turn, struggling to slash the tentacle with her dagger.

I still wasn't close enough for a regular sword strike, so I did the best I could. I threw my sword like a spear, and it struck the disgusting gullet stalk dead center.

And went right through. I heard it clatter against the hull on the far side.

Now *that* pissed me off. *Come on, LaCrosse,* I told myself. *You once killed a genuine fire-breathing dragon and faced down Gordon Marantz. You going to let a boneless sea monster get the best of you?*

I drew my boot knife and yelled, "Suhonen! Jump!"

He saw what I was about to do, bent his legs, and sprang up. The beak snapped shut, just missing his feet. Then I leaped and wrapped my arms and legs around the shaft.

It was like hugging a skinned deer that had been left out in the rain for a week: soft, slimy, and rank. There was nothing to hold on to, and I began to slip almost at once. I braced my feet on the hatch lip, buried my knife into the shaft, and began to saw. Most of it was pulpy and put up no resistance, and my hand sank into it up to the elbow. Suddenly, though, the blade bit into something solid, a tendon or shaft of gristle, and I viciously cut through it.

The ship rose beneath us. Whatever this thing was, it was big enough to push the whole vessel up above the water when it was hurt. It shook me off the shaft, which flopped to one side. Only half the beak now moved. The tentacles dropped Jane and Suhonen and rushed their tips to the beak, which oozed blue blood where I'd cut the tendon or muscle inside it. The tips fluttered around the wound like a grandmother's fingers.

The ship crashed back down into the water, bouncing us into the air. I got up and looked around; Jane and Suhonen weren't moving. Jane lay facedown in the bilge, and the water around her was already stained red. The white crabs were examining her, not quite certain she was carrion. I was coated in disgusting sea monster saliva, and wiping at it only spread it around.

I looked back at Duncan, still huddled on the bottom step, clutching his knife as if it were a child's sleep toy. "Duncan!" I yelled. "Get over here!"

The boy blinked, looked at me, and, despite the utter terror I saw in his eyes, jumped up and ran to me.

The ship continued to groan, and somewhere wood cracked. I realized we were descending. The injured monster was trying to pull the whole ship down with it. I didn't know if the hull would hold. Water surged in through the four portholes.

I turned Jane onto her back. She was alive, but her skin was wan and her lips faintly blue. It occurred to me that those tentacle claws might be poisonous. "We have to get them out of here, back onto the deck. You take her; I'll manage Suhonen."

"No one has to manage me," Suhonen said. He was on his feet, weaving but alert. Three punctures diagonally crossed his torso, oozing blood. The scar on my own chest twinged in sympathy; if one of those claws had gone deep enough to get to his lungs, I knew just how unlikely his survival would be.

Suhonen tossed Jane over his shoulder as easily as I might a sleeping child. "I think the party's over," he said, and made his way toward the stairs, battling the rolling ship.

I picked up Suhonen's dropped sword, then retrieved Jane's and handed it to Duncan. "Ready to go?" I asked. He nodded rapidly. "Then let's make sure nothing nasty follows us."

I watched ahead of us, while Duncan kept an eye behind. I had to trust him—more tentacles were squeezing into the portholes, seeking to touch the injured beak shaft. When one came too near, I slashed, and it withdrew at once. We got to the stairs and only then did I risk a look back. Duncan was right there, and from the fresh blue blood on the end of his sword, I knew he'd been busy.

Kaven lay where he'd fallen beside the stairs. His eyes were wide open, but he saw nothing; the impact had snapped his neck across the walkway's edge. I said to Duncan, "You go up first," but he shook his head. It wasn't the time to argue, so I clambered up the stairs and squeezed past the thick tentacle that blocked half the hatch, aided by its natural slime. Duncan followed.

On the pitching deck, Jane sat with her back against the mainmast. Her right leg was stuck straight out, and blood pulsed from the puncture in her thigh. She was conscious again, weak from shock and loss of blood. Her attitude hadn't changed, though. "Holy shit," she gasped when she saw me, "that was fucking close. I didn't think we'd get past that last tentacle."

Suhonen knelt at the rail, trying to haul in our boat. The ship was so low to the water that it bobbed at deck level. If it stayed this low, the water rushing into the big hold would sink it.

"Go help him," I told Duncan. The boy rushed to take the rope from Suhonen, who didn't put up a fight. Instead he flopped to the side, unconscious, as soon as the rope was out of his hands. Duncan put Jane's sword on the deck under one foot and began to pull with all the might his panic provided, which was considerable.

Across the way, the crew of the *Red Cow* waved at us. At first I thought they were cheering our success, which seemed odd; then I realized they were pointing behind and above us. I turned.

Three tentacles rose as high as the ship's foremast into the air. They wound around the masts and snapped the topmost lengths off. Splinters rained down on us. Duncan had almost gotten the boat to the rail, which was good because the monster now had us so low in the water, waves began to swamp the deck. "Come on!" the boy yelled.

I helped Jane to her feet and she hopped quickly to the boat, landing in an undignified heap across the bow seat. Then I muscled the unconscious Suhonen across my shoulders and rolled him in on top of her, eliciting a weak but outraged, "Ow! Watch it!"

A huge column of water shot into the air. I knew cuttlefish propelled themselves with water jets, and it seemed this one was no different. The ship groaned, more bits of mast fell off, and the wherry nearly capsized. I grabbed the rope from Duncan and said, "Get in the boat!"

He did as I told him, almost impaling himself on Jane's huge sword. I was less than a second behind him. Another jet of water pushed us rapidly away from the ship, accompanied by a surge of jet-black ink. The water smelled rancid now, and Duncan and I quickly began to row for the *Cow*.

As we pulled away, another tentacle appeared and reached for us. How many goddamned arms did this thing have, anyway? Before I could react, Duncan stood and whacked the tentacle with Jane's sword. A three-foot section dropped into the boat and flopped at our feet, spewing blue blood. The rest of the arm recoiled, knocking the sword from his hands and into the water. But by then the combination of waves and our own frantic rowing put us safely out of reach.

The creature's other tentacles enveloped the ship now, and the bow sank beneath the surface. "No way," Jane whispered in awe. "It can't possibly pull the ship down."

"I don't think it knows that," I said.

With a great unearthly cry—part scraping wood, part animal's shriek—the boat shot into the air as the monster lost its battle to pull the ship beneath the water. The vessel bounced, sending several waves toward us that pushed us toward the *Cow* even faster. Then it settled, the tentacles withdrew, and by the time we reached our ship, the strange vessel once again sat motionless in the sea, although lower, thanks to the water in its hold. Only the broken masts and ink-stained water indicated what had happened.

Jane looked up from tying a tourniquet around her leg. "That was a hell of a trap," she croaked.

"It was," I agreed.

She began to laugh.

I t took four men to carry Suhonen belowdecks, and three more to manage Jane. I had to coax Duncan out of the boat; he clutched his sword and stared at the other ship as if he expected the creature beneath it to come after us. Honestly, the same thought had occurred to me. I wondered if we'd dealt it a mortal blow, or just an inconvenience.

The ship's surgeon, a portly old man named Skurnick, judged Suhonen the more seriously injured and began working on him at once. Jane was carried unconscious to her cabin, but she was already pale and sweaty, and she began to mutter to herself without waking up. Dorsal waited outside the cabin and watched, wide-eyed, as Jane was tended, then slipped in when only I remained watching over her.

"She's hurt real bad," he said. It wasn't a question.

"Yeah," I agreed. I was still covered with slick, sticky monster spit, and it did not grow more pleasant as it dried. "Can you watch her until I get back? I need to get this gunk off. If you need me, holler."

"Sure," he said.

I undressed, went on deck, lowered a bucket, and washed as best I could with seawater. Around me, the crew worked in grim silence, aware of what lurked beneath the innocuous ship across the way.

Good-natured, secretly love-struck Captain Clift was as furious as I've ever seen anybody. He stalked the deck like a panther, snapping orders that Seaton did not have to repeat. He glared at me as I cleaned up, but I knew his anger wasn't personal. He'd narrowly avoided the fate of all those other ghost ships, and the nearness of it rubbed him the wrong way.

"Cap'n!" a sailor called. They were tying up the boat we'd used, and several men stared into it. One of them reached down and retrieved the dismembered tentacle tip. "Appears we have a souvenir."

Clift looked it over. He lifted one of the claws from the center of a suction cup, and muttered a curse I didn't catch.

I said, "Ever seen anything like that?"

He nodded. "Bigger than any of 'em, of course, but I know the type." He flicked one of the claws near the tentacle's end. It was only two inches long, but no less intimidating when you thought about it buried in your flesh. "Want to hear the worst part?"

"There's a worst part I don't already know about?"

He pulled the claw free. It was smooth, and with a wide ball at the base. Blue ichor dripped from it. "There's no barbs."

"What does that mean?"

"They don't get the barbs until they're full grown."

I was so tired, it took a moment for that to register. "You mean it's a *baby*?"

"More likely a teenager. But yeah, it's not full grown." He handed me the claw. "I hope we don't run into Mama before we're done."

WHEN Clift and I returned to Jane's cabin, Skurnick stood over her leg. Dorsal had vanished, no doubt chased away by the doctor. Skurnick had cut away half her trousers to expose a single puncture on the inner side of her thigh, dangerously near the big artery that ran there. The edges of the wound were crusted with scab, but the center was still dark red and oozing. Each time he wiped it, more blood trickled out.

"Not much I can do for her," he wheezed. "I've cleaned it, and the wound's closing on its own, but she's lost a lot of blood. She'll either survive or she won't." He looked at me. "She's tough. I was with her for three years before she left the sea. If anybody can pull through this, it's Captain Argo." To Clift, he said, "She shouldn't be alone. She might be delirious, and she could hurt herself."

Clift and I exchanged a glance. I said, "I'll stay with her until midnight. You can send someone to relieve me then."

"I'll relieve you," Clift said. "I don't want the crew to see her like this."

Skurnick said, "She's got a fever, and it'll probably get worse before it gets better. Maybe we should tie her down."

I shook my head. "I'll make sure she doesn't hurt herself."

He looked me up and down, measuring my apparent strength against Jane's. "If you think you're up to it, son." Then he left, chuckling to himself.

Clift looked at the nameless ship through the porthole. "Who does that, LaCrosse? I mean, it's one thing to catch a beast like the one over there, which I admit is impressive. But to allow it to do your dirty work, and then just sail in and pick up the pieces . . . Who *does* that?"

"Someone pretty smart. I bet every other captain rushed in to rescue his crew and never came back."

"I learned from their mistakes," he said with no irony.

Jane said something we didn't catch. Her eyes were open, and she licked her lips before speaking again. "I said . . . he'll be coming to check his trap."

Clift nodded. "I already figured that. I've got a plan." But Jane's eyes were already closed.

"What is it?" I asked Clift.

"You'll see." He turned toward the door. "I have work to do. We have to gather Veasely's and Kaven's gear and toss it overboard. Keeping it is bad luck, or at least the crew will think so. I'll see you at midnight, and I'll make sure Skurnick stays sober. If anything changes, yell good and loud."

"Aye," I said, and half saluted.

Dorsal slipped in before the door closed and joined me at Jane's bedside. "I hope she doesn't die."

"Me, too."

He touched Jane's hand. She gasped and jerked her hand away without waking. Dorsal took a step back, and I said, "Don't take it personally."

He looked up at me. "I don't."

"Thanks."

I sat down on the floor, my back against the wall. I was asleep within minutes.

THE sun woke me when it had crossed the sky and now shone through the porthole. I hadn't intended to sleep, but there was no resisting it. I got up, stretched, and opened the cabin door to allow what little breeze we could get. Dorsal sat outside the cabin and nodded at me. I saluted back.

Jane was breathing steadily, but sweat poured from her, soaking her hair and the bedclothes. I removed the blood-soaked bandage on her leg; the wound was now closed, but the scab was fragile, like the first ice on a pond. I decided to let it air out a little before I rebandaged it.

She opened her eyes. They were shiny with delirium and didn't focus on anything. "Miles?"

"No, it's Eddie."

"Eddie? Where's Miles? Is he here?"

"He's home. Safe."

"Are you sure?" Her voice was pitiful in its concern. "He's not a fighter, he gets hurt so easily. . . ."

"Absolutely," I said. "He's fine."

"Good," she sighed. Her eyes closed again.

After sunset, I lit the lamp, and again her eyes opened. This time they were clear, and they looked right at me. "Have you been here all day?"

"Yeah."

"How am I?"

"'Bitchy and foul-mouthed' seems to be the consensus."

She smiled. "I'm too tired to look. Have I still got my leg?"

"Yeah."

She chuckled weakly. "Skurnick usually doesn't wait to am-
putate. I think he keeps score; his bone saw has little notches
on the handle." She raised herself on her elbows, an effort that
took all her strength. "Goddamn if it isn't the same leg I broke
back at that conference where we met. Do you remember that?"

"I do."

"Can I have a drink of water?"

I found the jug and tipped it up for her. She was still very
pale, but her fever had broken and the sweat had dried. She
asked, "How's Suhonen?"

"Fine, the last I heard," I said. Which was true. Like Jane,
he'd either live or die based on his own innate toughness.

She lay back. "Who was that boy that was in here?"

"His name's Dorsal."

"Is he the cabin boy?"

I nodded. "But he thinks he's the captain."

"And the little girl?"

"I think you might have been dreaming her. There's no little
girls on board."

She laughed, weak but unmistakably Jane. "That figures.
Not sexy young men, just a strange little girl." She smiled and
lay back. "At least it wasn't the handmaiden again."

I remembered Clift's drunken assertions. "You dream about
her a lot?"

She nodded. "Don't you dream about your failures?"

"I used to. Talking to Liz about it has helped, believe it or
not. You ever talk to Miles?"

She snorted weakly. "What do you think?"

"You want to talk to me?"

She thought for so long, I worried she'd passed out with her eyes open. Then she said, "Close the door."

I did so and sat on the floor opposite her bunk.

She said, "You were a mercenary before you became a sword jockey, right? What made you change jobs?"

I didn't want to get into detail about the whorehouse massacre that left me the only survivor, with no idea who'd killed everyone else or why. It made me take a long look at myself and the life I'd chosen. "I saw who I'd become and didn't like it."

She nodded. "Me, too. I was a pirate, and a really good one. My crew made tons of money. Then one day we captured a ship with some noblewoman on board. She wouldn't tell me where her jewels were hidden. I told her I'd kill her if she didn't cooperate, but she was stubborn. That snotty kind of stubborn, you know? When I threatened to torture her, one of her handmaidens jumped to her defense. So I snapped the girl's spine across my knee."

I knew where this was going. I'd suspected something like this ever since I met Jane. "Did the noblewoman change her mind?"

She laughed, weak and without humor. "No. She didn't think any more of the girl than I did. Except after a while, I couldn't get the girl out of my mind. The look on her face, the terror . . ." Big tears welled in her eyes, but her voice remained steady. "Sometimes we have to be ruthless, you know? Show no mercy. But I killed that girl for all the wrong reasons, primarily just because I *could*. For the hell of it. I was fucking showing off." She wiped her eyes. "I didn't like myself much after that. I became a pirate hunter because I thought I could help balance the scales for that girl's life, you know? But they don't ever balance, do they? The past never goes away."

"No," I agreed.

"So I became a sword jockey. I make my own rules, decide who and how to help, and choose what lines to cross and why. No ship's crew to satisfy, no Anti-Freebootery Guild to boss me around."

I took her hand. It was as big as mine, and callused around the many rings.

She looked up at me. "Don't you get mushy on me, LaCrosse."

I didn't pull my hand away. "Stop telling sob stories, then."

"Yeah," she agreed. "Must be the blood loss talking. Gets me all light-headed."

I squeezed her hand. "I think you'll be all right."

She yawned and stretched. "Mind if I go to sleep?"

"Would it matter if I did?"

"Not a damn bit," she slurred, and in moments she was out.

SHE slept until Clift relieved me at midnight. I passed Dorsal on my way to the deck, lurking in the shadows by the ladder, and he nodded sagely. I wondered if he'd overheard Jane's story.

A very light breeze blew across the deck, and the moon illuminated the monster's ship. I got a drink of rum, found a spot to sit, and sipped it gratefully. My involuntary nap that afternoon had thrown me off, and now I was wide awake.

I spotted Duncan Tew trying to concentrate on unwinding and de-kinking the grapple line again, but he wasn't paying much attention to the job. Instead he kept glancing at the other ship, watching for any change.

I sat down beside him. "Weird to think what's out there, isn't it?"

"Yeah," he said without looking at me.

"You know, you did a great job. We wouldn't be sitting here talking about it without you."

"I pissed my pants," he said, eyes downcast. "When it tried to grab me out of the boat."

"I don't think anyone noticed. And you still did the job. Hell, I was scared to death, too."

"Then why didn't you piss *your* pants?" he demanded bitterly.

"Because I have more experience being scared like that."

"Is that all it takes? Experience?"

He said it sarcastically, but I answered him with the truth. "Yeah."

He snorted as if he didn't believe me.

I asked, "Did you ever hear the story of the colonel's red shirt?"

He shook his head.

"There was this colonel in the army of his kingdom, it doesn't matter who or where. Whenever he'd be about to go into battle, he'd say, 'Fetch my red shirt.' No one knew why, until one day a lowly private worked up the nerve to ask. Do you know what the colonel said?"

He shook his head again.

"He said, 'If I'm hurt, the bloodstains won't show on a red shirt. My men will think I'm invincible, and follow me into hell if I want them to.'"

Duncan smiled. "Clever."

"Yeah, until the day his army had to fight one five times

larger. You know what he said then? 'Fetch me my brown pants.'"

Duncan laughed for a long time. At last he settled down, worked silently for a while, then said, "You think my father is behind that ship and the monster?"

"I hope not, for your sake."

"I mean, being a pirate is one thing. But this is . . . so fucking cowardly. Letting a monster do all the dirty work."

"Can't argue with your take on it."

He didn't look at me. "Part of me hopes he *is* behind it. That way I can hate him with a clear conscience."

I put a hand on his arm. "Just wait until you know for sure."

He shrug-nodded the way some kids do. He *was* still half kid, despite being a father. He was struggling toward maturity all on his own, with no template to go by.

Seaton came on deck and blew his whistle. "Captain wants everyone here, now," he bellowed. "All hands on deck!"

The crew quickly gathered below the quarterdeck. Clift stood up there with his hands on his hips, looking over at the nameless ship outlined by moonlight. When there was reasonable quiet, he said, "Men, we narrowly avoided the same fate that befell those ghost ships we encountered. But whoever set that trap doesn't yet know that. So we're going to disguise ourselves as a ghost ship and wait to see who comes to salvage us.

"We don't know how long it'll take. There's no way for the villain to know his monster has snagged a victim, so he probably comes around on a regular schedule. We have to lie low and play dead, possibly for days. Maybe weeks. That means no one on deck during the day, no lights at night. We shift the weight so that the ship lists a little. I want some cut lines and spare canvas draped over the side, like they've fallen from disrepair. And here's the hard part."

He paused for effect. "We have to be ready to fight as soon as they appear. No matter how much time it takes. I'm asking a lot of your patience, and your courage, and your strength of character. But I promise you, the fight will be worth it. The Guild will reward us handsomely for capturing the bastards behind this. And we get the satisfaction of doing what no other pirate hunter has been able to do. Songs about the *Red Cow* will be sung in every tavern along every coast. What say you?"

A roar that might've disturbed the exhausted sea monster rose, along with fists and brandished weapons.

Clift smiled. "Aye, lads, that's the spirit. Now let's get the *Cow* ready for her date, eh?"

Another cheer rose from the men. Clift came down and walked among them, thanking and encouraging them individually. He knew how to command, that's for sure. At last he reached me, put a hand on my shoulder, and said, "I'd like to speak to you a moment."

"Sure."

He pulled me aside but stayed within view, if not earshot, of the men. "I left Skurnick with Jane. Her fever's gone, and she's sleeping normally. It looks good for her."

"And Suhonen?"

"We don't know yet." He paused. "When the moment comes, when the carrion crabs come around to see what they've caught, I'd like you to lead the attack."

"Me? I'm just a passenger."

"False modesty is still a falsehood, Mr. LaCrosse. You're also the man who got away from that sea monster with barely a scratch, as well as rescuing both our best fighter and my former captain. I know how good *they* are. You seem to be better."

"Just luckier."

He leaned close. "I'm serious. The men know what you did. If you don't lead them, they'll assume it's because you think we can't win, and then I've lost them. I need you."

I glanced past him at the crew. All of them watched with varying degrees of discretion. I'd fought on ships before, so I wasn't completely unfamiliar with it, but at the same time, I barely knew these men and, except for Suhonen, I'd seen little to impress me. If we spent our days cowering belowdecks, we'd have no chance to practice and drill so I could get to know them better, either. We were all on this ship together, though, and that meant I had a vested interest in how the battle came out. "Okay," I said. "But I want a third of my money back."

He nodded. "A man deserves a fair pay for a job. But only if we win."

I grinned, the kind of sideways grimace that has nothing to do with humor. "If we don't, Captain Clift, poverty will be the least of my problems."

chapter

TWENTY-ONE

One way to tell the true strength of any fighting force is by how well it waits. By this measure, the *Red Cow*'s forces were pretty good. Of course, it helped that we had to wait only three days.

Before we started hiding and waiting, though, we again disguised the *Cow* as the *Crimson Heifer*, just another derelict whose crew now filled the belly of the nearby beast. A spare sail was draped over the bow as if it had tumbled from the foremast, along with enough rope to mimic its rigging. Lines were dropped over the side, their ends ragged as if they'd broken loose from the monster ship. The deck was cleared of anything that could signal recent occupancy.

Jane continued to recover, although she remained too weak to move. Suhonen wasn't dead, but neither had he opened his eyes; he simply slept, like some animal in winter hibernation.

Bandages swathed his broad chest, with three small red spots where blood soaked through. The men gave his hammock a wide berth, except for Skurnick, who checked on him regularly. He lay in the dark, swaying with the ship's movement, like a statue that might come to life at any moment.

When I approached him, one sailor grabbed my arm and said, "I'd use caution."

"Why?"

"I've heard stories about Suhonen. They say that if he's hurt in a fight, he wakes up and thinks he's back in the middle of it. I saw him knocked out once, and when he awoke, his arm was still in mid-punch. Like to near flattened Mr. Greaves, who was standing just beside him."

"I'll be careful."

The sailor shrugged. "Your skull, sir, not mine."

I waited until I had some semblance of privacy, then leaned down and spoke into Suhonen's ear. "If you can hear me, I just wanted you to know Clift put me in charge of whatever fight we end up having. I know you won't be up to actually joining us, but you know these guys better than I do and I could use your advice."

There was no response.

ON our first day hiding in the hold, three fights broke out. Clift settled two of them quickly, but a third looked to keep brewing even after the men were separated. I understood completely: it was so hot, humid, and crowded that my own temper was on edge. I could've retreated to my cabin, but I wanted the men to see I was in it with them, not lording it over them. I had them move Suhonen to my bunk, where his huge bare feet hung off the end.

Jane was sitting up now, scandalously undressed in the heat. I had to avert my eyes whenever I went to check on her. This amused her to no end. "It's a pair of boobies, LaCrosse, they won't kill you."

"I've run into plenty that were quite lethal, thank you very much."

"How goes the preparations?"

"We're prepared. Now we just need for the bad guys to show up before we all skewer each other."

"How are you going to run it?"

"We're going to let as many of them board us as we can before we give ourselves away. They'll likely tie onto us, but they'll cut those lines right away if they start to lose the fight. We'll use the ballistae belowdecks to fire grapples up through the ports. Hopefully, since we'll be shooting up at their rail, by the time they figure out where *our* ropes are, we'll have taken their ship."

She nodded. "Smart."

"I also had the carpenter install another hatch aft of the main one. It's flush with the deck, so you can't see it unless you're right on it. When the bad guys come down the main hatch, we'll have a team ready to go out that one. That way we won't get bottled in."

She shook her head and smiled. "You're a clever SOB."

"I just want this fight to be quick and one-sided. If I'm right, they won't be expecting any resistance."

"And you'll take Marteen alive, right?"

"Yes. I've made that completely clear. Clift said any man who kills Marteen forfeits his shares for this whole voyage."

"That should do it. You don't mess with a pirate's money."

"Ex-pirate," I corrected with a grin.

"Oh, yeah," she agreed ironically. "Completely ex."

AS soon as darkness fell, we rushed on deck, grateful for the space and air. The monster ship was barely visible on the horizon, and we saw no other vessels. Men pulled buckets of water from the ocean and doused themselves with it to cut through the day's accumulated sweat. I took some rum to Jane, checked on the still-immobile Suhonen, and touched base with Clift.

"Not good," the captain said. "We're drifting. If we move too far from that other ship, they might not find us."

"They found the others."

"Aye, but I imagine they tied up to the monster's vessel before boarding. Then their ship stayed put."

"I suppose we could tie up to it," I mused.

"Unless you swear to me that creature's dead, I'm not risking becoming a ghost ship for real."

If I'd done permanent damage to its mouth, then it would eventually starve to death. But for all I knew, it had been catching fish outside and stuffing them through the portholes all night. Or perhaps it could simply wait a long time between meals. "I left it hurt, but that's all I can say."

"Then we'll just have to row in closer and hope Marteen doesn't spot us while we're moving."

So we did, using a launch to tow the *Cow* back to where she'd started. The next day was another scorcher, and again everyone was on edge. But this time, knowing that nightfall would eventually come and we would escape, they were able to contain it.

When we did emerge, Clift had to remind the men to speak in whispers; sound carried far over the water.

And then, on the third day, we sighted another ship.

SHE bore three masts, a flush deck, and no flag visible at this distance. She headed straight for us, taking advantage of the wind that slowly pushed us away from the monster ship. Clift and Seaton peered out the porthole, careful not to let the sunlight illuminate their faces. I stood with the crowd behind them, waiting for their word.

"That's the one," Clift said at last.

"How do you know?" I asked, fighting the urge to whisper, as if a ship miles away could hear us.

"A feeling," he said. I wondered if perhaps he was wrong, that this was just some passing merchant or naval vessel wondering if we needed help. But the closer it got, the more I shared Clift's intangible sense that this new vessel was dangerous. It was a sense that I, like the captain, had long since learned to trust.

I turned to the crew. The men stood ready, arms unsheathed, making last-minute adjustments to their leather armor and weapons. They all looked expectantly at me. It had been a long time since I'd been watched with that kind of eager, almost childlike reliance. I felt a surprising rush of what I can only describe as excitement.

"If I'm right, the ship will pull alongside and board us. I don't know how close they'll look us over; I hope that by now they're overconfident about their monster. But they may be on their guard because we're drifting and not tied to the other ship. We have to let as many of them get on board as we can, even coming down here without giving ourselves away. They'll be sunblind in the hold, so it'll take time for their eyes to adjust. Let them give the alarm: when they shout, everyone left above will have their eyes on the main hatch, and we'll come busting out the new one."

They all nodded excitedly. Again, like eager children.

"I'm going to split you into two squads. One of them will concentrate on defending this ship; the other will board theirs. I'll be leading that one. The ones staying behind, you'll answer to Captain Clift." I hadn't cleared this with him first, but he nodded agreement. "The danger is that the other ship might break away from us. If they do, the men with me will be trapped in the enemy's lap."

"Not for long," Clift said. "She can't outrun us."

I'd seen nothing to indicate the *Red Cow* had that sort of speed, but it seemed the wrong time to make an issue of it. I continued, "It may mean being taken prisoner, at least for a while. It may, of course, mean dying. So I want real volunteers, not people picked out by the first mate." I glanced at Seaton. "No offense."

"None taken," he said. "And I'll be the first to sign up."

"Me, too," said Duncan Tew.

In short order I had my team, twenty men ready to join me in boarding the other ship. I stressed two things: Watch your fellow soldiers' backs, and take the captain alive.

I went to see Jane. Her leg was noticeably better, and she was bright-eyed and rested. "Hey, boss," she said when I came in. I put a sword beside her. "What's this?"

"Not as big as you're used to," I said, "but big enough. We've spotted another ship closing in."

She tried to stand. "I'm not waiting in here—"

"Yes, you are. I'm leading the boarding party, and Clift's commanding the troops here. He claims this heap can outrun anything, so if they get away, you'll have to make sure he chases us down."

"He will. But I can still fight. Just give me a crutch and—"

I couldn't help it; I laughed. "You can't even put your pants on, Jane. Just stay in here until the fight's over."

She glared at me. "Could you?"

"I could if you told me to."

She started to snap back, but I added, "I'll get the carpenter to knock together a crutch for you. But it's only for emergencies. And I won't be here to watch your back."

She grabbed the collar of her tunic with both hands and ripped it open almost to her navel. "And they'll be too busy staring at my front. Go do your job, LaCrosse. I'll be fine."

Now the waiting had a purpose, so the men were silent and still. Clift and I risked peering through the porthole to watch the ship as it neared.

"Look," Clift said. "The banner."

It was black, tapered, and trailed like one of the monster's tentacles. Stitched in white was an image I'd seen before, on the letter Angelina had kept all these years: an angel holding a sword over a skull. And then, beneath it, the double *X*.

"And the name," Clift added.

Painted on the bow in large black letters were the words BLOODY ANGEL. A thrill I'd never expected to feel again went through me. I was about to lead men into battle, and damn it, at some level, I *loved* it.

"Ready, lads," the captain said as loud as he dared. "We've hired the band, now it's time to name the tune."

The *Bloody Angel*'s crew scurried into their sails like monkeys, gathering the canvas and slowing the big vessel as it neared. They were slower than the *Cow*'s crew, but then again, they were self-employed. She was a third larger than the *Cow,* and consequently her crew outnumbered us. I wasn't worried about that nearly so much as I was about having no real place to retreat. If my trap failed and they bottled us up on the *Cow,* all they had to do was set fire to us and watch us burn.

The ballista gunners stood ready at their weapons, the grapples pointed up as much as the ports allowed. They would arc over the *Bloody Angel*'s rail, fall to the deck, and then we'd yank them back until the hooks caught. Then we'd reel them in. If we were lucky, it would rock the *Angel*'s deck and confuse them even more.

"Swing across!" someone called, and a moment later there

were multiple thumps on our deck. I counted at least half a dozen; I'd hoped for more. That left an awful lot of them still on the *Angel*.

The boarding party walked around, inspecting the ship. If we'd inadvertently left anything on deck to betray our presence, we were screwed. Then a voice yelled back to the *Angel,* "Looks like a merchant ship. Lots of crates on deck. Tie us up."

"Not so fast. What's the cargo?"

I caught Clift's eye. Someone on the other ship was already suspicious.

"Fuck if I know," came the annoyed reply. "Think I can see through solid wood?"

"Open a crate and check it," the first voice said.

"You open it, I'm going to check the hold." To someone else in the boarding party, he said, "I hate these fucking empty ships. I keep expecting a ghost to jump out at us."

"Yeah, and this one wasn't moored to our trap," his compatriot said. "That's why the captain doesn't want to tie on to it."

"No shit. You figure that out yourself? I'll tell you what's happening: After all this time, the captain's paranoid. It just broke loose and drifted away, any idiot can see that. If anyone *had* been alive on board, they'd have been yelling to get our attention, thinking we might rescue them." He laughed. "Dumbass floating salesmen. Probably a hold full of damn women's shoes. Come on, let's get what we came for and send this heap on its way."

We moved back into the shadows so that the light from the hatch wouldn't reveal us. I crept to the top of the ladder beneath the new exit and made ready to throw it open.

Just below me a sword hit the deck, jostled from someone's

hand. The noise sounded like crashing cymbals. We all froze, waiting to see if there would be cries of warning, but apparently no one on deck heard. "Steady," Clift whispered.

"Wait a second!" a new voice said. "Here, look at this. These are ballista sockets."

Damn. It hadn't occurred to me to cover the holes where the weapons were mounted. I saw by Clift's expression that he was mentally kicking himself, too.

"It's another damn pirate hunter," the first man said. "Son of a bitch, disguised as a damn merchant ship."

"Don't be a moron, you headless eel," a woman's voice said. "Somebody too cheap to build their own ship just bought an old pirate hunter. Either way, it's empty now."

"She's right," a third voice said. "Let's find the—"

The noise of the main hatch cover being lifted drowned out the final words. A pair of boots appeared on the top step. The first one down was the woman, short and round and with one of those arrogant, vicious little faces you saw on a lot of criminal types. She had gray hair cut mannishly. Behind her were a half-dozen big, filthy men, also older than I expected. They all wore rags, except for the odd bit of newish gear they'd likely looted from ships like this. These were real pirates, the kind I remembered from my mercenary days, and as if to confirm it, the first wave of their stench reached me.

But one thing I hadn't expected: They were so confident in their monster's thoroughness that none of them had drawn their weapons.

The mean round woman reached the bottom of the steps. Tense sweat stung my eyes. A dozen men stood within arm's reach, but she couldn't see them, because her eyes hadn't yet adjusted.

"Fire," I said softly.

The ballistae *thunk*ed as their pronged bolts shot into the air.

I took a deep breath and bellowed, in a voice I thought I'd never again use, *"Stab at their balls, men!"* Then I shoved open the new hatch and led the charge up onto the deck.

Like the old days, I absorbed the scene in a glance. Dozens of men lined the *Bloody Angel*'s rail, but surprisingly few of them were armed. On the *Cow,* four men waiting to descend into the hold stared at us, frozen in surprise. The biggest surprise was that they were all *old,* with gray hair, white beards, and missing body parts replaced with wood or metal implements. That didn't make them any less dangerous; veterans were twice as vicious as even the most enthusiastic new recruit, because they had the skills to survive.

Then both ships rocked as the lines fired from below caught and our men pulled the hulls together. They hit with a solid thud that knocked down most of the *Angel*'s unprepared crew, as well as several of ours.

"To the other ship!" I shouted, stepped onto the *Cow's* rail, and leaped the short distance to the *Bloody Angel*'s deck.

There was no time to pick and choose targets, and I cut down unarmed men as well as those with weapons. Many died still struggling back to their feet. I fought off two men and a woman who had sense enough to attack together. They were good, but they didn't realize what they were up against, and I quickly overcame their sloppy technique. In moments, all three lay dead at my feet. My tunic was sticky with their sprayed blood. The woman had time to spit at me before she closed her eyes.

I glimpsed Duncan Tew battling a taller, older opponent. He wasn't making much headway, but he had his defensive moves down pat, and his opponent was getting pissed off. If Duncan could keep his temper while the other man lost his, he'd soon get an opening. Nearby, Seaton moved with the slow, methodical strokes of a veteran, blocking and thrusting as if it were part of his daily routine. He left a row of dead men on either side of his path.

By now Clift's men had emerged from the hatch and overcome the boarding party. About half the *Angel*'s crew swarmed onto the *Cow,* not quite noticing that their ship was simultaneously being boarded behind them. I took advantage of this confusion to rush the *Angel*'s wheel and cut down the helmsman struggling to turn his ship away from the *Cow.* I spun the wheel the opposite direction, and the two ships again slammed together. I heard screams and splashes as the impact knocked men overboard.

My foot slipped in the helmsman's blood. When I regained my balance and turned, a new man stood before me. He had the unmistakable air of command about him, wearing as he did a tricornered hat, red velvet coat, and boots either recently bought or stolen. He also looked nothing at all like Duncan Tew. I said, "Wendell Marteen, I presume."

He looked at me closely to see if he knew me. "That's Captain Marteen to you, you pox-faced parrot. You think you're clever, don't you?"

"Since you fell for it, I'd say I have the right to."

Marteen's eyes bulged with anger, and he swung his wide-bladed sword at me with both hands. I dodged and hit his blade with mine as it went past, making him spin and fall. His hat went flying. The big sword clattered to the deck, slid across the wood, and tumbled out between two rail posts. I jumped to put the tip of my sword at Marteen's throat, but he scrambled away and cried, "Men! Assistance!"

Four of his crew jumped—well, shuffled with alacrity—to his defense. I got one through the belly, but the second one seriously cut my right shoulder and the third barely missed decapitating me. The pain from the cut was monumental, and I shifted my sword to my left hand. The remaining two grinned and charged me. Overconfident old bastards.

I dropped and rolled at their feet. They fell over me, and one continued tumbling over the rail and into the water. The third hit hard, and his eyes cleared for just an instant before I stabbed him through the neck.

I looked around for Marteen. The decks of both ships were a chaotic mass of flashing swords and swaths of red blood, and bodies dotted the water around us. I spotted him near the *Angel*'s mainmast, and hacked my way toward him. When he saw I wasn't dead, he looked confused, then scared. I knew I had him.

I was so confident, in fact, that I failed to notice the knot of men surging toward me as they fought one another. They caught me up in their struggle and, before I could react, pushed me over the *Angel*'s rail and into the space between the hulls of the two ships.

I released my sword and grabbed one of the two grapple lines that held the ships together. The heavy, rough rope burned my palms. If the vessels slammed together again, I'd be squashed like a bug.

I held on with every bit of strength I had. My cut shoulder expressed its displeasure with pain like hot knitting needles jammed down my arm. Beneath me, in the churning water between the ships, bobbed the dead and dying from both crews. Distinctive triangular fins slid among them, turning the foam pink. That motivated me, and I climbed hand over hand up toward the *Bloody Angel*'s deck.

And then somebody cut the rope.

The instant of free fall made my heart try to leap out of my throat and into the sea. Somehow I held on, even when I smashed into the *Cow*'s hull and my boots dangled in the water. A huge shark's mouth opened beneath me, and I yanked up my feet just in time. Above me, men continued to fight, oblivious to my dilemma. There was no point in shouting for help. I tried to climb to the *Cow*'s porthole, but my arms and injured shoulder had no juice left. It took all my strength to avoid losing my toes to the eager jaws below.

The other ropes had been cut as well, and the two ships moved slowly apart. Men jumped the gap until the last possible moment, and a few even after that. One of the *Angel*'s crew smacked into the *Cow*'s hull, bounced off, and landed in the water. He grabbed the trailing end of my rope and held on until one of his overboard shipmates clutched at his legs and pulled him free. A half-dozen fins converged on them, and their high-pitched screams filled the air.

As the *Bloody Angel* pulled away, I saw Duncan Tew at her rail, looking helplessly at the *Red Cow*. Behind him, smiling with perverse satisfaction, stood Wendell Marteen. The *Angel*'s sails unfurled, caught the wind, and drove the vessel quickly away.

A ladder slapped the hull beside me. I switched my grip to it, but had no strength to climb. Eventually someone noticed and began to pull me up.

My strength was exhausted, but not my fury. I hoped Clift was right about the *Cow*'s speed, because I was not about to rest until I shoved that smug grin down Marteen's throat.

I crawled over the rail and fell limp to the deck. No one offered to help me up. I heard shouted orders and acknowledgments, and felt the thudding of urgent feet through the deck's wood. Finally Greaves knelt beside me and said, "Do you need the doctor?"

"No," I croaked, and pushed myself up with my good arm. Greaves helped me to my feet. "Are we going after them?"

"Aye, sir. The captain is—"

I shrugged off Greaves's concern and rushed astern, dodging the sailors hurrying to their tasks. The fake fallen sail had been cut away, and the false crates dumped overboard. Clift stood at the wheel, but instead of watching the departing ship, his eyes were on Estella at the foremast crosstrees. Greaves strode about, directing the lowering and trimming of sails, all of which filled with wind. Yet the *Bloody Angel* was leaving us behind despite our having every bit of canvas deployed.

"Still under full sail!" Estella called down. "Ten knots, maybe twelve!"

"Steady as she goes," Clift ordered, and Greaves repeated it. The captain looked at me grimly and said, "That didn't go as planned, did it?"

"Sometimes it doesn't," I agreed. The *Bloody Angel*'s wake sparkled in the sun.

"We've got seventeen of their men dead or captured below, and by best count, twelve of ours remain on the *Bloody Angel*." He nodded at my shoulder. "And you're hurt."

"It's a scratch." I clenched my fists helplessly. "And correct me if I'm wrong, but aren't they getting away?"

He smiled. "You had your shot, Mr. LaCrosse. Now just sit back and enjoy mine."

I wanted to punch that smirk from his tanned face, but I reminded myself I wasn't really angry at him. And besides, he was right. My plan *hadn't* worked; hopefully, his would.

Like the *Bloody Angel,* the *Red Cow* was soon running under all its canvas, but the other ship rapidly pulled ahead. No one seemed concerned with this, least of all Clift, who serenely steered his ship and frequently checked with Estella above us. The *Cow* seemed to be straining against something, and even with my limited nautical knowledge, I realized she ought to be going faster.

"How fast are we going?" I asked Greaves.

"About four knots," he said with no concern.

I said to Clift, "Is something wrong? Shouldn't we—?"

He nodded brusquely toward the rear of the ship. I looked over the rail and was astounded: the barrels I'd previously seen tied to the stern now dragged behind us, slowing us to a crawl no matter how many sails we deployed. Each barrel was connected by a rope to a central metal ring, which a single thick cable bound to the ship. I started to demand an explanation; then my weary brain comprehended it. It was a hell of a plan if the *Angel* fell for it.

Greaves asked quietly, "Did you happen to see the situation surrounding Mr. Seaton on the other ship before you disembarked?"

"He was holding his own. I got the feeling he's done this before."

"Oh, aye, he was once a madman with a cutlass. But he hasn't fought in a boarding action in years."

"Really?" I said in surprise. "Why did he volunteer, then?"

He shrugged. "No way of knowing. He's a mystery, Mr. Seaton is."

Before I could pursue this, Jane thunked her way across the deck on her new crutch. One leg of her trousers was cut away to reveal her bandaged thigh. The effort showed in her face, but when she reached me, she acted as if nothing were unusual. "I take it they didn't roll over and play dead."

"No. Most of the boarding party is still on the other ship."

"Was it Marteen?"

"Yeah. And a crew of white-haired old water dogs."

"What about Black Edward?"

"I didn't have time to ask."

She nodded at my shoulder. "You're cut."

"I've had worse. I've had worse on that shoulder, even."

"Uh-huh. Tomorrow I'm going to remind you that you said that."

"Ahoy, below!" Estella cried. "She's trimming sail!" The *Bloody Angel* didn't look any different to me, but her words prompted the crew to leap into renewed action and Clift to order, "Right, lads! Run out the flying jib and cut loose the drag!"

He grinned devilishly at us. "I'd hang on to something if I were you, friends."

Jane laughed, backed up to the mainsail shrouds, and threaded her arm through the netting. I did likewise.

There was a slight jolt as a flying jib billowed out onto the bowsprit. Since both the sail and the bowsprit were extra long, the ship strained even harder against the barrels holding it back. Then I heard a pair of sharp *thwock*s as someone cut through the rope that bound the barrels to the ship.

Freed of the drag, we surged forward. The change knocked me back against Jane. As she pushed me upright, she said, "Careful, or I'll tell that redhead of yours that you were all over me." When I got my balance and could again look ahead, the *Bloody Angel* was twice as close as she'd been before. We were slicing through the waves, and she didn't seem to notice.

"Boarding party, ready weapons!" Greaves called. He handed me a sword. "Care to join us, Mr. LaCrosse?"

"I think I can clear my calendar," I said. I looked back at Jane. "You'll be okay?"

"Don't make me smack you," she fired back.

"Remember, take the captain alive!" Clift yelled to the massing fighters. "If you don't, I'll see to it no one gets a shred of prize money for this whole voyage. That's no bilgewater, lads, see if I don't!"

It seemed to take no time for the *Red Cow* to overtake the *Bloody Angel*. Marteen's ship frantically tried to get back under way, but the crew wasn't nearly so sharp or well-trained as ours, and so it became a confused mess of people running through the riggings and scuttling up and down shrouds. The *Cow*'s ballistae had been returned to their slots on deck, and we fired grapples as we slowed and pulled alongside. The crews wound the lines, and once again our hulls crunched together. We vaulted the rail and started hacking.

This time it was a rout. Marteen's crew was panicked, terrified, and exhausted. They barely put up a fight despite his exhortations and threats from the quarterdeck. They no longer seemed like pirates, but tired old men and women exhausted by the day's battle. If this was the limit of their endurance, it explained why he needed his elaborate ghost-ship trap.

At last, Marteen gave up and ducked down the passageway toward his cabin. I pursued him, kicked in the door, and found him about to crawl out the stern window, although where he thought he'd go from there, I couldn't imagine. I leveled my sword at him despite my hurt shoulder and said, "Right there, Marteen. Your crew is worn out and needs a nap. You got nowhere to go."

He froze, halfway in and out. He looked at the sea below, where some of his men already floated facedown, then back at me. The fight continued on deck, but it was all one-sided and he knew it.

"You'll get more mercy from me than from the sharks," I said. "But not if you keep me waiting."

He pulled in his leg, tossed his sword on the floor at my feet, and said, "I saw you go over the side back there. How did you survive?"

"I can fly. Now, put your hands on your head and sit down."

He did so, in the chair behind the captain's desk. I knew that, like me, he probably had a weapon or two hidden on him, but at the moment they did him no good. We could search him more thoroughly once we had him bound and secured on the *Cow*.

"So Edward Tew's *Bloody Angel* didn't sink after all," I said.

He laughed. The genuine kind, both mocking and amused. "I didn't think you had the look of the sea about you, and now I know it for sure. Do you not think more than one ship might bear the same name? Especially if that name is so well known, men still tremble at its mention?"

"Then you *were* the lone survivor of the original *Bloody Angel*'s sinking."

Again, he threw back his head and laughed.

Through clenched teeth, I said, "I'm trying to find Black Edward for an old girlfriend. She just wants to know what really happened to him. If he's dead, just tell me."

Before he could answer, if he was even going to, Clift and three more sailors burst breathlessly through the door. One of them was Duncan Tew, bedraggled but apparently unhurt. They stopped when they saw me and Marteen. Clift put away his sword, smiled, and said, "So this is the fool who thought he could outrun the *Red Cow*."

"I could've if you'd played fair," Marteen said.

"To play fair with your crew, I'd have to wait until I was thirty years older," Clift said, then saw something. "Now, what in the wide ocean do you need all these for?"

I followed his gaze. Along the wall rose a waist-high stack of small crates and boxes, all of varying sizes but unmistakably of the same purpose: medical kits stolen from the various ghost ships.

"Those?" Marteen sneered. "We fuck so many women, we're worried our dicks will fall off."

"If your bunch can get two hard-ons among the lot of them, I'd be surprised," Clift said. The noise of battle on deck had faded to random sword clashes and groans. "Gentleman, please thoroughly bind Captain Marteen and make sure he doesn't have anything sharp and nasty hidden about his person. Then take him to my dayroom and secure him to something solid. We'll be along to question him shortly."

Duncan and the other two sailors moved to obey. Marteen put up no resistance, but he said, "I don't care what you do to me, I'll never give up Black Edward's treasure. You're wasting your time and mine."

"Perhaps my ship's surgeon just intends to use you for dissection," Clift said. "Ponder on that." Marteen was frog-marched out of his cabin. Clift turned to me and said quietly, "Again with the treasure you keep denying you're after."

I sighed. I was suddenly so tired, I didn't care if he believed me or not. "Look, if you want my help with the interrogation, we better get to it before I pass out."

"Oh, I think I'll be wanting to keep an even closer eye on you," he said, then turned and strode from the cabin. It took all my strength to follow.

I supervised as Marteen was tied to a chair in Clift's day-room. The chair wasn't nailed down, so strategic knock-overs were an option. He said nothing, staring into space as if we didn't exist.

Up close, he was downright repulsive. He had a sore-scarred nose and bald ringed patches in his hair from parasites. He smelled like a chamber pot, and I wondered if he'd deliberately wet himself. Beneath his red velvet coat, his clothes were tattered and often badly repaired. The sole of one boot revealed his toes through a split. He was older than me, probably close to fifty, but not so old as some of his crew. Still, even if we hadn't caught him, it seemed unlikely he'd make it to sixty in this level of decrepitude.

"Guess piracy isn't as lucrative as it was in our day," one of his jailers taunted. Marteen did not react.

When Marteen was secured, Duncan Tew put a cloth hood over the pirate's head. It wasn't airtight, but it certainly wasn't comfortable. I assigned one sailor to guard him, but made him promise to do so in absolute silence.

I retrieved a clean tunic from my cabin, where Suhonen still slept. My current shirt had grown stiff with dried blood and sweat, though thankfully most of the former was not my own. I almost made it on deck before Skurnick accosted me. Fifteen men rested in their hammocks, bandaged and stitched. Most were asleep, but a couple moaned in pain, and one whimpered for his mother. I spotted Dorsal gently touching an unconscious man's dangling hand. He caught my eye and looked at me with too much sadness for such a young boy. I wondered how many friends he'd lost in his brief life. The doctor said, "Let me take a look at that shoulder."

"It's nothing."

"I saw you fighting left-handed, so it must be something."

"I was making it a fair fight."

"Uh-huh. Off with your shirt."

The difficulty of obeying that command convinced me that Skurnick might be right. He efficiently cleaned, sewed, and dressed the three-inch cut with a surprisingly light touch that did absolutely nothing to keep the needle from stinging like a bastard. When he was done, he gave me a sling to wear so I wouldn't accidentally rip open the wound.

"How long until I can use my arm again?" I asked.

"Try moving it around in a couple of days. If it starts bleeding, then it's too soon."

I went on deck and found it was sunset. The *Bloody Angel*'s deck was empty save for three of our men readying it for the trip to Blefuscola. Hopefully the capture of that ship, as well as the account of its defeat at our hands, would lift the self-imposed embargo cluttering the harbor.

Clift and Jane stood over a body on deck. When I got close, I saw it was Quartermaster Seaton. He was wounded in three visible places; the deep furrow bisecting his skull looked to have been the fatal blow.

"What happened?" I said.

"He got killed," Clift said simply. "He knew the risks when he volunteered."

"Yeah, why did he do that?"

Clift shook his head. "He was a good quartermaster, for sure. He sailed with me for ten years. I think he found the life of a pirate hunter too tedious. You saw that play he wrote about Black Edward? I believe deep down that's the kind of end he secretly wanted, but that he could never get on this side of the law."

"That's a shame."

Clift nodded. "He had a job. He did it the best he could. He chose the method of his passing."

It struck me that such an epitaph would suit me as well. I'd have to remember to write it down and give it to Liz.

Clift draped a large piece of sailcloth over the body. He said, "Sew him up, gentlemen," and two sailors who specialized in mending sails bent down to enclose Seaton in his burial shroud. The captain turned to me and said, "How's our prisoner?"

"Stewing in his own juices. And I mean that literally."

"Well, he'll not smell any better if we wait," Clift said. "Mr. Greaves, continue repairs and make sure we haven't left any of our wounded on the *Angel*."

"When they're wounded and unconscious, pirates and hunters tend to look a lot alike," Jane explained.

"And bring me every scrap of paper from the captain's cabin—logbooks, maps, notes, everything," Clift added.

"Aye, Captain," Greaves said, and rushed off to his duties.

"Mr. Dancer!" Clift called, and the gunnery master appeared before him. "We'll be sinking that ship with the monster beneath it. Ready your men to fire flaming bolts."

"Aye, sir," Dancer acknowledged.

We followed Clift down into the hold. He paused to speak to the wounded who were conscious, thanking them for their work and promising they'd be compensated for any lost extremities. Then we stopped to draw a bucket from the piss barrel. It said something that the odor of blood, death, and sweat meant the smell from the bucket didn't bother me at all.

Clift walked into the dayroom and threw the bucket's contents into Marteen's covered face. He yelled, sputtered, and madly tossed his head to dislodge the clinging wet burlap.

Clift yanked off the hood. Marteen spit, looked around, and realized his situation. His brow knitted and he fell silent.

"You're a prisoner of Captain Dylan Clift, representative of the Anti-Freebootery Guild," the captain said. "You and your crew will be taken to Shawano for trial and hanging. Do you understand this?"

"What's the point of the trial if you already know the verdict?" Marteen snarled. "Does that help your head rest better on your soft lace pillow?"

"You have one chance to avoid that fate," Clift continued. "I might intercede and recommend a life sentence in the Mosinee Prison if you help out my friend here."

"That's some trade," Marteen sneered. "Death either way, one fast and one slow. Why don't you pick for me so I'll be surprised?"

Jane, who had remained by the door, now stepped forward. "Do you know who I am, Marteen?"

"Some whore passed around by these scurvy trolls?" he said, and smacked his lips at her. "You been spreading your legs so much, you need that cane to walk with 'em closed, eh? They must like 'em tall on the *Cow*. Do you diaper them like little babies, too? I've known some men who paid well for that."

"My name is Jane Argo."

Marteen's smile, and attitude, faded at once. Even his face turned pale beneath his tan. "Captain Argo," he whispered. "I heard you left the sea."

She backhanded him so hard, I worried she'd broken his neck. Her rings left cuts along his jaw. He sat there for a moment, recovering, and when he turned to us again, his teeth were coated with blood from his ruptured lips.

"As you can see, I'm back on the waves," Jane said. "Now, Captain Clift has made you a generous offer. I'm here to sweeten it. If you answer my friend's questions, I won't spend ten minutes alone with you." She returned his blown kiss.

He spit blood, but was careful not to get any of it on Jane. Then he looked at me. "Since you haven't done or said anything, I assume you're the friend with the questions."

I nodded. "It's the same one I asked you earlier. What happened to Edward Tew?"

He frowned in apparent concentration. "Tew?"

"Yes."

Then he grinned. "Why, one and one equals two."

His laughter rang out in the little room. When he finished, I said, "Let's try again. What happened to Edward Tew?"

"I'd sooner hang than give up my comrades," he hissed. To Clift, he said, "How does it feel to betray your friends and your oaths, joining up with Queen Remy against your brothers?" He looked at Jane. "And you? Are you his whore now? Queen Remy know she's supporting a floating brothel?"

Jane smiled. If Marteen had any sense at all, he would've started begging for mercy right then, but he didn't. She said, "Marteen, I've got a hole in my leg thanks to your little pet, and it pisses me off. Eddie and Dylan here have this thing, what's it called? Oh, yeah. A conscience. They have one of those. I don't." And with that, she drew a dagger and stabbed it into Marteen's left thigh.

His howl could've summoned wolves, had we been on dry land. It grew even louder when Jane pulled the dagger out, wiped it on Marteen's shirt and put it back in her belt. I winced in sympathy; even Clift seemed a little startled. Blood surged up from the wound.

"Fuck!" Marteen said, his voice raw.

"You've got a lot of other things we can stab," I pointed out. "Now, what happened to Edward Tew?"

Marteen's eyes dripped tears of pain, but he said, "You might as well kill me. I'm not going to tell you anything, and there's nothing you can do to make me. Keep torturing me if you think you have to, but you'll just be breaking a sweat for nothing. I'm not afraid to sail with the White Captain off the edge of the world. Once I'm dead, I'll be far beyond your grasp."

I'd seen men scared of torture try to bluff their way through before, but there was something calm in Marteen when he said this that made me believe him. As a last resort, I said, "Would it help if I said please?"

Marteen looked up at me in astonishment, then began to laugh.

I nodded toward the door. It was time to regroup.

Clift put the wet burlap sack over Marteen's laughing face and cinched it tight around his neck. Blood from his thigh wound had soaked his pants and started pooling at his feet. Clift brought a belt from his cabin and tied it tight around Marteen's leg.

We stepped out into the hall and closed the door. I spoke softly so Marteen couldn't overhear. "Any other ideas?"

"I haven't even gotten warmed up on him yet," Jane said. "Wait until that thigh starts throbbing like mine did."

"I could threaten to hang him right here, before we even get back to Shawano," Clift said. "We could string up a couple of his dead shipmates, make it look like we'd executed them."

"That's an old one, he'd never fall for that," Jane said. "Now, some pliers to his testicles—"

"If we hurt him too much, he'll just tell us what we want to hear," I pointed out. "He's our only source. If we can't get real information out of him, we're at a dead end. Or at least I am."

I looked around in the shadowy corners to make sure Dorsal wasn't lurking there. I didn't want him to overhear anything too brutal.

"What're you looking for?" Jane asked.

"Making sure the cabin boy's not here."

Clift asked, "What cabin boy?"

"Dorsal. You know. His real name's Finn."

In utter disbelief, Clift whispered, "You've seen Dorsal Finn?"

"Yeah. Why?"

Even Jane asked, "Dylan, what's wrong?"

Clift could barely speak. "Dorsal Finn died of a fever over a year ago. I was holding his hand when he passed. We buried him at sea five hundred miles from here."

And despite the heat of the tropical night and the stuffy warmth of the ship's hold, a shiver went through me.

TWENTY-FIVE

I t was near midnight. I lay on Jane's bunk and stared at the wooden ceiling. The swaying lamp made shadows seem to crawl across the grain. After three days of enforced rest, Jane was far too fidgety to sleep anytime soon, so she was on deck with Clift. With Suhonen still slumbering away in my cabin, hers was the only refuge I had. And I needed it.

We'd ignored Marteen since our earlier session. He sat in the chair in the captain's cabin, the wet bag still over his head, his injured leg still untended. A guard stood, or rather sat and slept, outside the door. I didn't blame him; it had been a hell of a day.

Besides, there was no doubt Marteen was still there. He seemed to be running through an unending repertoire of bawdy sea songs:

They were humping on the quarterdeck
And humping on the stairs
You couldn't see the tiller
For the pile of pubic hairs. . . .

I put the pillow over my head and tried to stuff it into my ears. How many verses did this song have?

EARLIER, when we'd come on deck after Marteen's first interrogation, I begged off from Clift's questions, claiming I needed time to think. After the revelation about Dorsal Finn, that was certainly true. Clift said, low so no one else would hear, "I think if my ship is haunted, Mr. LaCrosse, I have a right to know."

"Look, I can't answer that. Really. Maybe I dreamed the whole thing, or I've gotten smacked in the head too many times. So if you'll excuse me, I'm going to go sit somewhere and try to think of something we missed." When Jane started to follow me, I said sharply, "Alone. Okay?"

Neither was happy, and I couldn't blame them, but I was too tired after the day's battles to deal with it. I found a place by the tiller where I could see the *Bloody Angel* across the way, lit by lanterns. Shadows moved across the deck as occupying crewmen from the *Cow* passed in front of the light. There *had* to be something we'd missed.

We did have one actual, physical clue: that stack of medical crates taken from a variety of ships. Clift had planned to send them back to Blefuscola, but suddenly I wanted to check them before they left in the morning. I got Duncan to row me over, since my shoulder wasn't up to it, and he lit the lamps in the captain's cabin so I could see.

"What are you looking for?" he asked.

"The reason why these were all that they took. Think about it: They had undefended ships loaded with goods and money, and they took only the medicine chests. Why?"

"They were old and sick?"

"Old, yes. But did they fight like they were sick?"

"Well, no." He scowled, thinking.

I opened several of the chests. All appeared completely intact. I began removing the contents of one, pausing to examine each item. There were knives and razors for surgery, irons for cauterizing wounds, pliers for pulling teeth (and, according to Jane, other things), scissors for bandages, needles and line for stitching wounds, and in carefully organized slots, various dried substances that could be combined and reconstituted into medicines.

I pulled one bottle from the box and held it to the light: poxbinder, an herb used to deaden injuries so they could be repaired. It took barely a pinch of it to be effective; slightly more than a pinch would ensure the injured party had no subsequent worries about anything. It was expensive, and could be found only along the tree line of the Galick Mountains. Its drying and preparation were a fiercely guarded secret, and only a licensed buyer could purchase it. That explained why the bottle was so small, and held so little actual poxbinder.

"I don't suppose you know," I mused aloud to Duncan, "how common it is to carry poxbinder in a medicine chest?"

"I've never been on a ship before," he said. "And luckily, so far I've never needed to see the inside of a medicine chest."

"Help me check. See how many of these have poxbinder in them."

With Duncan's help, it didn't take long. They all did, some in tiny vials smaller than my pinkie. Many shared some of the other contents as well, but poxbinder was the only thing common to all of them. It might be a clue, or just as likely a coincidence. Because even if I was right, why would Marteen go to all this trouble just to collect poxbinder?

"Did you find what you wanted?" Duncan asked after I'd silently stared at the bottles for a long time.

"What? Oh, yeah. Let's put things back like we found them." As we returned the boxes to the stack, I asked casually, "Do you believe in ghosts, Duncan?"

"Ghosts? No. I mean, I've never seen one. Some people told me the ghost of my mother roamed the dunes looking for my father, just like in the play, but now I know that's not true. Why?"

"Oh, I was just thinking about the play, too," I lied as dismissively as I could. No sense making him think I was a lunatic.

"Do you think the captain of this ship knows anything about my father?"

"Definitely. The trick is getting him to talk. And the better trick is getting him to tell the truth."

"Will you tell me what he says?"

"Of course. And if your father's out there, we'll keep looking for him."

"And if he's dead?"

I shrugged. "Then my job is done. I report back to my client."

"My mother." He said it flatly, with neither disdain nor affection.

"Yes."

After that, he was silent. As we approached the *Red Cow,* I scanned the rail for any sign of Dorsal Finn. I wondered if I'd ever see him again.

I must've dozed, because when I tried to shift my position, every joint in my body protested, especially the cut on my shoulder. When I was Duncan's age, I never woke up achy after a fight. Marteen was still singing in the background. Then from inside the room, a familiar voice said, "Your pardon, Cap'n."

The pillow was still over my head. I slowly pulled it away. I knew what I'd see. I also knew the cabin door was locked and there was no other way into the room.

Dorsal stood against the wall, hands behind his back, one foot twisting on the floor. He looked like any other kid caught in a lie, except *his* lie crossed the veil between life and death.

I studied him closely as I sat up. He looked exactly like a little boy. The light from the flickering lantern fell on his skin, and when he moved his foot, I heard his callused toes scrape faintly on the floor.

I said at last, "You're a ghost, aren't you?"

Eyes downcast, he nodded.

The urge to try to touch him, to see if my hand would go through him, was overwhelming. I thought about all the times I'd seen him dodge around people or slip through doors just before they closed. I thought he was just being discreet or sneaky. Now I realized he was hiding his true nature. "You could've told me."

He shrugged.

"Okay, so you're dead. Why are you still here, then?"

He looked up and met my eyes. There was nothing otherworldly in his gaze. "Cap'n Clift needs me. Especially with

Cap'n Jane around. He feels like me dying was his fault. Like he should've paid more attention to how sick I was. But it wasn't nobody's fault, things just happened. I know that. When *he* realizes that, I won't need to watch him anymore."

I nodded. That made as much sense as anything. "But he can't see you and I can. Why is that?"

"I didn't show myself to you. You just saw me. You must've crossed the line once yourself. You died, and then came back. Otherwise, you'd never have seen me, either, unless I'd wanted you to."

"Yeah," I said, and felt a tingle in the scar over my heart.

"Besides, you've met this lot. If I showed myself to any of the crew who knew me, I'd scare them to death. They'd go screaming over the side like parlor maids with their hair on fire. You just thought I was the cabin boy. I missed that. Cap'n," he added deferentially.

I nodded, then yawned. My catnap had been a tease. I rubbed my eyes, and when I opened them again, Dorsal wasn't alone.

I jumped and hopped back on the bunk. Now a little girl, younger than him, stood beside him. She wore a simple sleep gown and had curly brown hair. In one hand, she carried the same doll Jane had fished from the bilge on the monster ship.

"This is Aggie," Dorsal said. "Her father was Captain Verlander of the *Vile Howl*."

My mouth was dry, but I managed, "Hello."

"You look like my daddy," the girl said. "He has a beard, too."

Like Dorsal, there was absolutely nothing about her to give

away her supernatural status. "I'm sure he's very handsome," I said.

"I can't find him," she said sadly, and looked down.

"The monster on that ship killed him," Dorsal said. "And her, too."

A chill that came from somewhere other than a fear of ghosts ran through me.

"The mean captain found me hiding," Aggie said. "He made me go down into the bad ship. He told me my mommy and daddy were there, but they weren't, at least not anymore. The monster ate me." She paused. "It hurted a lot."

Her round little face was impassive as she said this. It made the horror of her words that much more vivid.

"She's too angry and scared to move on," Dorsal said.

"I can imagine," I said. "I'd be angry, too."

"She has a favor to ask."

He nudged the girl. She asked, "Is that the mean captain I hear singing?"

"Yes."

Without looking at me, she said, "Can you kill him for me?"

I was speechless for a moment. Then I said, "No, not in cold blood. I'm not that kind of guy. He is, but I'm not."

She nodded, as if it was the answer she expected. "I'll just wait for him to die, then."

"Why?" I asked.

"When he dies, I can hurt him. I was innocent. He was evil. Over here—" Then she looked up and smiled, a sweet expression made terrifying by her words. "—I have more power than he does. I can hurt him back. Forever."

I swallowed hard. I really didn't need to know this much about how the universe worked. I'd already encountered a goddess masquerading as human and a face-changing sorceress. That was far too much cosmic insight for a simple guy like me.

Then I had an idea.

"Look . . . Aggie . . . I can't kill him for you. It's not that I don't believe he deserves to die, because I do. But it's not my place to do it. Can you understand that?"

She nodded.

"But . . . he knows something I need to know. He won't tell me. I'm not sure we can make him; he's pretty tough. But I think *you* can."

Aggie wiped her nose as if it could still run. "How?"

"Just go see him and tell him what you told me. That you're waiting for him, and what you plan to do to him when he does cross over. Can you do that?"

She looked at Dorsal. He nodded. She looked back at me and said, "Yes."

"And afterwards . . . I think it'll be okay if you go on to your father and mother. I know they're waiting for you." I didn't, but under the circumstances, it seemed a little enough fib.

"Okay," she said.

Dorsal looked at me. "Thank you, Cap'n."

"You can go, too, you know."

He shrugged. "Maybe."

"Captain Clift would want you to. He'd be very sad if he thought he was the reason you stuck around."

His little face creased with concentration as he thought about that. At last he said, "I'll ponder on it."

"Wait a minute first, though," I said. "Marteen's got a bag on his head. I want him to be able to see you."

I stood, and they scooted away from the door just like any real, corporeal people would do. I went past the sleeping guard and into the captain's dayroom. When he heard the door, Marteen stopped singing.

"Well, what brilliant trick do you plan to try now?" he said mockingly. If possible, he smelled even worse. "Or do you have a request for my next number?"

I yanked the hood off his head without a word and went back out.

"An attack of conscience?" he yelled after me. "You'll never make it as a pirate, you know that? You're soft as a cookie fresh from the goddamned oven, that's what you are!"

I went back into Jane's cabin. It was empty.

I sat on the edge of my bunk and waited.

It didn't take long.

chapter

TWENTY-SIX

Wendell Marteen screamed in true, pure terror. There was no secondary emotion, like anger or frustration. It was the kind of scream that gave nightmares to the people who heard it, as their imaginations tried to conjure the source. I knew the source, and it still sent chills through me.

I left my cabin just as the guard snapped awake and jumped to his feet. He looked around, blinking in confusion. "What was that?"

"Your prisoner," I said.

"Oh, crap," he said, and preceded me into the dayroom.

Marteen's demeanor was entirely, completely different. All the arrogance and defensiveness were gone, replaced by the kind of gallows terror you see only in men who know they are about to die. "Please, don't kill me," he whimpered when he saw us, his words rushing out all at once. "I'll tell you anything, I'll take you to Black Edward, just please, don't kill me, I'll do anything you want, please, I don't want to die."

Clift burst into the room, followed by Jane. Others gathered just outside, all summoned by the unearthly shriek. "What's going on?" the captain demanded.

Marteen bent forward, bowing in as much supplication as his bonds allowed. "Please, Captain Clift, don't let them take me, I'll help you, I'll gladly go to Remy's prison, just don't let me *die*!"

Clift looked at me; I shrugged.

"He was alone in here when he screamed, Cap'n," the guard volunteered. "Mr. LaCrosse came in with me."

"I'll tell you where Edward Tew is," Marteen said in a tiny voice. "I'll tell you where his *treasure* is, just don't let me die. Please, promise me you won't kill me."

Clift quickly closed the door on the watchers. He glared down at Marteen and demanded, "What do you think will happen if I do?"

Marteen stopped talking, and for a moment, I was afraid he'd even stopped breathing. Then he sagged against his ropes and began to cry. It was oddly touching, and I was annoyed at the sympathy I suddenly felt for the guy.

Jane looked questioningly at me. I touched my lips and winked, a signal that I'd fill her in later. She nodded slightly in acknowledgment, then pushed in front of Clift and snarled at Marteen, "All right, prove you mean what you say. What heading should we take?"

"Southwest," Marteen said through tears. "Straight due

southwest. Bring me a map, and I'll show you. We're about eight days away. It's an island with a pair of mountains, and a long sandy peninsula on one end."

"And Black Edward is there?" she pressed.

"Yes, I swear. Now, please, promise you won't kill me."

Clift smacked him on the side of the head. "I will if you don't stop blubbering."

Marteen immediately fell silent. His lower lip trembled like a child's, and tears cut through the dirt on his face.

Clift then turned his full authority on the guard. "Your name is Carrisimo, right?"

"Yes, sir," he said, standing straight.

"You heard what this worm-riddled piss pot said about Black Edward Tew's treasure, right?"

"Yes, sir."

Clift stepped nose to nose with the younger man. "You breathe a word of that to anyone other than the people in this room, and I'll have your balls for castanets, understand?"

Carrisimo gulped. "Yes, sir."

"Good. Now cut him loose, but don't take your eyes off him." Clift went the short distance into his cabin.

As Carrisimo followed his orders, Jane sidled up to me and said, "What the hell did you do?"

"Nothing, I wasn't even in here."

"Bullshit, I know that smug look of yours."

Before I could say anything else, Clift returned with a handful of maps. Marteen was rubbing his wrists where the ropes had bitten into them. Clift unrolled one map, held it in front of Marteen, and said, "Show me."

Marteen unhesitatingly pointed to a tiny dot among a cluster of other dots. "Here. He's here."

"Now show me on this map," Clift said, switching them quickly. Marteen immediately pointed out the same island. Clift made him do it twice more on two additional maps before he was satisfied that Marteen wasn't making the whole thing up. "How long has he been there?"

Marteen laughed ironically. "Twenty years. For the last fifteen, you couldn't get him on a ship again if you chained him up and had a whole brigade to drag him."

"Why?" I asked.

Marteen looked at me, swallowed hard, and pointed at Jane. "Because Black Edward has that thing she said you and Captain Clift have. A conscience. He was so horrified by what he did to secure his treasure that he swore never to sail again."

"What did he do?" I asked.

"He sank his own ship, with all his crew on board," Jane said. "After he took the treasure off. Didn't he?"

Marteen nodded.

AT dawn, the *Bloody Angel* left for Blefuscola with a hold full of chained prisoners and about a third of the *Red Cow*'s crew to mind them. It said something that our ship didn't seem significantly less crowded. We then returned to the monster's vessel, which waited in the sunrise as innocent as a child opening a birthday present.

"Bring Marteen up here," Clift said. "I want the son of a bitch to see this."

We smelled him before he appeared. He'd been manacled

again, and Carrisimo escorted him with a knife to his back. He moved heavily, like the life had already gone out of him. He watched impassively as the ship's largest ballista was positioned and the bowstring was winched back. The head of the bolt was lit, and when the fire was burning well, the gunner shot it over to the monster's ship. It struck the middle of the empty deck and stuck there, the flames slowly catching. Two more bolts joined it, and a fourth was being prepared when Clift said, "That'll do it."

And it did. The ship was fully aflame now, and all at once, the monster's tentacles burst from the water and tried to somehow fight the fire. Big bursts of water came from the creature's siphons. It snuffed some of the blaze, but by then, the hull was compromised.

With one last desperate effort, the monster rolled the ship belly-up, trying to use its own pulpy weight to drive the burning vessel into the water. We saw how it was attached to the bottom: the huge round head was encased in a net, fastened to the hull so that the animal's mouth was forced against the hatch. The ship sank, taking the monster with it, and leaving only a roiling sea of foam, black ink, and blue monster blood.

"And now," Clift said, "head southeast, Mr. Greaves."

Greaves, promoted to quartermaster since Seaton's death, said, "Aye, sir." He walked the length of the deck, calling orders up to sailors in the riggings.

Clift turned to Marteen. "I don't have to tell you what will happen if you're lying to me. I don't care if the biggest ambush in world history is waiting for us, I assure you: You'll die first."

"It's no trick," Marteen said listlessly.

"Who's on the island besides Tew?"

"Just a few sailors. The ones too old or sick to be of use. Most of them came with me."

"Uh-huh." Clift didn't believe Marteen, and I didn't blame him. "Well, I want my cabin back. Mr. Dawson!"

The ship's carpenter came running up and saluted. He had forearms as muscular as some men's legs. "Yes, sir."

"Build a cage big enough to hold this gentleman. We're going to hang him off the stern until he airs out a little."

"Yes, sir," Dawson repeated. He bent at the waist, touched the tips of one finger to the deck at Marteen's toes, and reached the other arm straight up, measuring the pirate's height. "Have it for you this afternoon, sir," he said before he rushed off.

"Tie him to the mainmast until then," Clift said to Carrisimo. "And keep an eye on him. Your health is directly tied to his."

"Yes, sir," Carrisimo said.

Clift strode off, and Jane took advantage of the moment to pull me to the rail. "Okay, talk. What did you do?"

I didn't want to keep things from my partner, especially after berating her for doing the same thing. "Just between us, right?"

"Sure."

"I sicced a ghost on him."

She stared at me. Then in a whisper, she said, "You mean there really was a ghost?"

I nodded. "You saw him, too. When you were delirious. The little blond cabin boy."

She let out a long, low breath. "Fuck me."

I had nothing to say to that, so I added, "And you saw his friend, the little girl."

"You said I hallucinated her."

"I thought you had. I hadn't seen her yet. She said she was killed by Marteen's monster."

"She spoke to you?"

I nodded.

Jane shook her head. "Does this sort of thing happen to you a lot, LaCrosse?"

I recalled a freakish little man who'd been kept alive by magic for over five hundred years. "More often than you'd think."

THAT night, we had dinner in Clift's cabin. There was still a lingering hint of Marteen in the air, but Avencrole the cook had put together a suitably pungent dinner to cover it. The main course was a fertilized chicken egg cooked and eaten in the shell, known as the "treat with feet."

As we ate, Clift said, "We need to clear the air about the treasure."

"Yeah," Jane said.

I said, "I told both of you, if we find it, I have no interest in it. You two can have it."

"Will you sign something to that effect?" Clift pressed.

I was still tired and sore from the battle yesterday, and the experience with the ghosts last night, and this was the final straw. I stood and slammed my fist on the table, rattling the dishes. "Yes, I'll sign anything if it means you two will stop asking about it. In case you've forgotten it, you both work for me right now. I'd appreciate a little more diligence in that and a little less counting imaginary gold pieces in your head." I threw my napkin on my plate, as petty a gesture as it sounds, and slammed the dayroom's door behind me as I went on deck.

There, the night wind cooled me off and I immediately regretted losing my temper. It was a sign of how exhausted I must actually be, and I decided to have Suhonen moved back to his hammock. After all, having room to stretch his legs hadn't appreciably sped up his recovery.

Then it occurred to me that I hadn't asked Marteen about the poxbinder. Certainly he'd know what it was for, and at this point, he'd probably tell me more than I ever wanted to know about it. I found Celia Zandry in charge for the night shift and said, "Can I get a couple of strong backs to pull Marteen's cage up? I need to ask him something."

She narrowed her eyes at me. "Does the captain know about it?"

Despite everything, I felt a flash of anger, which I did my best to choke down. "He doesn't. If it'll make you feel better, I'll go tell him." I was careful not to say, *go ask him*.

"No, I suppose it's all right, you being the paymaster and all." She sent three sailors with me, and they wound up the winch that pulled Marteen's cage up from where it hung. The boom holding it creaked under its weight.

When it rose into the light from the deck lanterns, though, it was immediately clear Marteen was dead. He slumped in the floor of the cage, one arm hanging out through the wooden slats. I grabbed the cage with my good arm, swung it over the deck, and by the time it landed with a thud, I had the lock off and the door open.

I dragged Marteen out. There wasn't a mark on him, just a

look of absolute terror on his face. Flies already clustered around his wide-open eyes.

"Son of a bitch," I muttered. The news spread in whispers through the crew.

Clift appeared from below, followed by Jane. He pushed through the crowd and knelt beside Marteen. "What happened?" he demanded.

"I wanted to ask him some more questions," I said wearily. "He was dead when he came up."

Clift examined him as well, and like me found no sign of injury. "That stinking bastard," he seethed.

"He wasn't a young man," I said. "And he was terrified. Maybe his heart just gave out."

Clift got to his feet. "Well, he's no good to us anymore. Throw him over the side."

Two of the men who'd helped lift the cage did as Clift instructed. The splash as Marteen's body hit the dark water was barely audible on deck. Clift kicked the cage in frustration.

"I sure hope he wasn't joking about that island," he snarled. "For everyone's sake, but especially yours, Mr. LaCrosse." Then he turned and marched off.

Jane came close and said, "You're doing a real good job of pissing off the people you should want on your side."

"You mean the ones that are only interested in treasure?"

Jane looked around to see if anyone had overheard the T-word.

I rolled my eyes. "You're a piece of work, Jane."

I turned, and Suhonen stood right behind me, towering over me as always. I jumped. So did most of the others on deck;

somehow the gigantic sailor had slipped up on all of us. He wore only a loincloth and the bandages around his chest.

"We need a new piss barrel, I overflowed this one," he said. "How long was I out? Did I miss anything?"

I looked up at him and began to laugh. So did Jane. After a moment, so did Suhonen. It spread to everyone. And by the time we finished, I wasn't angry anymore, just eager to finally reach the island and confront the other Edward.

chapter

TWENTY-SEVEN

Eighteen days later, I stood with Jane and Captain Clift at the bow, staring ahead through fog so thick, it was like pastry frosting. The cool damp felt nice after the tropical sun, but it also had us on edge—we wanted to find Marteen's island, but not by crashing into it.

We found the archipelago he'd indicated on the map, but we'd hit it at the far southern tip. The first island was big, and fires told us it was occupied. The one Marteen specified was in the middle of the group, so we thought we'd have no trouble locating it. We passed all the others, and knew Marteen's should be next, slightly to the west. Then the fog closed in. We sat at anchor for four days until it lifted enough for us to get our bearings, but it was only yanking our anchor chain. Now we were wrapped in it, sailing at a crawl, and everyone was on edge.

"No bottom at twenty!" someone called from amidships, where he constantly played out a knotted line. If the sea floor started to rise, it meant land was near. Usually.

"This is inconvenient," Clift said. Then he called up to the lookout, "Anything?"

"Nearly got decapitated by a seagull who looked as lost as we are," Estella called back.

"We're not lost," Clift said. "We're exactly on course; we just can't see where we're going." He turned to me and said more quietly, "I'd have bet Marteen was too scared to lie to us, but now I'm not so sure. Think he plotted us into a trap?"

"How could he?" Jane said. "He sent us to a real island. It was on all your maps. Everything else was accurate."

"It was *an* island, maybe not *the* island," Clift said. "Maybe he sent us to an island always cloaked in fog, with a ship's graveyard waiting for us."

"He thought he'd be along for the ride," I pointed out.

"Might have been worth his own death to ensure ours," Clift said.

"No," I said with certainty. "He would *not* have done that."

"Let's have some optimism, gentlemen," Jane said. "I think it's just bad weather."

Clift nodded. "And bad timing."

I looked back, where the fog was so thick, it hid the ship's stern. There was very little wind, and we bounced over wave crests instead of slicing through them. Men lined all the rails, watching as intently as Clift, as if they, too, bore responsibility for the ship's safety. The faces I could make out were serious, even a little frightened, with none of the jocularity they displayed even in the middle of a fight. I wondered where in the haze I'd find Duncan Tew; knowing we closed in on his hated father must weigh on him at least as much as the weather.

Suddenly the lookout cried, "Voices ahead!"

Jane looked at me. "Voices?" she repeated.

I heard it, too. It sounded like the crowd in a castle's great hall after the wine started to flow. There had to be at least a hundred people talking all at once to make that much noise. I tried to catch some of the words, but I didn't recognize the language.

I heard swords, knives, and cutlasses being drawn all around me.

"A few people left behind, my ass," Jane said. "The little dung beetle *did* send us into a trap."

"Steady, lads," Clift said. He had not moved or reacted. "Don't cut off your shipmate's head in your eagerness."

"It sounds like quite a crowd," Jane said.

"Well," Greaves said casually, "we may not know what we're about to face, but then again, neither do they. Shall I summon Mr. Dancer?"

"Not yet," Clift said. "We know it's a bunch of people—we don't know if they mean us harm. Steady, lads," he repeated.

"Bottom at twenty!" the sailor amidships suddenly called. I felt movement through the deck as the rest of the crew scrambled into action. Sails were drawn up to slow us, and everyone without an actual task crowded around us to watch for land, and for whoever waited to greet us.

"I lost my sword to that overgrown squid," Jane said.

"I've lost two," I said. "I gave you a new one."

"A toothpick," Jane snapped dismissively. "I need something big enough for a full-grown woman."

"Try this," Suhonen said from behind me. I jumped, as always. The big man handed Jane a huge sword that I would've needed two hands to swing. She handled it easily with one.

"Nice," she said with genuine appreciation. "Where's it from?"

"No idea. Claimed it off a guy last year. He didn't need it anymore. The balance is good for such a big blade."

"I'll say. But what will you use?"

He gestured at his waist, where he carried two normal swords in scabbards, one on each hip.

"You're okay with two?" Jane asked.

He nodded, then smiled and winked at her. "Actually, there's three. But the third one might startle you."

She laughed in delight and experimentally swung the new sword. A couple of sailors had to jump back out of the way.

"Fog's breaking ahead!" the lookout called. "Land ho! *Really* ho!"

"Look!" someone beside me practically shrieked.

We followed his outstretched arm and pointing finger. Two huge shapes emerged from the fog, gathering details as they did so, dark gray in the haze. The blue sky behind the island made these twin mountains stand out plainly. By the time we could see the jungle greenery that covered the two mountains, the fog bank was entirely behind us. Directly ahead lay a wide, gently sloping peninsula with a white sand beach, just as Marteen described.

"Drop anchor!" Clift called, and we heard the heavy splash followed by the chain's rattle as it played out. When it hit bottom, the ship lurched slightly as it stopped.

We saw no one. Yet the voices continued, louder than before.

"There's your welcome party," Clift said, and pointed at several huge offshore rocks. They were covered with nesting seabirds, all squawking loudly in an uncanny imitation of drunken human revelry. Without the fog to mask it, the scent of accumulated bird dung reached us as well.

"Smells like a couple of parties I've been to, all right," Jane said with a laugh. "Not on deserted islands, though."

"It's not too deserted," Suhonen said. "Someone lives here."

Clustered along the beach was a complex shantytown of small huts. As the fog dissipated, we made out gardens, pens for animals, and what looked like a small well located beside a common walkway. The dwellings were made of rocks mortared together with mud; roofs were mats of vines over old pieces of sail canvas. Pieces of ships poked out of various structures, as if the builders had cannibalized whatever vessels brought them here.

A long dock stretched out past the low tide mark. Three small boats were tied there, bobbing in the waves.

"No cooking fires," Jane said about the dead chimneys. "No animals in the pens. This place is deserted."

"I don't think we can tell that looking from the safety of the forecastle," Clift said.

"No," I agreed. I looked at Jane. "Is your leg up to it?"

She threw her crutch overboard, winked, and said, "Try and stop me."

"I think I'm ready, too," Suhonen said.

Skurnick appeared from behind him. "I told him he's not strong enough yet. You're not a barrel, son. We can't just plug the holes and pour more blood into you. Your body needs time to make it."

"I've got a lot left," Suhonen said. "And I'm as strong as I need to be, like always." Then, more softly, he added, "I need to win a fight, okay?"

Clift looked at Skurnick. "I could use him. But I won't go against your recommendation. It's your call." When Suhonen started to protest, Clift silenced him with a glare.

Skurnick sighed. "What the hell. If he says he's up to it, maybe he is. Might be the best medicine."

Suhonen smiled. "Thanks, sawbones."

"You can thank me by not needing my attention again," Skurnick said dryly.

Clift said, "Get a boat ready. I'm going, so is Mr. LaCrosse, so are Captain Argo and Suhonen. I want two other volunteers."

"Try to keep me away," Duncan Tew said as he stepped forward. He clenched his sword tightly in his hand, and the blade reflected sunlight onto his grim face.

Clift shook his head and pushed the sword blade until it pointed safely down at the deck. "Sorry, Mr. Smith. You've done great work so far, but I need a more experienced sword arm."

I said, "He'll do. I'll vouch for him."

Clift's eyebrows rose, not so much that I'd stood up for Duncan, but that I'd contradicted the captain on deck. That was a no-no in any organization. I quickly added, "With your permission, of course."

"Glad to know I still have some authority," Clift muttered. "All right, you're in. One more. Who'll it be?"

A squat fellow with a barrel chest and arms that hung almost to his knees said, "I'll come along."

Clift looked at the man dubiously. "You're volunteering, Dietz?"

He nodded at Suhonen. "I'm the only man on the ship who can beat him at arm wrestling."

"And that's only when he's drunk," Clift said. "But all right, you're in. Mr. Greaves, is our boat ready?"

"Aye," the new quartermaster said.

Clift gestured grandly at the ladder hung over the side. "Gentlemen, lady—shall we get our feet dry?"

THE beach was silent except for the distant birds and steady crash of waves against the sand. We tied up beside the other boats, none of which showed any sign of recent use. If Marteen was right, and most everyone in the village had been aboard the *Bloody Angel,* then we were safe enough. He'd said that the ones left behind would be the sick, old, and/or infirm, but I wasn't prepared to concede that.

We stopped at the foot of the dock, looking at the buildings and the jungle beyond them. Here the whoosh of waves on the beach drowned out most of the birds' cacophony. A few hovered overhead, hoping we'd drop something edible.

"A pirate haven," Jane said. "I've seen these on other islands. When regular ports are too dangerous for them, they just set up their own. They take supplies from the ships they capture, and kidnap girls to serve their other needs. No rules, no laws, no gods."

"No soap," I added.

"You and your hygiene issues," she shot back.

"Marteen did say I'd never make it as a pirate."

"He also said someone would be here," Clift said. "I don't

see anyone. Who would these people be, anyway? Black Edward's original crew all drowned, didn't they?"

No one, least of all me, had an answer for that.

"Which house does Black Edward live in?" Duncan asked.

"None of these," I said.

Jane nodded. "No, these shanties are for sailors, not captains. The lord of the manor doesn't dwell among his serfs."

"We'll still check these houses and see if anyone's hiding," Clift said. "Make lots of noise. I don't want to lose anyone to a misunderstanding."

As we walked up the sand, my legs tried to convince me that I was still on the ship's rolling deck. I knew it would happen after all this time at sea, but I hoped it would wear off soon.

I estimated fifty dwellings made up the settlement, most no bigger than my cabin on the *Cow*. The ground between them was a mix of dirt and sand, and the marks of hundreds of footsteps had been set into the sun-baked soil when it was wet following the last storm. My own boots barely left a scuff.

I opened the door to the first hut. It wasn't really a door, just a woven straw mat attached to the doorframe by rope loops. The smell made me wince. I peeked inside and waited for my eyes to adjust to the dimness.

It was a one-room dwelling, with space for a single bed, a stove, and a sea chest in the corner. Shelves went up one wall and held souvenirs of the owner's life, mostly knickknacks from various ships. The room was trashed as if someone had gone on a mad search through it. I suppose the men left behind might've gotten drunk and done this, but it was impressive destruction for sailors Marteen had described as too old and sick to serve on the *Bloody Angel*.

An unmistakable rust-colored smear on the wall got my attention. Someone had bled here, and recently enough that the stain was still faintly sticky.

I stepped back to the door, tried to banish my preconceptions and take a fresh, open-minded look at the hut. Two things struck me as odd. One was that the damage was confined to the floor, and rose no higher than my waist. The shelves below that line were knocked aside and their contents scattered; above it, they were intact.

The other odd thing was the clean square spot on one wall above the damage line, where a picture had clearly hung until recently. It was nowhere amongst the debris.

I moved down the line to the next dwelling. The second hut had identical damage, down to the missing picture from the wall. And the third. But in that one, I found something else: a ship's bell, still highly polished as if it were a treasure and carefully displayed on a high shelf. Engraved on it were the words BLOODIE ANGELLE. It was the first actual confirmation that Marteen had told the truth.

I emerged at the same time Jane did from across the way. She said, "Every place I've checked has been trashed, but low to the ground, like drunk midgets had come through. I found some bloodstains, too. And there's a space on the wall where someone took down a picture."

"Same here," Suhonen said as he rejoined us.

"And me," Clift agreed.

"And me," Duncan said.

"Likewise," I said.

We all looked at Dietz. He said guiltily, "I, uh . . . didn't notice."

"Go back and check," Clift said. As Dietz skulked away like a guilty child, he added, "And put back anything in your pockets. We're not pirates anymore, remember that." To the rest of us, he said, "What else did you find?"

"I found an old bell from the *Bloody Angel*," I said.

"But no signs of life or bodies," Jane said. "And not enough blood to indicate a real fight." She shook her head. "Man, this stench will stick with me. Who lives like that?"

"Pirates," Clift said.

"We never did," she insisted.

"I think your memory is turning rosier with time," he said.

Dietz returned. "Yep, there was a picture missing in every house. Why would somebody take them?"

"We don't know that anyone took them," I corrected. "We just know they're not there."

"Oh, that's right," Dietz said dryly. "Here in the tropics, the art migrates this time of year."

"We're migrating, too," Clift said. "Let's see what else the island's got for us."

A triangular pile of stones, like a cairn, stood at the edge of the jungle. It marked the head of a trail that led off into the thick growth. I dismantled the rocks to see if anything was hidden inside. There was not; it was a mere marker. I glanced at the trail, a dark tunnel into the thick forest of the interior.

"If Black Edward lives here," I said, "it's probably at the other end of this."

"I don't see any smoke coming from the interior," Suhonen pointed out.

"If he's spotted the *Cow*, I doubt he's cooking us dinner," Jane said.

"Unless we're the main course," Dietz said. "Man in desperate enough straits isn't picky about his table fare."

"Given everything else we have to worry about, Dietz, I'd appreciate it if you'd stop looking for new things," Clift said. Then he strode off down the trail, the rest of us following.

chapter

TWENTY-EIGHT

The trail took the path of least resistance and meandered over the uneven landscape. It went around rocks, fallen trees, and changes in the terrain. Originally, it had been wide enough for two people, but the greenery had encroached on it. In six months, the jungle would close it up, like a healed wound.

By noon, we were exhausted, overheated, and deep in the island's interior. We stopped at a clearing cut by a spring-fed stream, where we drank and rested in the shade. Strange sounds told us of many curious animals lurking just out of sight. Birds with cries like mocking laughter watched us from high in the trees. Hungry biting insects sought our skin.

"He's probably dead, you know," Jane said. She reclined against a tree with her eyes closed. A spot of blood had soaked through the bandage on her thigh, and she kept one hand waving to chase the flies away from it. If she was in pain, it didn't show.

"Who's probably dead?" Duncan asked as he took off his tunic, dunked it in the creek, and wiped his face with it. He had scars along his lower back and, by implication, his buttocks. I'd seen those kind of marks before: the physical sign of his foster parents' tender care.

"Black Edward," Jane said. "That's our luck. I bet he died yesterday."

"Now who needs some optimism?" I said.

She was undeterred. "If we're extremely lucky, we'll find his corpse. Although the maggots have likely made short work of him in this heat. He's probably mostly liquid."

I nudged her. "You're a ray of sunshine, you know that?"

She laughed, but her voice was tight. "I'm ready for this leak in my damn leg to stop, that's what I am."

Duncan checked to make sure Clift and Dietz, the only ones unaware of his parentage, were too far away to overhear. "I hope he's not dead. I've finally worked out what I'm going to say to him." I waited, but he didn't elaborate.

"Just bloody great," Dietz said as he emerged barefoot from the stream, holding his battered boots. "No one to fight and nothing to loot. Tell me again why I volunteered for this chicken-shit boarding party?"

"Because you thought there'd be someone to fight and something to loot," Clift said. He stood watchfully in the shade while we rested. He was on alert, but hadn't said why.

"I'm not sure no one's around," Suhonen called. "Look at this."

We joined him beside the stream. In an open patch of mud,

there was a bare human footprint. None of us but Dietz had removed our boots, and his feet were much broader.

"Fresh, all right," I said. The sharp edges and imprinted skin detail told me that. "Made since this morning."

Jane looked around for additional prints and quickly found them. "Here. And here. And look, he pushed through that tangle of vines. He's headed toward the beach."

"But he didn't take the trail," I said.

"Why?" Duncan asked.

"We spooked him," Suhonen said. I nodded.

"So either he went somewhere else on the island, or else he's probably watching us right now," I said.

Jane nodded. So did Clift. Duncan clenched his jaw in frustration. I leaned close to him and said, "I don't think Black Edward would be running around barefoot and hiding from every little noise."

I wasn't as quiet as I thought, because Dietz said, "Unless he's gone crazy here all by himself. All this heat, the bugs, might drive anyone seal-shit nuts." When we all glared at him, he demanded, "What?"

I shouted to the jungle, "Hey! We're not here to loot or fight. Angelina Dirnay sent us to find Black Edward Tew. Can you help us? We can pay you."

We stood very still, but there was no response. In fact, there were suddenly no sounds at all, no birds or insects or wind. Even in the bright sunlight it was spooky.

"I knew it," Clift said as he drew his sword. "I had a feeling."

"Hey," Duncan asked softly, "is this an ambush?"

Before he could reply, there was a loud *hiss* from the jungle to our right. It sounded like an old man clearing his throat. A very, very large old man.

Instantly we were all armed. Jane and I reflexively stood back to back, to cover all sides. I glanced at Duncan, but he showed no sign of panic. Except for Dietz frantically putting on his boots, no one spoke or moved.

The sound came again. I watched the undergrowth for any sign of movement.

Jane whispered, "Thar she rustles."

I followed her nod. At the edge of the undergrowth, something blue, forked, and as big around as a child's arm snaked out, touched the ground in a couple of places, then drew back. A moment later it reappeared and repeated the motion. It was far too big for a snake's tongue, even the huge tropical ones you might reasonably expect here.

"What the fuck?" Dietz barked, hopping up and down to settle his boots on his feet.

"Quiet!" Clift rasped.

Suhonen drew both his swords and took a step toward the strange sight.

"Wait!" I whispered urgently. The image had suddenly clicked into place. "We might consider running."

"No," Suhonen said, and spread his feet. "Whatever it is, I'll face it."

"Yeah," Jane said, drawing her own enormous weapon. "It's just some animal. How bad can it be?"

Only Clift took my warning seriously. "If LaCrosse thinks it's bad enough to—"

I looked behind us and saw another blue tongue flash in

and out of the jungle shadows. "The one in front will get our attention," I interrupted. "The one in back will attack first."

"There's one in back?" Dietz cried, and tried to watch all sides at once.

Then the first one emerged, and even Dietz fell silent.

It was a lizard. It had gray-black skin that seemed to be the same color and texture all over. Four squat legs lifted the upper body off the ground, while the tail dragged behind it, deceptively limp. The blue tongue continued to check its environment, and its black eyes showed no interest in us at all. Its thick, goopy saliva trailed in strings along the ground, collecting bits of dirt and leaves.

And it was fifteen feet long.

And it wore a metal collar.

"Holy shit," Dietz whispered, mesmerized.

I knew Jane watched for its companion, so I kept my eye on the one in front. The collar threw me: who would keep this sort of animal as a pet? Even right out of the egg, they'd snap a chunk out of you. But pet or not, its casual stalking behavior told me it was far from tame.

It turned its huge head and looked right at us. Then it opened its mouth and hissed. I saw the hole in its lower jaw where the tongue retracted, and rows of even, very sharp teeth. The saliva in its mouth made a wet smack when it closed.

"Get ready," I said. "This one's just for show."

As I predicted, the one behind us burst from cover hissing like a newly forged lance head dropped in a bucket of water. It undulated side to side as it ran straight for Duncan, who yelled in terror but stood his ground. The problem was that from head on, the lizard presented virtually no target. It would be on the boy before he could get into position for a blow. I yelled, "Duncan! Run!"

Fortunately, Suhonen covered the distance between them in two steps and, coming in from the side, brought both swords down on the lizard's spine.

One blade bounced off. The other broke.

I caught this peripherally, because the one in front now had my complete attention. It moved slowly toward us, not giving away until the last moment that I was its target. It lunged between Clift and Jane and snapped sideways at my legs. I jumped back, simultaneously jabbing my sword toward that open mouth. I hit some of the soft tissue, because it hissed and arched its back in pain. Clift swung at it and sheared a layer of skin and flesh off one shoulder. The muscle beneath it was white and ropy.

"Nice," I said gratefully.

"There's a reason I sharpen my sword every night," he said.

The one Suhonen whacked had turned and charged him, and he now lay on the ground beneath it. His legs were locked around its belly and those huge hands dug into its throat, holding the jaws just out of reach of his face. It snapped all around his head and tore at him with its claws, leaving great deep scratches. "Is that all you got?" Suhonen screamed at it. "Is that it?" Then man and lizard began to roll around the clearing, neither releasing its hold on the other.

Jane looked for a vulnerable spot while Duncan tried to stab the thrashing tail. That was a mistake: suddenly the tail cracked like a whip and knocked him ten feet through the air.

The one I'd stabbed saw this and rushed for him. I dropped my sword, leaped, and grabbed its tail. It was cool, dry, and the muscles inside it were hard as stone. I dug in my heels. At first it didn't realize what had happened, and kept straining toward Duncan.

Dietz stuck his sword in the ground and drew his knife. "Well, I said I wanted a goddamned fight," he snarled, then jumped on its back and drove the knife deep into it. Duncan scrambled out of range, still trying to catch his breath.

Clift and Jane rushed over to help, since against all common sense Suhonen was strangling the life out of the second lizard. Just then mine realized I was there and swung back to snap at me. It snagged part of my tunic and tore away the fabric, its teeth stroking but not breaking my skin. But that was nothing compared to the flash of silver as Jane used the huge sword Suhonen had given her to slice off the lizard's head, and a lock of my hair as well.

The sword buried itself in the ground and the head rolled, jaws still snapping. The body began to thrash; Dietz and I let go and scrambled away. Jane yelled at it, "You're a pair of boots now, ya bastard!"

I got to my feet and checked to make sure she hadn't also gotten an ear. "A little close there, wasn't it?" I yelled, my voice higher than normal. I'm sure it was just the exertion.

Jane wrenched her blade free of the ground and said, "Close only counts in venereal disease, LaCrosse."

With a great roar, Suhonen heaved the now-lifeless lizard off his body. He lay there gasping, his arms and legs bloodied but a huge grin on his face. "Now that . . . was what . . . I needed. Worth breaking a sword for."

"Not your third one, I hope," Jane said, and the big man began to laugh.

I knelt to examine the collar on the strangled lizard. It fit snugly, as it would have to, since the creature's head was about the same diameter as its neck. There was a lone loop welded onto it for a leash or, more likely, a chain. And a name was engraved in the metal: BUTTERCUP.

"Someone's pet, all right," I said. "Or watchdog."

"Stand aside," Jane said, and when I did, she decapitated this one, too. "Always pay the insurance," she said, and draped the huge bloody sword across her shoulders.

Now that the crisis was over, the cut on my shoulder suddenly announced itself, and I winced as pain ran through my whole right arm. I gingerly lifted the collar of my tunic and checked it; the stitches were intact, and it wasn't bleeding. That was good news. It did nothing to ease the pain, of course.

Clift knelt and cut open the lizard's belly. "Let's see what this thing's eaten lately," he said, then lifted the carcass from behind. He wiggled it until its organs fell out with a splat.

"I've had to shake the lizard before," Dietz said, "but never like that."

Clift let the corpse fall to one side and used his sword to push aside coils of intestine and cut open the stomach. In addition to fur and feathers of their normal prey, there was a severed finger, a belt buckle, shreds of clothing, and a sailor's pipe. "I think we know what destroyed those huts. And where the ones who stayed behind have ended up," Clift said, wiping his hands on the grass.

"Except for whoever left those footprints we found," Duncan said.

"And who wants to bet that Mr. Footprint is also the one

who let Buttercup and—wow, this one's named Pansy—off their leashes?" Dietz said.

We exchanged a look. The idea that Black Edward might have gone crazy now didn't seem so unreasonable. If, of course, he hadn't also become lizard food along with everyone else.

I said loudly, "We killed your lizards. You can't possibly kill us all before we find you, so you might as well come out and talk to us."

I was bragging about our prowess, of course, but it seemed an appropriate bluff, given what we'd just done. It didn't impress our unseen watcher, though, because he didn't appear.

"Well, if there are answers," Clift said, "they'll be at the end of the trail." So we resumed our hike. Behind us, smaller specimens of the same lizards ambled from the forest and began fighting over the corpses.

TWENTY-NINE

The trail grew more treacherous as it climbed the nearest mountain's slope. Here the greenery had gotten a better grip, and in a couple of places we had to stop and seriously look around to figure out where the path continued. Suhonen, in a giddy mood despite the slashes covering his arms and legs, whistled and cut through anything that blocked our way.

No more giant lizards attacked us, and despite our best efforts, we saw no sign that anyone secretly pursued us. It wasn't a big island, but there were plenty of hiding places, especially for a lone man familiar with the terrain. If Black Edward *had* left those bare footprints, this case could turn especially ugly. The only real way to find a single person on an island like this was to use what the Pontecorvans called *Kayhemadda:* set fire to the greenery and let it burn the island clean. It was a literal scorched-earth policy that would be a very last resort.

The trail ended at the base of a flight of stone stairs. They weren't ancient, but neither were they recent: lichen and moss had already encroached. They rose above us to a small plateau. The stream we'd crossed earlier tumbled down beside it, making a narrow waterfall. The spray from the pool felt wonderful.

"Who goes first?" Clift asked, wiping his face.

"I will," I said. The idea that Black Edward Tew was up there, whether in a castle or hiding in the bushes, filled me with impatience. After all this time and distance, I could be close to getting my answers. Why had he sunk the *Bloody Angel*? What did he do with the treasure? And most important, my actual job: Did he even remember Angelina Dirnay?

Then I felt cold steel at the back of my neck. A voice said, "Wait just a minute."

I turned. Dietz moved his sword's point to the hollow of my throat, and his square face creased in concentration. "We've all heard about Black Edward's treasure, Mr. Sword Jockey. Some say it's on the bottom of the ocean; some say it's not. And if it's not, what better place to find it than under Black Edward's own bony ass?"

"Dietz," Clift said, "put the sword away now."

"You just hold on, Captain, I'm looking out for you here, too. I think we need to make Mr. LaCrosse swear a blood oath that whatever we find, we split. Just among us, of course. The rest of the crew, well—" He smiled. "—what they don't know won't hurt 'em much, will it?"

I stood very still. I was too tired to be scared. Mainly I was just annoyed. I had suspected the veneer of respectability was thin on a lot of these former pirates, and here was the proof.

But he was keeping me from the culmination of my search, and that was pissing me off.

"Dietz," I said, "put the sword down like the captain said, or die. It's that simple."

Dietz pushed my chin up with the blade's tip. "You think you're fast enough to get me before I get you, old man?"

"I won't have to do a thing. Last chance."

His smile grew. "Not a one of your friends could get me before I get you, and I bet they're all considering my offer just now. Besides, the blood oath I want from you requires *all* your blood."

I knew from the way he'd leaped on the big lizard that he was brave and tough, but smarts hadn't been a factor then. Now he looked suddenly surprised; his arm dropped and his sword fell to the ground. A moment later, he fell atop it. There was a gash across the back of his neck that had severed his spine, and a matching bloodstain on Clift's ultra-sharp sword.

"Dumb bastard," Clift said, and used Dietz's tunic to clean his blade.

Jane said in annoyance, "Well, *I* was going to do that, show-off."

"Sometime today?" Clift deadpanned. "Or when your calendar cleared?"

Jane laughed. I said to Clift, "Sharpen that thing every night, huh?"

"Every night," he assured me. "He's not the first one to turn his back on his pardon."

"Will you get in trouble for doing that?" I asked.

"We have a standing policy for recidivism. You just saw it."

"Of course. My mistake to doubt you."

I suddenly felt very tired. Dietz's eyes were still open in surprise, and his sword lay beside him. I should've tried to reason with him and get him back on our side, even if it required trickery. Instead, I'd stood by while he'd been killed, knowing it was going to happen, because I just couldn't muster the energy to care. Whether he deserved it or not was immaterial. I wasn't worried about his soul; I was worried about mine. I'd have to be more on guard against that kind of complacency.

I looked at the steps again. "I'll go up and see what's there."

"We'll be waiting," Clift assured me.

"Be careful," Jane said.

I asked, "Are you worried about me?"

She grinned. "About my money."

The climb was a bastard. The stairs were so steep that I had to use my hands as well, crawling up like a jungle bug. Tactically they were brilliant: no one could mount them with a weapon in hand, and by the time you got to the top, you were too winded to be much of a threat.

About halfway up, I had to stop and wait for a snake to finish crawling across one step. It was as big around as my arm, and in no hurry. I glanced down at the others, which was a mistake. The stairs were so close to vertical that my head began to spin, and it wasn't hard to imagine toppling down them to my death. At last the snake's tail appeared, and in moments it was gone into the weeds.

When I finally reached the top, I knelt on the last step and rested my upper body on the plateau's ground, waiting to catch my breath before taking a detailed look around. My shoulder throbbed something fierce, but I didn't have the heart to see if that was sweat I felt or blood. I momentarily closed my eyes, and when I opened them, an enormous hair-covered spider bigger than my hand sat looking at me, its dozens of eyes gleaming in the sun.

I stared. It stared. I said, "You can try it, pal, but you ain't got enough ass in your web to handle me today."

The spider seemed to agree. It turned and scuttled away into the undergrowth.

The plateau was really a flattened foothill of the island's nearest mountain. The stream ran across it and disappeared into the jungle on the other side. A stone path led from the top of the stairs to a small wooden house, bigger than any of the huts below but still nothing grand, certainly not the castle of a pirate king. One huge tree loomed over it, casting it in shade. The windows were dark and curtainless. In fact, there was no sign of any movement or life at all. Somewhere a jungle bird squawked in amusement.

I pushed myself to my feet and walked toward it. Despite being hot from climbing, I shivered. There was something hostile in the air, as if invisible forces sought to stop me. Halfway to the house, I called out, "Hello? Anyone in there? I'm looking for Edward Tew. Angelina Dirnay sent me."

The house remained dark and still. A steaming tropical wind stirred the boughs of the tree, and it reminded me of some enormous beast awakened by a foolish traveler.

On the off chance I was, in fact, being watched, I took off my sword and put it on the ground. Seldom have I felt so naked without it. I raised my hands. "Look, I'm unarmed. I just want to talk. Okay?"

There was still nothing. Whoever, or whatever, might be in the house wasn't coming out. Several bright red birds launched from the big tree and sailed out over the jungle below the plateau. From here I could see the *Red Cow* in the harbor, and the persistent fog bank beyond.

I also spotted the remains of a large bonfire in the open space away from the trees. In it were rectangular wooden frames. Now I knew the fate of the pictures taken from the huts below. But what did they depict that caused someone to hate them so much?

I picked up my sword and went back to the top of the stairs. Far below, the others looked up expectantly, and I waved for them to join me. Whatever I was walking into, I'd feel much more secure with them at my back.

LIKE me, everyone needed a moment to recover after the climb. The bloodstain on Jane's leg was bigger now, but she neither mentioned it nor limped. Suhonen stood motionless, staring intently at the house. Clift said, "No sign of anyone?"

I shook my head. "No. I shouted when I first got here, but there was no response. I don't think anyone's in there."

"No one's crawling up the steps after us, either," Jane said as she checked. "There must be another way off this high ground. Pirates like to drink, and those steps would kill a drunk."

"Maybe that was the point," Clift mused. "Well, shall we?"

We strode down the stone path to the house. The hot wind blew back our hair, and seemed to moan through the distant rocks above the tree line. Unruly vines and weeds had claimed the edges of the clearing, and it looked as though the primeval forest would soon regain possession of it, just like the path that brought us here.

I knocked on the door. The wood was laden with moisture, and mold clung to its edges. It made a wet smacking sound instead of the sharp rap I expected.

I pushed the door; it was unlatched, and swung open with a high-pitched creak. The tree's shade made the interior dark despite the numerous windows. Jane, sword in hand, flattened against the wall on one side of the door, Suhonen on the other. Clift stayed behind me, his sword still on his belt. Duncan stood beside him.

With my hands loose at my side, I stepped into the house, ducking low at the last moment in case someone waited to take off my head. Nothing happened. I stood up and waited for my eyes to adjust.

As they did, something extraordinary happened. It was like I'd entered some sort of spellbound cottage. From the sun-blasted jungle outside, I now trod the darkness of a rain forest hidden in perpetual dusk. I sensed great ancient forests around me, with its naked inhabitants peering out around the trunks of the great trees. I blinked a few times, and the images resolved into things painted on the walls and ceilings.

I forgot to breathe. The detail, design, and execution of these images was extraordinary. The trees began with spidery root patterns that extended from the baseboards onto the floor, and their trunks climbed the walls until limbs branched out across the ceiling. The colors were vivid, brighter than life and yet somehow pulsing with it. Birds of red, orange, and yellow sat among the leaves, and here and there were parts of snakes, lizards, and insects. Behind the trees, simple blurred lines suggested the rest of the forest, with occasional faint beams of sunlight implying depth.

As a baron's son in Arentia, I'd been taught the basics of art appreciation, and I knew without a doubt I was in the presence of genius. I turned slowly, taking it all in. Who the hell *did* all this?

There were people there, too. A bare arm here, a naked breast there, dark hair obscuring faces . . . It was the kind of tribe that you might find on an island like this. Had there been one before the pirates arrived? If so, where were they now?

"Eddie?" Jane called from outside. "You okay?"

"Yeah," I answered numbly. "It's, uhm . . . all clear."

They joined me in the house, Suhonen having to duck to get through the door, and were equally startled by the art. "Good grief," Jane said at last. "Somebody had a lot of free time."

Clift touched one of the paintings. It had begun to flake off the wood. "It won't last much longer."

I felt a sharp pang of anguish that this wonder might not be long for the world, but I brought myself back to the moment and looked past the art at the house containing it. This was the big main room, with a stove in one corner, a desk in another, and nothing else. A door led into a second room, where only a rumpled bed remained. On the bedroom floor, though, several recent bare footprints had marked the dust. Our watcher in the woods?

"Eddie?" Jane called. "You better come see this."

I joined her. They all stood in front of one section of the wall, where the artist had painted a nude woman leaning seductively back against a tree. In one hand she held some sort of fruit. She was depicted larger and more prominently than any of the others, who were shown hiding and peeking out.

When I didn't react fast enough, Jane said, "Look *above* her neck."

I did, and got my biggest surprise yet. It was, without a doubt, *Angelina*.

It wasn't just the detail, which he got right—well, at least on the parts of her body I could personally verify. He'd captured something ineffable about her, so that anyone who knew her couldn't fail to recognize her. Her expression was one I'd seen many times, a mixture of annoyance and amusement that, coupled with her nudity, made her almost unbearably sexy. My mind involuntarily conjured up the memory of our one kiss all those years ago, and I felt an uncomfortable arousal building in me.

It lasted until Duncan quietly asked, "Is that my mom?"

I nodded, the momentary spell broken. I'm pretty sure I blushed, too, but it was too dark for anyone to see.

"Your mom?" Clift repeated. "Is there something here I should know about?"

It seemed pointless to keep the secret now. "He's Black Edward's son."

Clift looked at Duncan. "Really," he said with a mix of annoyance and disbelief.

"He's never met him," I said quickly. "Black Edward may not even know he exists."

"The man's got a good memory, though," Jane said. "If he hasn't seen Angelina in twenty years."

Yeah, I agreed to myself, *a very good memory.* Or Angie had flat-out lied to me. She occasionally went away for weeks at a time without telling anyone where or why; did she meet her pirate lover in secret? Hell, did she come here and pose for him against that huge tree outside?

"Look at this," Suhonen said. He stood over the desk, nodding toward something but careful not to touch it. My God, he was a quick study. We gathered around him.

He'd found a book, with wooden covers and vellum pages bound between them. Painted on the cover was a sailing ship halfway sunk beneath the stormy waves, the water around it filled with drowning men. Below this was the title.

"It looks like a logbook," Jane said.

"Yeah," I agreed distantly. Everything receded except the words painted on the cover by the artist's steady hand.

"I can't read the language, though," she added.

"Me, neither," Suhonen said.

"I can," I said. My voice was barely a whisper.

She noticed my attitude. "What's the matter with you?"

"Nothing," I said, snapping back to the moment. "I can read it," I repeated.

"What language is it, then?"

"Arentian," I said.

"You're from Arentia?" Suhonen said in surprise.

"Originally. And not for a long time."

"Do you think it'll tell us what really happened to his ship?" Clift asked.

"I'm absolutely certain it will."

"How do you know?"

I tapped the lettering on the cover. "Because the title is *The Wreck of the* Bloody Angel *and What Really Happened.*"

The same title as the official book back in Watchorn Harbor. The irony was as sharp as Clift's sword.

I wanted to read it. They wanted me to read it to them, although they hadn't said so. It was clear in the way their gazes flicked from me to the book and back. I tried desperately to think of a legitimate reason to avoid it, though. I wanted to read it first in private. Although we had the same name, nothing had prepared me for the realization that we also shared a nationality.

I lifted the cover. This was no government document; the handwriting was a bit sloppy, but it still showed the traces of Arentian school penmanship. The first sentence beckoned me, and I saw no way around it: *All this treasure—*

Then Duncan saved me by asking, "What's that out there?"

He nodded out the window toward the yard opposite the one we'd crossed. Most of it was shaded by the huge tree, which kept the weeds from growing too high. The terrain sloped slightly down toward a round hole about the size of a tavern table. Directly above this, hanging from a thick tree branch, was a block and tackle. Clearly something had been lowered into, or lifted out of, the opening.

"A well?" Jane suggested.

"Wouldn't need a well with that stream going right by the house," I said.

"Looks like just a hole in the ground to me," Suhonen said.

"Yes," Clift agreed. "And we all know why pirates put holes in the ground."

I was grateful to have something other than the journal to think about, so I led us outside to the edge of the hole. I got as close as I dared and peered down; there was nothing but darkness.

"Hey!" Jane yelled down the hole. "Black Edward! Are you down there?" There was no response. She shrugged. "Well, sometimes it's that easy."

"Not this time," Clift said. He looked up; the wind was starting to pick up, and on the other side of the mountain, we saw the first dark gray hints of storm clouds. "Weather looks touchy."

"Too touchy for me to go down and have a look?" I said.

"I'm no weather wizard. I see gray skies, I get nervous. But they might go right past us with nary a sprinkle."

Duncan picked up a chain that lay on the ground. One end was attached to a loop driven deep into the tree trunk. The other had a heavy-duty snap that might clip on to a particularly large collar. "This must have been where those big lizards spent their time before they got loose: guarding that hole."

I examined the snap. It was solid and intact. "They didn't get loose, they were *turned* loose."

"Here's the rope they must've used for the pit," Suhonen called. He'd found a long coil of thick line hanging from the stub of another branch. "It's pretty stiff. Hasn't been used in a while, but it seems strong enough." He paused. "That pulley's heavy-duty, too. Whatever they lowered into that hole wasn't a feather pillow."

"Or pulled out of it," Jane added.

"Yeah," Suhonen agreed.

I stepped away from the hole and examined the ground. There had once been a worn path from the house to the hole, but grass had begun to overgrow it. I saw no sign of the bare footprints we'd seen earlier.

I looked at Jane. She said, "We have to know what's down there."

"Or what *was* down there," I added.

"Yeah," she said. "The pile of unanswered questions just gets bigger and bigger, doesn't it?"

"I'm the smallest," Duncan said. "I'll go down."

"No, it's not your place," I said, and when he started to protest added, "This is my case, not yours."

"Is your shoulder up to it?" he challenged.

"It works just fine." I left out the part about it hurting like a bastard.

"And if there *is* treasure down there?" Clift said.

"Eddie will tell us," Jane said with the kind of certainty that brooked no further questions. "And then we'll decide what to do next."

Duncan proved to be useful, though. He shimmied out onto the branch and threaded the rope through the block and tackle. I tied a loop in one end for my foot, and some knots to give me handholds. After the lizard fight and the climb up the steps, I didn't want to rely on just my fading strength to keep me safe. Finally, I sat on the edge of the hole, arranged the rope, and looked back.

"Two tugs means pull me up now," I said. "Three means I've hit bottom. Depending on what I find, I might tie something to the bottom of the rope and send it up first. If I do, I'll tug four times."

Suhonen nodded. He'd wrapped the rope around the tree's trunk, then around himself; he would be in charge of playing it out as I needed it. "How long do we give you before we send someone else down?"

I looked at Jane. "Captain Argo will determine that. If you lose contact, she takes over for me." I turned to Clift. "If that's all right with you."

"Seems my opinion and three gold pieces will buy you a nice dinner," he snorted.

The sky was turning darker behind the mountain. The storm could pass us by as Clift said, but I didn't have that kind of luck. I took a deep breath, peered down into the blackness, and yelled, "Anyone down there, don't panic. I'm coming down, and I just want to talk."

"Would you believe that if you were down there?" Clift asked Duncan.

Duncan, self-conscious at being so casually addressed by the captain, merely shrugged.

I kicked off the lip, then braced my feet against the edge of the shaft. If I straightened my knees, my back pressed against the opposite wall, which made stopping very easy.

The sides of the shaft had once been shored up with wooden

planks. Many had fallen, and roots poked through the dirt. Insects and other vermin clung to the walls near the surface, but as I descended into the darkness, they grew fewer and fewer.

"See anything?" Jane called down.

"Bugs and tree roots," I answered. "If I run across Miles, I'll give him your regards."

Her laugh echoed in the shaft.

Close spaces didn't typically bother me, but something about this one did. The tropical heat and humidity had me sweating, but some of the perspiration was ice cold. It wasn't just the physical narrowness, it was the same dread I'd experienced going in the opposite direction to question Rody Hawk. I'd had just enough contact with the supposedly unreal to let my imagination conjure all sorts of things below. After all, I'd encountered ghosts within the safety of the *Red Cow;* anything could be at the bottom of this hole.

The bugs didn't help. I couldn't see them, but I felt them as my hands brushed the sides of the shaft. There was no wooden shoring here, and whatever lived this deep crawled with impunity until I shook them off. Ordinarily bugs didn't bother me either, but this wasn't an ordinary situation, and I kept anticipating painful bites that thankfully never came.

As the circle of light above grew smaller, I saw a dim pinpoint far beneath me. And when I was equidistant between the two, I felt a light breeze rising through the shaft. It grew stronger as I descended, until it was whistling around me.

"Seems to be open at the bottom," I called up. "There's light and wind." I waited, but no one replied. I might have been too far down to hear it, or something might've happened to them. I tried mightily to believe the former.

Then I was there at the bottom, my feet hanging into open space. Diffuse sunlight shone on a flat patch of rock. Planks and dirt that had fallen from the shaft still lay piled there. I braced my legs and back against the shaft's bottom lip and waited. Beyond the wind, I heard the sound of waves and running water. When I looked up, I could not see the top of the shaft.

I took a deep breath, bent my knees, and let myself drop through the hole. I hoped Suhonen was ready to take my whole weight. I felt the jerk as the rope snapped tight, and my cut shoulder protested. I spun in place, quickly at first and then more slowly. The cooler air felt wonderful. Finally, I was lowered through the open space toward the ground twenty feet below.

It was a sea-cut cave, big enough to hold a dozen ships. Along one wall was a huge, jagged horizontal gap through which I saw the gray overcast sky. Outside, birds hovered in the wind, and I heard that same faint squawking we'd all mistaken for a party. Rubble beneath this crack showed where the outer wall had collapsed to form the opening—quite recently, if the debris was any indication.

A dark pool took up a third of the cave floor, the water deep beneath the still, glassy surface. One section of the wall was huge and smooth, and the image of a ship had been painted on it as part of a mural. I couldn't make out the details as I slowly corkscrewed my way to the ground.

At last, I touched bottom and took my foot out of the loop. I gave the rope three hard tugs and hoped Suhonen remembered our cues. Then I tied it to the base of a stalactite so that it couldn't be pulled up. That wouldn't stop anyone at the top from throwing down their end, but I had no control over that.

I put my hands on my knees and took several deep breaths. I hadn't realized how truly creepy the shaft was until now, and my chest hurt from breathing shallowly on the way down. My shoulder throbbed from my neck to my fingertips. Here the air smelled of salt and damp, and the wind swirled in and out of the cave like water. There was another smell, vaguely familiar, but for the moment I couldn't place it.

When my head was back to normal, I looked at the mural. It depicted a ship on the bottom of the ocean, skeletons half buried in the sand around it. I recognized the same hand that had painted the hut's interior and the cover of the mysterious book. Along the bottom were the words THE FATE OF THE BLOODY ANGEL, and beneath it a list of names. The postscript read, SENT TO THEIR DEATHS BY THE TREACHERY OF BLACK EDWARD TEW.

And all this was written in Arentian.

I drew my sword. The strange man in Blefuscola assured me I'd find my quarry alive, and I didn't want to do it just before he drove a knife in my back.

"Black Edward Tew!" I called. My voice sounded thin and distant over the ever-present wind. "Angelina Dirnay sent me to find you! I don't want your money, she just wants to know what happened to you."

I waited. Except for the wind, there was nothing. The clouds outside grew thicker, which dimmed the light in the cave. It was so eerie that if Dorsal and his little girlfriend had stepped out of the shadows, they would not have seemed out of place.

A man-made divider of stacked rocks stuck out from the wall at a ninety-degree angle and hid one corner of the cave from view. I moved toward it carefully, making as little sound as possible. It was ten feet high, and the end reached nearly to the pool, with just a narrow space to squeeze around. There was nothing alive in the water: no algae, no fish, no small crustaceans along the edge. I picked my way around, trying to watch every direction at once, including up.

On the other side of the wall, in the shadows, I saw the opening of a small sub-cave. I stayed by the edge of the pool and waited for my eyes to adjust to the comparative dimness. After weeks on the *Cow* going from deck to hold and back, it didn't take long.

This secondary cave was closed off with iron bars. Thick as my arm, they were stuck deep into the uneven floor and the smaller cave's ceiling. I couldn't see past the bars into the shadowy interior, but what they guarded wasn't much of a mystery.

An iron wall sconce held an old torch. I turned my back to the wind and struck flints until it lit. I waited for the flame to settle. When it did, I knew I was in the right place.

Behind the bars, the cave held a pile of treasure as big as my bedroom. Maybe larger: I had no idea how far back it extended. Wooden chests were stacked to the ceiling; those closest stood open, the torch light sparkling off the gold and jewels within them. No dust could fully hide that kind of glimmer. I couldn't conceive of how much this would be worth. More, certainly, than the whole national treasury of a backwater kingdom like Neceda. More than my old family fortune back in Arentia. More than I'd ever earn as a sword jockey in a dozen lifetimes.

I'm a little bit ashamed to say I was so dazzled by this that I didn't notice the other thing behind the bars. On the floor, one hand in an open chest, lay a dead body. He was facedown, and had the same distinctive black hair as Duncan.

"Hello, Edward," I said softly, the disappointment so heavy, I could hardly stand upright. I made a mental note to slap the guy in Blefuscola if I crossed paths with him again. I leaned my forehead against the bars. "Looks like Jane was right. Let's keep that between us, okay? She's insufferable enough."

Then the body *moved*.

This was the second time, after Rody Hawk, I'd thought someone dead who wasn't, and I almost let out a shriek like a startled girl. But when he rolled onto his back, I saw that his cheeks were hollow from starvation, and his eyes sunken into dark pits. They were open, though, and despite their milky glaze, they slowly moved to look at me.

I wasn't sure he could hear me over the pounding of my heart. "You . . . you're Black Edward Tew."

He nodded. I swear I heard his bones creak. One thin hand raised itself imploringly in my direction. Around his arm—so loose, it dangled to his elbow—was a golden bracelet. I saw the angel wings engraved in the band.

His jaw worked, but no sound came out. His lips were thin, and his gums had drawn back from his teeth. Then the hand fell limp to the floor and the head lolled to one side. His eyes closed. This time I knew he was truly dead. Both Jane and the crazy old man had been right.

There was a door as well, with a heavy lock mechanism and a socket for a lone key. I tried it; it was shut tight.

Fate gave me little time to mourn my loss or Tew's death. Something bubbled, and it took me a moment to wrench myself back to the present and look around for the source. The middle of the dark pool churned and roiled, and waves rolled out and slapped against the flat rocks. The water rose so that it swamped the narrow path around the end of the divider. It surged toward me and I backed up to the bars. I returned the torch to the sconce to leave my hands free.

And then the source of the disturbance appeared.

"Shit!" I yelled. I'd walked right into the same goddamned trap *again*. On the plus side, I *had* learned where Wendell Marteen got the idea. So I wasn't a total failure as a sword jockey.

Maybe instead of Clift's noble quote, *that* would be my epitaph: *Not a total failure.*

It was the same kind of sea-living killing machine Marteen had chained to the bottom of his ghost ship, but if this first glimpse was any indication, Clift had been right: That one was a mere juvenile. What rose from the pool, slimy skin gleaming in the light, was bigger than the *Red Cow* herself.

It had the same bulbous head with at least one round eye. The oblong pupil, black as Rody Hawk's soul, was big enough to reflect me full-length, which it was in fact doing. I froze, hoping that if it saw no movement, it would think it had been mistaken, but that was futile. This was a staring contest I'd never win. It knew damn well I was there and had nowhere to go.

The odor was ghastly as well. The creature on the ship had smelled like this, but here it was a thousand times stronger, and my gag reflex barely held on. This was what I'd smelled but couldn't identify: the stink of the monster.

Two thick tentacles rose from the water, weaved a bit in the air, and then grasped a pair of thick stalactites. The creature lifted itself farther from the pool. For the first time, I wondered if it might not be just aquatic, but amphibious as well.

Not that it mattered, because its tentacles were plenty long enough to reach me. It was in the process of illustrating this, as a half-dozen arms unrolled their way across the cave floor, guided by that looming, all-seeing eye.

I desperately rattled the treasure vault door. Alas, the lock was sturdy. I slashed at the first tentacle tip near me, and it withdrew like a burnt finger. The others halted their advance. I glanced at the hole in the ceiling, using all my will to conjure a battalion of Suhonens dropping through to save my ass. They did not appear.

I couldn't get over the partition wall, or behind the vault's bars. I couldn't attack a vulnerable spot on the monster, because none were within my reach. I thought of throwing my boot knife at the enormous eye, but I figured the last thing I wanted to do was seriously piss this thing off. If I was very lucky, it would crush me to death quickly before stuffing me into the shiny black beak that waited below the water. If I made it mad, though, it might toy with me.

More tentacles appeared, grabbing the edge of the pool and providing more leverage. The creature surged up even more, sending a wave at me that soaked me to the waist. The good thing was that if I wet myself like Duncan, it wouldn't show. I'd be squid food with the appearance of dignity.

The water went through the bars and shifted Black Edward's corpse. I could see his skull-face now, grinning at my predicament. A fine way to treat a fellow Arentian in trouble.

By now, the monster's bulk blocked most of the light. If it rose much higher, all it would need to do was fall on me. There seemed to be no way out; I seriously considered cutting my own throat just to get this over with. But I knew that no matter what, I'd go down fighting.

Then a woman's voice said, "Don't hurt it again!"

I looked around. I saw no one, and it was such a ludicrous request, I called back, "Okay!"

"If you make it mad, I can't stop it."

That sounded reasonable, even though I had no idea who was speaking, where she was, or what she had planned. "So what do I do?"

"Just stand there and be quiet."

I did. The tentacles did not attack again. In fact, they withdrew into the water. The ones attached to the ceiling released themselves as well. Slowly, so that very little water was disturbed, the massive monster sank back into the pool. It managed to keep that lone spooky eye above water until the last moment, looking at me with crustacean malevolence. Then with a ripple, it was gone. The water around me receded.

I waited until every last wavelet had vanished from sight before peeling myself loose from the bars. I crept around the end of the wall, the whole time watching the pool. When I reached the other side of the partition, I finally saw my rescuer.

She squatted by the pool, two big empty jugs beside her. She wore a man's vest and ragged pants cut into shorts. She was barefoot, and her skin was deeply tanned. Her hair was wavy and untamed, and bits of leaves and other debris clung to it. I couldn't see her face; she concentrated all her attention on the water.

"Just stay there," she called. "This stuff puts it to sleep, but not for long and not if it's agitated. You're luckier than you know." At last, she said, "I think it's gone." Then she stood and faced me.

I was speechless.

She put one hand on her hip. "Come on, I know I'm not the ugliest thing in the world, but you don't have to make *that* big a deal. Or have you just not seen a woman in a while?"

My voice entirely escaped me.

"Okay, you're making me nervous. I know you can talk. Say something."

I took a breath, and forced out the only word that seemed to matter at the moment, because this woman standing before me, on an island thousands of miles from Neceda, was unmistakable.

"Angelina?"

chapter

THIRTY-TWO

I t wasn't Angelina, of course. The resemblance was strik-ing, but the voice was completely different. It took a minute for that to register, though.

The woman laughed. "No, I'm . . . My name is . . . My name is . . ." She seemed to be struggling to remember. "Barbara. My name is Barbara." She shook her head. "But he called me Angelina. Or Angie. Or Angel. And made every-one else do it."

I really needed to sit down now, but made do with leaning against the wall. I said, "Are you the only person on the island?"

"Except for him," she said with a gesture toward the trea-sure cave.

"It's just you now," I said.

She blinked a couple of times, and her face went blank. Then she grabbed me by the hair. When she snarled, "What?" I felt spittle on my cheek. "What did you say?"

I didn't try to break free. At the moment, it didn't seem to matter. "I said, he's dead. Just now."

"Oh, no," she whispered, and let me go. She walked a few steps away, quietly repeating, "No," to herself.

I didn't know what else to say, so I said, "I'm sorry."

It was the wrong thing.

"Sorry?" she yelled as she whirled on me. "For a month, I've been sitting outside that cage, waiting to watch him die! I've given him just enough water to keep him alive, watched him wither, listened to him beg the way he made me beg! And now you tell me I missed it?" She began to laugh. Then it changed to sobs. Then it exploded into full-blown hysterics that rang off the ceiling.

I glanced nervously at the pool, but the surface was motionless.

I couldn't just sit by and listen to this, so I stood up and put my hand on her shoulder. "Look, is there anything I can—?"

At the moment of contact, she drew a knife from her belt and spun at me. I reacted reflexively, blocked her thrust with my forearm, and hit the point of her chin with the heel of my other hand. Her head snapped back and she dropped to the ground. The sound of her skull hitting the rocky floor rang like a lone drumbeat.

The whole altercation happened so quickly that it was over before I really comprehended it. She sprawled on the rocky cave floor as if she'd fallen from the sky. "Shit," I whispered to myself. I seriously worried that I might have killed her.

I picked up the knife and waited for the shakes to stop and

my breathing to return to normal. When my fingers were steady, I checked her neck for a pulse. It was there, and she moaned when I pulled my hand away.

I carried her to the wall and propped her against it. There was nothing to cover her with, but the tropical breeze wasn't exactly chilling. I tore a strip from my tunic and risked dipping it in the water, but again, there was no sign of the beast. I returned and wiped her face until, at last, her eyes opened and focused on me.

"You didn't kill me," she said.

"Hell, I didn't even mean to hit you. It was a reflex."

She looked down at herself. "I've still got my clothes on."

"Why wouldn't you?"

She smiled wryly, without humor. "You've never been a woman captured by pirates. Even old pirates." She gently felt the back of her head. When she pulled her fingers away, there was no blood. "There's a lump, but it doesn't seem to be serious. What's your name?"

"Eddie."

She laughed, again without any humor. "No."

"Yeah. Eddie LaCrosse."

"Another one. Two Eddies. Well, he's an Edward. Was an Edward." She paused, took a moment to compose herself, and said, "Is he really dead?"

"Yeah."

"Can I see? I need to see it for myself."

"Sure, if it won't wake up Grabby." I nodded at the pool.

"Cherish," she corrected.

"Cherish? That thing's name is Cherish?"

"Everything needs a name. Wendell picked it; he said she was an old girlfriend who went crazy on him."

"Wendell Marteen?"

"Yeah."

I wanted to ask her more questions, but the desperate need in her eyes was hard to ignore. I helped her to her feet, led her around the wall, and showed her the corpse of Black Edward Tew.

After giving her a few moments to take it in, I asked quietly, "How did he end up in there?"

She kept her eyes on the body. "A comedy of errors. He dropped the key to the treasure chamber out here and didn't realize it until the door slammed shut behind him."

"So where were you when that happened?"

She smiled, again with no warmth. "Right here. He took me everywhere, and I mean that literally. One of his favorite places was bent over his precious treasure. This time, though, he told me to wait outside while he filled the box. His last and best mistake."

She knelt and reached through the bars toward his nearest hand, too far away to touch. "You have no idea what that man did to me. You can't imagine. And all I wanted in revenge was to see him die. And I missed it."

"Where were you?"

"Where do you think? Following you. Didn't you see my footprint in the mud? I didn't have time to go back and cover it up."

"Did you sic the lizards on us, then?"

"No, they don't need me to help them find meat."

I looked at the way the door was constructed. There would be no removing it easily, and picking the lock would take time. "So the door just happened to close when you were out here and he was in there?"

"Think whatever you want," she said wearily. "I threw the key into the pool when I realized he was locked in. It was the only one; no copies. There's no fishing it out, and there's no way to break into the cave without stirring up Cherish, and she's so big and pulpy, weapons don't hurt her. Which means you've wasted your trip."

"I'm not interested in the treasure."

She laughed. It came out as a sharp little snort.

"I'm serious," I insisted. "Why does nobody believe that?"

"Are you a monk?" she taunted.

"No, I'm a sword jockey. I was hired to find Black Edward Tew, nothing more."

She looked up. "Then . . . did my husband send you? To find me and bring me back?"

"No," I said. "But I will take you back, if you want."

She just stared at me. I couldn't imagine the feelings going through her, so I just waited. At last, she said, "You really are just looking for Edward? Not the treasure?"

"Yes. Someone wanted to know what happened to him." Now I laughed without any amusement. "You reminded me of her, actually. That's why you startled me so much."

"The other Angelina?"

I nodded.

"So I do look a lot like her."

"A lot," I agreed.

She gazed down at Edward's haggard face, now gray with

death. His wet hair lay plastered across his cheeks and forehead. "Edward kidnapped me from Kontis, where I worked in my husband's tavern. He said I reminded him of someone, and I guess it was this Angelina woman. He brought me here . . . my God, fifteen years ago. My husband barely knew I was around when I was underfoot all the time; wonder how long it took him to notice I was gone?" She paused. "Of course, that was before Edward went crazy."

"Crazy how?"

"You know how every ship has a bell with its name on it? He took the bell from his ship before he sank it. He used to say he could hear it ringing still, even when it sat there on his desk, collecting dust. Finally, he gave it to one of the old men in town."

"The ones you released the lizards to get?"

"They got what they deserved. And if the lizards kill some of Wendell's crew when they get back, that's even fewer people around to hurt me."

"So who were the people that lived here? Not Tew's original crew."

She snorted. "No, they're dead. You know, even after he gave away the bell, Edward swore he could see their ghosts accusing him of treachery and murder. He painted that mural to try to quiet them, to give them a memorial. But they only lived here," she said, tapping her temple.

She shook her head back to the moment. "The ones in the huts were people Wendell accumulated whenever he left the island. For years it was just me, Edward, and Wendell. Then when Wendell would leave, he'd bring someone back. They were harmless, or so I thought; just bums too lazy or old or injured to make a living at sea, and wanting nothing more than a beach to lie on and enough rum to make them forget. They were afraid of Edward, so they mostly left us alone. But Wendell gathered enough of them that he finally made a crew after Edward's accident. If you stay long enough, you'll get to meet them. They should be back soon."

"Wendell's crew isn't coming back."

Her eyes narrowed suspiciously. "What happened?"

"The ship in the harbor is a pirate hunter I hired to help me find Edward Tew. We captured the *Bloody Angel* and sent the survivors back to Blefuscola to hang. Wendell's dead."

Now her lips twisted in a little smile, one very Angelina-like. "You expect me to believe you got away from his trap?"

"Sank it right on top of the monster."

"Without poxbinder?"

Many things clicked into place in my head. "Is that what was in those jugs you used?"

"Mostly water. Just a tiny bit of poxbinder."

That explained the cache on the *Bloody Angel*. Marteen wanted enough poxbinder to tranquilize or kill Cherish so he had time to break through the bars and get to the treasure. "So how did Marteen get the other monster to cooperate? Did he drug it, too?"

"Yes. He called that one Abigail. Cherish is too big to leave the cave, but the males are smaller and they get in through some underwater passage. She lays eggs every year, and they grow fast. He caught Abigail when she was no bigger than his hand, raised her until she was the size of a rowboat, and then chained her to the bottom of an old ship he stole. She kept growing, and when she was big enough, he towed the ship out into the ocean, figuring any ship that stopped to check on it would get its crew eaten. Then he could raid the poxbinder from their medicine chests."

"Never occurred to him to just go buy the stuff?"

"Did you meet him?"

"I see your point."

She turned and leaned back against the bars. Eyes closed, she said, "So Edward's dead. And Wendell. And everyone else."

"Except you."

She let out a deep, long sigh. "Does the real Angelina know about the treasure?"

"She's not interested in it, either."

"So what happens to it?"

I thought about Jane, Clift, and Suhonen waiting above. I thought about dirt-poor, dirt-farming Duncan. It was better for all of them if they never knew. "You and I are the only ones left alive who know about it. Do you want it?"

"No," she said emphatically. "I've been raped on top of it, and now that he's dead, I never want to see it again."

"Then if you don't mention it, I won't."

"You can really walk away from all that?"

"Doesn't seem to have done anyone else very much good, does it? Besides, I did what I was hired to do. I found out what happened to Black Edward."

Her expression changed to one of almost little-girl desperation, disconcerting on such an obviously grown woman. "So you'll be leaving soon?"

I nodded.

She licked her lips nervously. "And you really will take me with you, like you said? Off the island?"

"Of course."

She ran her hands through her hair, trying to straighten and arrange it, and arched her back so that her breasts strained against the leather vest. "I'll do anything," she said demurely, her assertiveness gone. "Just please don't hurt me."

"You don't have to. And I won't. No one will."

I saw gratitude like I never imagined I could see in a human being's eyes, shaded with the skepticism a life like hers demanded. "You swear?"

"I swear. We'll get you back home."

"Not home," she said quickly. "It's been too long. Just . . . somewhere else. Somewhere away from the ocean."

"Okay. Now let's go catch up with my friends. They're probably getting worried by now. And I'd rather not be here when Cherish finally wakes up."

"I'll show you the quick way."

"Quicker than the shaft from the cottage?"

She laughed. "There's an easy path up the hill outside that crack."

"Really? Then what was the shaft for?"

"Oh, the crack is recent. It opened up just after Edward got locked in. Before that, they had to use the shaft to bring up the gold he sent off with Marteen."

"He sent Marteen off with the gold? It looked like most of it was still there."

"Most of it is. He just sent a single box at a time. He did it a couple of times a year, but never told me why. I asked once, and he tied me to a tree and beat me. I never asked again."

I suddenly knew exactly where the gold went, but I said nothing. I was too tired for more epiphanies. We climbed the hill just as the rain began, and by the time we found Jane and the others, it fell steadily. It was not a storm, though; it was a hard shower, washing clean the years Barbara had been forced to live here under another woman's name.

It took a long time to get back to Neceda. I told no one but Jane that I'd found Black Edward. Clift and the rest believed I'd discovered only a cave and Edward's former concubine.

Barbara had learned a lot of useful nautical skills during her time as Tew's captive, and she quickly fell into the shipboard routine. She was okay with anyone who spoke to her, but she reacted violently if someone deliberately touched her. This quickly became common knowledge, and she was treated with the deference her experience on the island demanded. She and Jane spent a lot of time together talking, and I think having another woman to confide in, particularly one as self-possessed as Jane, helped a lot. I didn't know where she'd end up, but I felt good about her chances.

At Blefuscola, harbormaster Moleworth presented Clift

with a medal and a certificate of appreciation from Queen Remy herself. She had been monitoring the shipping crisis, and when Clift's crew arrived with Marteen's *Bloody Angel,* she was informed at once. I could tell it bugged Moleworth to deliver this praise, but he did so with professional efficiency. I wondered if it also meant Clift got a raise. Most of the *Red Cow*'s crew was there to witness the ceremony, and Moleworth let Jane pin the little ribbon on Clift's tunic. Clift clearly enjoyed getting the award from his old captain.

As we left the ceremony in the harbormaster's office, Suhonen said behind me, "Got a minute?"

This time I didn't jump, although as always, I had no idea he was there. "How did you get to be so good at sneaking up on people?"

"I'm the runt of my family. I had to learn to disappear if I didn't want my brothers to kick my arse."

"I see. Well, what can I do for you?"

"After all we've gone through, I wondered if you thought I'd make a good sword jockey."

"Sure. Lots of it isn't very exciting, though. And it's easy to lose your way, morally speaking."

"Easier than when you're a pirate?"

"Okay, maybe not. But you still have to keep a close watch on yourself."

He nodded, thinking hard. "Would you like an apprentice?"

"Me? No. I'm not a good team player."

"You could've fooled me. You led that boarding party like you'd done it all your life."

"And you'll remember, the other ship got away."

He laughed. "Okay, thanks, Mr. LaCrosse. I'll keep what

you said in mind. I owe Captain Clift my sword until the end of this tour, but after that, we may be working the same side of the street. Mind if I come by occasionally to ask your advice?"

"You're way too big for me to refuse."

We shook hands, and then followed the rest of the *Red Cow*'s crew to the nearest tavern.

I bought a round of drinks for everyone, and we all toasted both Clift's award and the successful voyage. Songs were sung, tales were told, and a few noses bloodied. Mostly we laughed. I realized that I'd actually miss these former lawbreakers, and came closer to changing careers than I can truly blame on the alcohol. But my anchor was already set back in Neceda, my home port.

I kept an eye out for the strange man who'd prophesied that I'd find Black Edward alive. There was no trace of him, and no one else in Blefuscola remembered him. Like the ghost of Dorsal Finn, he'd quietly vanished, his job done.

BEFORE the *Cow* departed, I managed to get Duncan alone on shore. We stood at the rail along the dock, gazing out at the harbor. When it wasn't packed to the gills with terrified ships, it was a beautiful place. "So what are your plans?" I asked him.

"I haven't gotten paid yet, so I can't go back to Watchorn. Guess I'll keep working until I can."

"Do you want to go back?"

"I miss my boys."

"And your wife?"

"More than I thought I would. But not as much as the kids."

I paused. I was about to light the fuse. "I need to tell you something. Back on the island, down in that hole . . . I found your father."

He turned to look at me. "Really," he said flatly.

I nodded. "He was dead. He'd been dead for a while." It was a small lie for comfort's sake, and I could live with that.

He chewed his lip. "Well . . . I guess that's that. You don't get answers to every question, do you?"

"Sometimes none at all," I agreed. Then I handed him a pouch of gold, cut from Angelina's advance. "Here's a bonus. Don't say anything about not deserving it or just doing your job. You left Watchorn a whiny little boy, and I'd call you a man now. A man who needs to get home to his family."

He tried not to let his pride show as he took the money. "Thanks, Mr. LaCrosse. And when you see my mother . . ."

I waited for the rage and fury.

He smiled. "Just give her my regards. Tell her where to find me. If she wants to see her grandsons, that's great, if not—" He shrugged. "—I won't hold my breath."

"Probably a good idea."

JANE and I left the *Red Cow* in Blefuscola and booked passage to Mosinee on a passenger ship. Compared to what we'd had on the *Cow,* these quarters were palatial, and we both slept soundly for about three days straight. Subsequently, she spent most of her time in the ship's bar, regaling tourists with tall tales of adventure in return for free drinks. Her laugh carried from bow to stern. By the end of the first week, most of the men on board thought they were in love with her.

I had a grimmer task. I had put off reading Black Edward

Tew's journal, diary, or whatever the hell it was as long as I could. I knew it would probably answer most of my remaining questions, and Angelina would want those answers. But I was sick of this whole case by now, disgusted with the people who would do such horrible things for such petty, selfish reasons. I'd had my fill of the Brotherhood of the Surf.

Still, I was a professional. I ordered some ale, locked my door, and arranged the journal so that the light from the port-hole shown on the pages. The cover promised I'd know why Black Edward had done the awful things he had done. I opened it, saw the neat words written in my own native language, and began to read.

He told about his past: the son of a well-to-do merchant, educated and trained for the family business but enamored of the sea since childhood. I didn't know the family he said he came from, but socially they would have been a tier or two beneath me. I recognized the place names, though, and the descriptions. He was Arentian, all right, just like me.

And in a short time, I knew pretty much everything else about him, too.

WHEN we reached Mosinee, I paid Jane what I owed her and added a healthy bonus, which used up the last of Angelina's gold. Our horses, kept in reasonable shape by the stable, showed no overt sign they'd missed us. Baxter seemed just as annoyed as he always did when I climbed onto his back. I was equally uncomfortable after being out of the saddle for so long. I could tell my butt was going to really hurt for a while.

Outside Tallega, we stopped where the road divided. "Well, LaCrosse, this is it," Jane said. "A hell of a trip, I'd say."

"Yeah," I agreed. "Hell of a one."

"You still won't tell me what was in that logbook?"

"Nothing that changes anything for us. The bad guys are all dead, the good guys are few and far between, and everyone left alive is on their way home." I paused. "So how'd you leave things with Dylan?"

She rolled her eyes. "Dylan had it bad for me, LaCrosse, not the other way around. I think he finally realized I wasn't who he thought I was. Or at least, not anymore."

"So it's back to Miles, then?"

"Yep."

"What're you going to do about him?"

"LaCrosse, I'll tell you a secret. There's only one thing worse than a husband you can't control."

"And what's that?"

"One you *can*." She winked, nudged her horse, and headed toward home. Miles wouldn't be there, but wherever he was, she'd find him, drag him back, and chain him to a bigger rock. And then they'd resume the life that worked for them. For a long time, I believed that Jane was trapped in her marriage by her sense of honor, but now I knew better. She was exactly where she wanted to be. Like me.

Well, not yet. I wanted to get back to Liz. Angelina could damn well wait.

"WELL," Liz said between gasps for breath, "good to see you, too. Need to fix that shaky leg."

"It always does that at that particular, uhm, moment."

"I meant the shaky *table* leg."

I let her down off the dinner table, and she moved her clothes back to their appropriate positions. I pulled up my pants and dropped heavily into one of the chairs. We could've made it to the bedroom, I suppose, but at the time, we'd had other priorities. I think the bards call it a "lusty bedding," even if technically no bed was involved.

"If I never get on a ship again, it's fine with me," I said. "You have no idea what it smells like after you've been at sea for a month. They use piss to wash their clothes, Liz. Seriously."

"Such lovely people you meet in your profession." She poured us both some ale from the bottle we kept in the kitchen. "You got a nice tan out of it, though. And you lost weight." She sauntered back with our drinks and sat in my lap. "And I assume, given your enthusiasm of the last few minutes, that you kept your hands off Jane."

"It was a struggle, but we managed to control ourselves."

She kissed me. Her face gleamed with the sweat of our exertions, and her short red hair was mussed. I thought she looked more beautiful than the sunrise over a tropical jungle. She said, "Does Angelina know you're back?"

I shook my head. "I'm not quite ready to give her my report. I need to sort things in my head first."

She kissed me again. "Want to tell me about it?"

"Eventually. But not yet. It's not that I'm wondering what I'll tell her. I'm just wondering what to do about it. We may have to leave Neceda." I looked at her. "Or at least, I might have to."

"You had it right the first time," she said. "'We.' As long as I'm with you, I'm home. Wherever we are."

I drank my ale and kissed her some more. There were few things I enjoyed doing more than those two. I couldn't believe I'd gone so long without doing one of them.

★ ★ ★

DESPITE a subsequent encore of my welcome home that should've left me too exhausted to think, I couldn't sleep. I left Liz in bed and wandered out onto the landing in the middle of the night, where I again found Mrs. Talbot at the bottom of the steps, this time pouring something from a large jug into a row of smaller ones.

"Poxbinder for killing sea monsters?" I said when she saw me.

She looked confused. "What?"

"Nothing. Cutting elderberry wine for street sale?"

"If I didn't, I couldn't sell it," she said. "Those mountain folks make it strong enough to melt you all the way down to the soles of your feet. When did you get back?"

"This afternoon."

"Did you find your pirate?"

"Yeah, I found him."

"After all this time, that's quite a feat. You should be proud of yourself."

"Yeah, well, it wasn't what I expected. Not at all."

She stopped, straightened up, and rubbed the small of her back. "You're not paid to expect things, are you? You're the legs and the eyes; the heart and the brain are the person who hired you."

I smiled. "That's what the training manual says. I think I forgot."

"Sometimes you have to relearn the basics."

"Sometimes. Good night, Mrs. Talbot."

"Good night. You two going to keep it down now that you've had your welcome home meet-and-greet?"

"Not likely."

"Well, make her scream once in my honor, then."

"No, that was me," I said.

She cackled.

I went inside, stretched out beside Liz, and kissed her bare shoulder. She snuggled back against me. Eventually I fell asleep. When I awoke, I knew what I had to do.

chapter

THIRTY-FOUR

I was leaning against the wall beside the tavern door when Angelina came down the street just before dawn. The mist was heavy off the river, and she emerged from it slowly, first a dark blob and finally an unmistakably feminine silhouette.

Neceda's various businesses were getting ready for the day as well. Both the area farmers and the crews on the riverboats got early starts. A local boy swept the wooden porch outside his family's shop and watched Angelina as she passed. She was old enough to be his mother, but some kinds of sexiness did not lessen with age.

When she saw me, she stopped. "You're back."

"I am."

"You look different."

"Weeks in a tropical paradise will do that to you. I have my report."

The normal seen-it-all haughtiness left her face. She desperately wanted to ask me if he was alive, but she didn't. Instead she calmly unlocked the door and I followed her inside. She locked the main door behind us, then went into the kitchen and unlatched the back door so Rudy the cook could get in and start the fires he'd need. She used flint stones to light a couple of lamps, then stopped at the bottom of the stairs leading up to my office.

"After you," I said, and gestured that she should precede me. I did my best to stay neutral, to give away nothing.

Inside my office, I found four messages had been pushed under the door, all the envelopes sealed with wax and embossed with various crests. One, from its weight, contained gold. There was an arrow as well, with a note wrapped around it. I knew what it said: *Not today. But someday.* A local gangster I'd once pissed off, my own little Rody Hawk, sent me one periodically to remind me how tough he was. I put them on my desk, sat down, and waited for her to do the same.

She still wore her shawl, and when she removed it, I saw the line of her bare shoulders. For some reason, this struck me as unbelievably sexy, and my resolve faltered. Then I wondered if she'd done it deliberately to distract me. Finally I realized the rather strange truth: I'd missed Angelina, too. Not in the same way as Liz, obviously, but neither in the sisterly way I usually felt about her, either.

"You're staring at my boobs," she said.

"No, at your shoulders, actually."

"Did you miss them?"

"I did," I admitted.

"Have they changed?"

"Not a bit. You're a really beautiful woman, Angie."

She looked at me oddly. "Are you all right?"

There was nothing for it now. "I found Black Edward, Angie. He's dead."

She looked down and nodded. This wasn't a surprise.

"Yeah," I said, and charged forward. "I also found his treasure, but then, you knew about that. That's where all your money comes from. Two shipments a year, each one in a little wooden box but worth a very big fortune. All tucked away in your attic. But he missed both shipments this year, didn't he? That's why you wanted to know what happened."

She did not move, but her eyes filled with tears. "I don't care about the treasure. How did he die?"

I kept my voice even despite the rage building in me. "Slowly. And ironically. He accidentally locked himself in with his gold, and he starved to death."

Her lower lip trembled. "So he died all alone?"

"Not entirely. He'd kidnapped a woman who looked a lot like you to keep him company. She couldn't rescue him, but she stayed with him while he died. And before that, he painted things. He wasn't a bad artist. You were his favorite subject."

"You mean her."

"No, it was you. Jane Argo saw it, too. There was no doubt who he was painting. And according to the woman, there was no doubt who he was fucking all these years, either."

That was cruel, but I didn't care. The sun had risen above the horizon by now, and the light came through the window. It made the tears dripping from her cheek sparkle as they fell.

"I thought at first that he'd gone a little crazy," I said. "He lived on an island with a bunch of other pirates, including his old first mate Wendell Marteen. You know Wendell, right? He's the one who brought you the gold twice a year?"

"I never knew where the gold came from for certain," she said. "It would show up here, on the back step, on the spring and fall equinox. I just couldn't imagine anyone else who'd send it. But he never included a note or anything." She sighed, and wiped her eyes. "I guess if he was crazy, that explains some of it."

"He wasn't, at least not in the way you'd think. It wasn't the heat or the isolation that got to him. He *wanted* those things. It was his own conscience he was trying to hide from. He'd been a pirate for exactly one voyage, but he'd done something so horrible, he couldn't live with it. For twenty years, it chewed at him, but it never quite drove him crazy. And I think the reason he didn't go nuts is because ultimately he believed it was all your fault."

I tossed the journal onto my desk. Its wooden cover struck with a thud loud as a thundercrack in the morning silence.

"He came to see you after he'd captured King Clovis's treasure ship and hidden the gold and jewels on his island. He sneaked into Watchorn and found you in that cottage on the dunes. He doesn't mention that you were pregnant, so I figure you weren't showing yet and you didn't tell him. He didn't know what to do with so much money, and his crew was getting anxious to have it divided up. Most of them were veterans, and they'd been dreaming of a score like this all their lives." I paused. "*You* suggested he sink the *Bloody Angel* with everyone on board except him and Marteen. Marteen would

be the sole survivor, making sure everyone knew the treasure
went down with the ship. When a suitable amount of time had
passed, he'd send for you to join him in his island paradise."
I tapped the journal. "It's all in there."

She sat quietly and did not respond.

"But he couldn't stand the thought of what he'd done at
your instigation. He wanted to take care of you, so he sent you
boxes of gold twice a year. He hated you, but he also still loved
you. So he abducted a woman who looked like you to keep him
company. All those contradictions chewed at his insides for the
past two decades."

My chest felt tight from the emotions battling to escape. I
continued, "I knew you had secrets, Angie. I knew you had
money you didn't use, and never talked about your past. Long
Billy once warned me about how dangerous you were, but I
thought he was just bitter because you'd kicked him to the
mud. I thought at some level I knew the real *you*."

She still said nothing. She might have been a statue for all
the emotion she showed.

"That's my report. Edward Tew is dead. His treasure is lost.
The fate of the *Bloody Angel* is no longer a mystery." I waited a
moment, then said, "You can get out now. It's still my office,
although I don't know if I'm staying here. I told you before that
leaving out something really important counts as lying. I'd say
you left out plenty."

Still nothing.

"And you could've said he was from Arentia. Two Eddies,
both connected to you, both from the same kingdom. That
was just spooky." When she did not move, I said, "The door's
right there."

"I was a girl," she said at last, her voice flat. "I wanted to escape from that stupid town. I didn't think about them as real people. Hell, *I* wasn't even a real person yet. I thought I was being clever. One simple act, and the biggest treasure in the world was ours. But when I found out he really did it, that all those people died . . ."

Now I said nothing.

"That's why I never spent any of the money. I just stuck it away. I live on what I earn here. I lie awake at night sometimes, thinking about what all that gold could buy, then I remember how much blood is on it."

I still said nothing.

"I don't know what the right thing to do in this situation is. I never have. I ran. I hid. I loved the wrong man and made a terrible mistake because of it, so I don't let anyone get close, just in case I have another terrible mistake in me. I keep things to myself when I probably shouldn't, because that's *how* you keep people from getting close. Beyond that, Eddie, I haven't got a clue. Does the past ever go away?"

A little jolt went through me. I'd done the same thing after Janet was murdered, although it took me years to admit my own culpability in her death. You could make the case that I was still doing it, since I'd left behind my Arentian heritage for good. Then I realized Jane Argo had done the same thing. And in his own way, Duncan Tew.

And Black Edward.

Two Edwards, both from Arentia, both of us sent running from our pasts by horrible events that were, at some level, our own faults. He loved Angelina the way I loved Janet, and that love led us both to make terrible decisions we could never make right. He hid from the world and wallowed in his guilt, kidnapping some poor woman to take Angie's place. I became a mercenary and killed people for money.

And now I was berating Angelina, who had been my friend for as long as I'd known her, whom I'd trust with my life with no hesitation, for doing exactly the same thing I and everyone else in this case had done.

I went around my desk and took her hand. She stood, I put my arms around her and kissed her. I held her close against me, marveling at the way she felt. When the kiss ended, she stayed very close and looked up into my eyes.

"What was that for?" she said in a voice so quiet, so soft that I could hardly believe it was her.

"I love you, Angelina," I said. "Not like Liz, but I do."

She put a hand on my chest. "Liz wouldn't understand this."

"She'd understand, but she probably wouldn't approve. Hell, she's jealous of Jane Argo."

Angelina giggled, then said, "We'll keep it between us, and never speak of it after this." She was so close, I could feel her breath on my face. "Do you remember the first time we met? I kissed you then."

"I remember."

And she kissed me the way she had that night. When our lips parted, she said, "Anything?"

I knew that I wasn't leaving Neceda. She knew it, too. "Still not. You?"

"Not a thing. Come on, sword jockey, I'll make you break-fast. And I won't add this one to your tab." She threaded her fingers through mine and led me out of my office.

She released my hand at the bottom of the stairs and went

into the kitchen, where Rudy was already working his culinary magic. A few early risers sat at the bar, nursing cups of hot tea.

I still needed to tell her about Duncan's offer, but that could wait. I couldn't imagine her slipping into the role of belated mother and grandmother, but perhaps some of that blood-soaked gold in her attic might find its way anonymously to him.

Angelina, Jane Argo, Dylan Clift, Duncan Tew, and I all chose badly for love and suffered the consequences. So far, I was the only one Fate had granted a real do-over. This might be the start of one for Angelina; I'd do what I could to at least make her see the opportunity. But I knew the answer to her question, and I suspected she did as well: The past never goes away.

"Hey, handsome," Liz said, breaking my reverie. She sat down on the stool beside me at the bar, leaned over, and kissed my cheek. Quietly she asked, "How'd it go?"

"As well as it could have."

She smiled, squeezed my hand, and lay her head on my shoulder. I hoped that someday Angelina, Jane, Clift, and Duncan all reached this same sort of peace. And wherever he sailed now, I sincerely wished it for the other Edward.

TELL THE WORLD
THIS BOOK WAS

Good	Bad	So-so

Great ✓ 😊

Fun! 😊

yes